HIS MAJESTY'S HIGHWAYMAN

Books by Donald Barr Chidsey

His Majesty's Highwayman

BY DONALD BARR CHIDSEY

WILDSIDE PRESS

HIS MAJESTY'S HIGHWAYMAN

1 *ALL THE WORLD WAITED*

THE HANGMAN HAD THE SITUATION WELL IN HAND. HE WENT about testing ropes. He adjusted the ladder. This half-hour was his.

The portable galleries were packed. Every tree, every rooftop for half a mile around, like the whole of the route from here to Newgate, was black with humanity. Ah! not Ranelagh nor Vauxhall, nor yet the gardens at Kew, could draw such crowds as Tyburn when it came time to kill in the name of the king.

The hangman moved with a deliberate and not ungraceful ease. He managed to give the impression that he was perfectly at home—that the enraptured stares of thousands were nothing to him. A large man, he wore black shoes, black stockings, brown doeskin breeches with somber silver buckles at the knee. He did not waddle as he walked. He was naked to the waist, and his muscles rippled like satin. His arms were exceedingly long. His hands, apelike, pale at the palms, hung low. Over his head and fastened around his neck was a black silk hood. He was aware of the dramatic appearance of this mask, and indeed had personally selected the material and cut the eyeholes; but he wore the thing only as a sop to prejudice: left to his own devices, he would have showed his face.

Now he was ready. He wiped his hands on a fine cambric kerchief, which afterward he thrust behind the top of his breeches. He folded his arms, sank his chin to his chest, and became still, a statue, ignoring the sallies of the crowd. It was better that way. More dignified.

Though he centered it, serving as a boss to its shield, the hangman did not take any part in the holiday spirit that prevailed this louring April day in 1755. Motionless, and without seeming to, he listened. Not for his ears the giggling, the loud flirtation, the singing, cracking of nuts, shouts of orange vendors. He waited for something else.

And suddenly he heard it. The corners of his mouth twitched slightly, though he gave no other outward sign.

He heard the faraway whoops of delight, the cheers.

They were bringing the victim.

2 *I WHO AM ABOUT TO DIE*

WHEN HIS SHACKLES HAD BEEN KNOCKED OFF, THE YOUNG MAN WHO was about to die walked somewhat unsteadily around the cell, rubbing his wrists. He had been chained to the floor for almost a week. The money in his purse at the time of his arrest had been soon spent on the most usual things—for everything here was sold—and after his trial, he'd had nothing left with which to purchase lighter gyves.

He looked at the ordinary, the keeper, the two turnkeys who would take him to Tyburn. There was also present, though in the background, the physician, a small, snuff-dusty man.

Despite his confinement, the young man did not cut a bad figure. His clothes, while not pretentious, were good. He was tall, and stood straight.

The keeper, perhaps out of the kindness of his heart, but more likely because of a certain professional prudery, had taken some trouble over this youth's appearance. Since it had been obvious that, when his time came, the prisoner would not be able to afford a hackney, as wealthier murderers did, but must make use of the common cart, and would be seen by thousands at close range even before he reached the scaffold, the keeper had caused a hairdresser and a barber-surgeon, both conveniently incarcerated at the moment, to be sent up from the yard. These worthies had not permitted the prisoner to touch their scissors or razors—and indeed he had not been unfettered, even briefly, lest he slash his own throat—but they had done a good job of work on him. He was by no means unhandsome, as he stood there rubbing his wrists.

"Once again, gentlemen, damn your eyes," he said, "my name is Thomas Savage, I come from Lincolnshire, I have lately been in France, and through all my life long I never robbed anybody. *I am not Harry Tewkes.*"

The keeper heaved a sigh. He drew forth a bottle of gin.

"Here, lad. You couldn't afford the laudanum, but this'll help."

Tom Savage shook his head.

"No."

The keeper, a much disliked man, was defensive in his manner.

"It isn't me! This was brought together a bit from here and a bit from there. The boys down in the pressing yard asked me to pass it on to you."

Tom's eyes burned with tears, but he blinked them away. He knew none of his fellow prisoners, having been led through the yard but a few times; but from glimpses and from hearsay he took them to be a pack of subhuman rascals, as unsavory, yes, and as mean, as any on this earth. There was no window in his cell and he could not see them, though he had heard them through most of the daylight hours, and what he heard was three-fourths filth. He did not hear them now. The yard was quiet. Were they waiting for a glimpse of him? Would they cheer him as he left?

He knew what gin must mean down there, where so many men strove to forget, and he knew, too, that in a place where money was everything, it cost twice as much as it did outside the walls. He was, truly, touched. Yet he shook his head.

"I go to the gallows an innocent man," he said, "and I might as well go a sober one, too."

"Don't be a beefwit! Get blind! They'll expect you to!"

"So, like some actor, I should be aware of my duty to the

4

public, eh? No, thank you. I never asked for this part, but since I have it I'll play it my own way."

The keeper looked at him with concern, as anxious as a mother who dresses her child for confirmation. It distressed him that the young man had no wig. Newgate itself, its administration, he knew, was this day on parade.

"You look well, lad. But if you should faint—"

"I'll not faint," coldly.

The keeper shrugged, and put the gin away.

"I'll allow you to walk unbound to the cart," he muttered.

"How kind of you."

"Nay, there's no call for high-and-mightiness. You were chained because your gang's outside. I never knew when they might rush the gate. But the soldiers take you over when you reach the street."

Here was a new thought, and Tom found it comforting. *Somebody* wished him out! During the two weeks since his arrest, he had been living in an unreal world. He could not call on the associates he had left in France: there was neither the time nor the cash. His lawyer had been unable to locate any acquaintance from Lincolnshire, a place the prisoner had not visited in five years. Tom's own mother and father were long since dead, nor did he have any brothers or sisters. Closest to him were three cousins, Earnest and Edgar Savage, and John Goodridge, all of them boyhood companions who could not possibly have been mistaken in his identity and who, in addition, could produce copies of the contract he had made with them at long distance, by means of couriers. This contract provided that monies from the sale of Tom Savage's Lincolnshire heritage should go toward a New World adventure in which all four should share equally, in coin as in services. They were to have met in Plymouth the first day of April and there to have embarked aboard the *Seraphis* for New England. Foul weather in the Channel delayed Tom, who had been passing through London on the day of the rendezvous—when he'd been most unexpectedly seized. Three days later, he was to learn that the *Seraphis* had already sailed, a day late. This was crushing news. He did not reproach his cousins. While they might have heard in Plymouth of the nabbing of Harry Tewkes, they would have had no way of connecting this with the non-appearance of Thomas Savage, their partner and relation, who, they might well have concluded, had given it up and decided to remain in France. There was the tide to consider; there were the other passengers, and the fact that time meant money. In short, they'd gone. They were now on the high seas, the three who could beyond all contest have proved that this prisoner was Thomas Savage. It might take six months, nine months, even a year, to get their depositions. The Crown had no intention of waiting that long.

Yet the prisoner, downcast as he was in the days just before his trial, could comfort himself with the reflection that if, through a freak of luck—and a lack of funds and of friends—he was temporarily unable to prove that he was Thomas Savage, at least nobody could prove that he was Harry Tewkes, the nation's bloodiest highwayman. Here he made a mistake. A dozen persons had visited him in his cell to stare a moment, refusing to talk, and no fewer than four of these later had taken the witness stand to swear that yes, the prisoner was beyond all doubt the same scoundrel who had held them up the night of such-and-such. These witnesses undoubtedly tipped the scale; but the recognition, as loot, of two objects found in Tom's pocket—a monogrammed silk handkerchief and a gold watch—neither of which he had known to be there, quite likely would have been enough to hang him in the first place. The jury had been out only a few minutes. The appeal for a reduction of the sentence to one of transportation had been rejected. He was to die.

"*Ave Caesar, morituri te salutamus!*" he cried.

"Eh?"

"Nothing."

The ordinary came forward. He was young, and he was not oily. His fine blue eyes, if weak, were kind.

"My son, your immortal soul—"

"La, I've no time for immortal souls!"

Then the physician took charge. A malodorous small man, he held a watch. He prodded Tom, peering into his throat. The watch, a grisly reminder, clacked on: the sounds were like hammer blows. In part to drown these, but also because he regretted his rudeness, Tom turned again to the ordinary.

"Forgive me, padre."

"It is not for me to forgive."

"I was—curt. *Omissis jocis,* padre, I am not at my most courtly today. But—*omnia munda mondis.* I'm sure you will overlook any disrespect to your cloth."

He could almost feel the startled chaplain roll the Latin over.

"It is no longer possible to plead one's clergy, my son."

"I know that."

"Nor is there time left for joking."

"Or for anything else, eh?"

"There is always a time for prayer."

Tom Savage looked around, his lip curling.

"In this place?"

"My son, God is everywhere. He can hear the lowliest."

"So we have been taught." Tom rather liked this timorous young priest, who at least was clean. "But I think I would prefer the open air. I'll be given a chance to pray at the—uh—the scene?"

"Of course. But—there will be thousands to watch."

Tom winced. Open air? To pray while half of London, slack-jawed and slavering, goggle-eyed, gaped? He shook his head.

"You're right," he said simply, and got to his knees. "Should I repeat the words after you? or what?"

"Just as you wish, my son."

The ordinary, though unhurried, was brief. His voice was firm and low, and sincerity seared it. Moved, Tom Savage

7

swallowed hard before he could echo the "amen" and get to his feet again.

He brushed his coat. The time had come. He straightened his cravat. He cocked with care the tricorn they'd restored to him. He nodded.

"Very well," he said.

One of the turnkeys, a slab-sided, rat-faced fellow, swept into a bow, his arms extended toward the door.

"The carriage awaits, m'lord!"

3 *LOOK THIS WAY, LADY*

NOBODY KNEW THOMAS SAVAGE WELL. AT HOME AND IN PARIS it was the same story: his nose was seldom out of a book. He rode, he fenced, on occasion he even drank and sang with fellow students; but most of the time he read. He minded his own business, as the saying is, personally, but he seemed incapable of minding the wool business his father had left him, and this had fallen into the hands of an uncle even less efficient, where in time it perished, leaving the scholar, then on his way from Oxford to the Sorbonne, with little but land. This land he had, piece by piece, sold through an agent. Not until the last field went, and it became imperative that Tom Savage quit his academy and face up to the world, did he consider the proposal put to him by his cousins—the New World adventure.

In Lincoln, those who remembered him at all were not likely to see him as a merchant in the American colonies. They were even less likely to see him as a condemned felon.

He had told the keeper he wouldn't swoon. He was not so sure of this once he had mounted the cart. The street, splotched with slops and garbage, was scarcely less fetid than the prison itself. The atmosphere was scarcely less noisome. Despite the chill, people, packed too tight, perspired. Men who had been waiting all night relieved themselves openly on the pavement.

9

The sky was dark, low. There was a muggy threat of rain. Thunder bumbled.

He thought: Some such approach as this Hell must have.

Here was pandemonium—an upsurge of faces, the mouths open, eyes aflame, distended like balloons. As Tom climbed into the cart, his ears were assailed by frenzied screeches. It was like a gale of wind, that sound. It caused him to rock, to walk a bit bent, as though wading knee-deep through water.

From Newgate to Tyburn was about two miles. But the passage would be very slow, the delicious pleasure of expectancy prolonged. Like a huge uncertain beetle, the cart inched its way across to where Newgate Street met Giltspur Street and the Old Bailey, and there, before St. Sepulchre's, as though bewildered, blinking, it came to a halt.

Suddenly, from the porch of the church, somebody threw something at the prisoner, and it landed with a "splop!" at his feet. He was thunderstruck when, looking down, he saw that it was a knot or nosegay of spring flowers. Oxeyes and cowslips, largely. This was early in the year even for those humble blooms. Somebody must have stayed up late and looked hard to gather them.

Then another knot was thrown, and another, until with a great gulp of astonishment, Tom Savage came to realize that these folks were not cursing him. They were cheering! They were wishing him luck for the rest of his life—the full twenty minutes!

"Keep the old chin up!"

"It won't be long now!"

"Awr, ain't 'e the darlin'! Look at 'im!"

It was heart-lifting. It was also droll. These sturdy, misled, unscoured, but exuberant subjects of George II were shouting themselves hoarse in praise of a myth. It would have been macabre enough, in all conscience, if they had had the right party. Somewhere in the realm (yet possibly outside of it by now?) was a man named Henry Tewkes, more popularly Harry the Horsepad, who had treated males with ferocity, females with an elaborate politeness, the while he filched from both; who, dashingly dressed, always wore a purple mask, a bright yellow cockade. Somewhere this being existed. But the citizens of London tonight were hurrahing a mild, apologetic person, a middle-class Midlander who was more interested in Plutarch than in the price of stolen pearls, and who had been about to embark, somewhat distastefully, upon a mercantile career in Massachusetts.

The jest was bitter. It merited a smile; and it might be that he did smile as he stood in that jolting cart.

" 'And 'im a potful,'Arry-me-boy!' "

"Keep a strite fice!"

They lurched to the left and started down Snow Hill.

Tom's head was clearing. His vision steadied. He regarded the faces—some above him, peering over the edges of the roofs; others below, undulating like a cream-colored wave; while still others, at windows, were almost on a level with his own.

As he had lain (literally) at Newgate, his thought had seldom dwelt upon the possibility of this ride. He had then been unable to believe that such a monstrous thing could happen. He had persisted in the belief that some day, somehow, somebody would come rushing in with the announcement that it all had been a ghastly mistake. Nightmares don't last forever. Sooner or later, he would wake up.

However, on those occasions when he had permitted his imagination to stray to the last ride, he had pictured himself shaking his fists while he shouted, *"I am not Harry Tewkes!"* In the event, stunned, he did nothing of the sort. The cart was seatless, and he shared it only with the two turnkeys, who at first made a show of gripping his arms, one on each side, but soon were caused to quit this by the indignation of the mob. These turnkeys doubtless had looked forward to the ride, for them a time of triumph. There were soldiers before and soldiers behind, though in truth the likelihood of even a rat's wriggling its way among the jammed-together spectators was slim. For this reason the turnkeys made but a feeble pretense of holding the prisoner. They were more interested in waving, slanging, or exchanging bawdy remarks. It was a great day for them, and they made the most of it.

Tom did not deceive himself. He knew that even if he had done all the deeds attributed to Harry the Horsepad, it yet wouldn't be he—the person, the man—that these cheerers had come to see. It would be Death—deliberate, public, *legal* Death, complete with pageantry. This, to Tom, was abhorrent. He himself had witnessed hangings. Who hadn't? But it was a vulgar business at best, and why should it be exploited? He sniffed. The crowd went wild.

There was no driver of this cart. There were no reins. The horse was led by a couple of grinning jail attendants. The pace was that of a turtle. Eight mounted soldiers were immediately assigned to the vehicle, four ahead, four behind, though whenever the way permitted, some of them rode alongside as well. They were guardsmen, very brave in their back- and breast-plates. Their sabers were drawn. Their high-stepping steeds were trained. Even so, this procession crept.

At the gate, there had been a squabble about who should ride with the condemned man, a lusciously public post. A couple of soldiers had believed that the privilege was to be theirs; but the turnkeys had waved papers and called for the keeper, and in the end won. Thus there was little love lost between the crew of the cart and the disgruntled guardsmen.

Two things Tom might have done. He could have lain on the bottom of the cart, or he could have stood grasping a three-foot, upright square post, which was smooth on top and to which, seemingly, the reins on an ordinary journey would have been snubbed. He elected to grasp the post. If he lay down, he would be called a craven. This consideration did not weigh heavily with him. But, the chains at Newgate being short, he had been lying down for a long while; and to be upright was a relief. Also, the floor of the cart would be damnably hard, for there wasn't a wisp of straw.

Yet it was not easy to stand with feet and hands bound. Three times within the first five minutes he was thrown against the side of the cart. While they righted him, the turnkeys were hooted for dirty dogs. Just then the mob meant little to Tom Savage, but it meant a great deal to the turnkeys; and when, after the third fall, they heard a turnip slap against the cart, and this was followed by a not-fragrant egg, they decided to wax humane. For the mob loved this prisoner, as it always loves its victims. So the turnkeys loosened, and then entirely took off, the cord that had tied Tom's ankles, and they greatly loosened the cord at his wrists. The crowd roared its approval, and the turnkeys bobbed like applauded acrobats. How pleased they were! Tom gave a grunt.

This, then, was the state of affairs when, somewhere in Lincoln's Inn Fields, the cart reached a maze of alleys and small streets, where it came to a halt. A jurisdictional dispute? These rides to Tyburn were as meticulously laid out as any coronation parade. Property owners fought for the privilege of being on the route, since window-space and roof-space could fetch a pretty rental. It was all arranged in advance, after much haggling. God help the guardsmen if they took a wrong turn!

It must have been somewhere near Little Turnstile. After this cramped, confused neighborhood had been cleared, they would turn left and cross the Fleet by a stone bridge. Then, the way widening past St. Andrew's, they would start the long climb up Holburn Hill, to the gallows.

The cart poked hesitantly into the first of these narrow streets. It was scarcely more than an alley, and the cart's sides all but scraped the old-fashioned, cantilevered, upper-story bays. The shouting within this chasm was immediate, intimate. And for the first time Tom Savage picked a single face to look at.

This was the face of a young woman who leaned from a window a short distance ahead, on the left. What must have drawn his eyes was the circumstance that it contained the only closed mouth he had so far seen. All the others had been oh-ing or ah-ing, or they had shouted obscenities. This girl only gazed at him.

The mouth pouted naturally, and was small. The eyes were amethystine, set rather close together, but clear and bright. It was a somewhat triangular face, the chin small, the forehead unfashionably broad. It was framed with tousled, dark brown hair, and it surmounted a neck and breast of surpassing loveliness.

The companion of this girl was so large that he filled all the rest of the window. In addition to his size, he was remarkable for the fact that he seemed to pay no attention to anything but a huge pewter box, from which he was endeavoring to lift some snuff. He failed woefully in this, and the powder fluttered down over his waistcoat and his huge rust-colored coat. There were many in the crowd who were drunk, for this was a memorable occasion; but the man in the window next to Violet Eyes was exceptional in that he appeared to have forgotten why he had come. His nose was bulbous, his cheeks crisscrossed with purple-red lines. He was blubbering to himself, his puffy lips twisted doggedly. His eyes, froglike, were rolled high.

Beauty and the Beast, thought Tom Savage.

Vanity is a curious thing. Tom Savage had his share of it, and he was rocked by the realization that Violet Eyes was not, after all, looking at *him*. Within a few spits of Tyburn itself, he thought of such a trifle! He could have sworn that a moment ago, like everybody else in that street save the overdressed oaf with whom she shared a window, she had been gazing upon the man who was soon to swing. But now, undeniably, it was not at Tom that she stared, but at one of the turnkeys. This was the same slab-sided brute who had executed a mock bow when Tom was about to quit his cell. A more ill-favored lout it would be hard to conceive; yet the lady gawped like one entranced.

This attention was not lost upon the turnkey, who began to smirk in salacious glee. He wriggled and giggled.

The giant in brown continued to fumble with his oversized snuffbox.

As the cart inched closer, the turnkey redoubled his flirtation, dancing and jigging like a man who feels an acute call of nature.

The lady dropped her glance, sighed, and distinctly colored.

It should not be supposed that anybody else noticed this byplay, which yet fascinated the center of their attention, Tom Savage.

I am leaving a world of fools, Tom thought.

The cart was exactly alongside the window now.

"What about a kiss, chuck?" and the turnkey thrust his face forward.

"Oh, sir . . ." she stammered; and then she snatched the snuffbox from her companion's hands and threw it with all its contents right at the turnkey's eyes.

The turnkey squealed in pain.

At this instant the giant in brown came alive. He heaved himself halfway out of the window. He reached far over the cart—and he was in truth a tall man, as he was a strong one, not a mite drunk now.

Hamlike hands were chunked under Tom Savage's armpits.

"Hop it, Harry," the giant whispered.

Tom never could have told why he sprang. But spring he did, his legs, at least, being free.

The sill was low. Tom went over it like a hunter, to land with a thump on the giant, who was by that time flat on his back inside the house.

A shot rang out. Glass was smashed. Somebody screamed.

4 A CORPSE SHOULD KEEP QUIET

TOM WAS SEIZED BY HALF A DOZEN HANDS AND HAULED TO HIS feet. He heard a solicitous whisper of "Harry," but for the most part the business was done in silence. He could barely see these men as they hurried him to a door at the rear of the room. Just before he passed through that door Tom Savage turned.

A guardsman showed head and shoulders above the sill. He must have been standing on the back of his horse. His casque gleamed, and the plumes jogged and leapt, a striking contrast to his no-nonsense face. Somebody had shut and locked the window. The guardsman, with his gauntleted fist and the butt of his saber, was smashing pane after pane.

The tinkle of glass, the splintering of wood, the hubbub, all were shut off when the hall door slammed. The last glimpse Tom had of the guardsman, that worthy had slapped his saber between his teeth and was crawling in headfirst.

The stair was narrow, the hallway below bare of furniture. There was an imperious pounding on the street door. They ignored this. They scurried to the back of the house, where, after lowering themselves through an open trap, they came, not to a cellar, as might have been expected, but to the end of a tunnel. It was narrow and damp, smelling of fresh-shovelled earth; yet it had been stoutly timbered.

Here they were met by a boy who carried a horn lantern,

and for the first time Tom got a look at the men who had saved him—though not much of a look. They were busy. They were closing the trap door, righting the ladder, prowling ahead to make sure that the tunnel was clear. Moreover, they paused but a moment to assemble themselves, to count noses.

There was nothing dim-witted about the guardsmen. They had been tricked; but after the deed was done, they did not sit their horses, "o"-mouthed, while the prisoner made the best of precious seconds. Tom and his comrades had scarcely started down the tunnel—of necessity in single file—when they heard the street door crash in.

The footing was treacherous, and the trip took a long while, perhaps ten minutes, though they hurried as well as they could. All Tom was able to see during this time was the rump, an enormous one, of the man before him, Brown Coat. They were all bent over like baboons.

This was a pity. Tom had the liveliest admiration for the men around him. What organization! What cunning, and cool nerve! If this had been planned, launched, and carried through by the followers of Harry Tewkes, what manner of paragon was *he*?

It was plain that he, Tom Savage, bore a striking resemblance to the outlaw. Yet—they could not look *exactly* alike. And Harry's cronies, here, soon would learn their error. What would they do then?

Tom did not trouble himself overly with this or other teasing questions. What did that girl have to do with such a gang? If they had gone to all this trouble, why had they not engaged their own lawyer to work for him and to visit him at Newgate? No matter. Just now, doubled over, Tom felt fine. The escape was exhilarating.

They came into a stable, where they could stand. The place was as dark as the tunnel, but the smell was unmistakable.

"Here you are, Harry—*up* she goes!"

Somebody lifted Tom's foot in cupped hands, and he was

hoisted to a wagon where, in the dimness, his fingers found a long box.

"Lay right down, captain. You ain't as dead as they'd like t've had you, but you'll do for a while, eh?"

He got into the box. It was padded, and though narrow, it was by no means uncomfortable.

Almost immediately the wagon started to move.

Tom Savage knew an instant of panic; no more. After all, he was among friends. They wouldn't let him suffocate.

Besides, the air was fresh, and there was a certain amount of light. He turned his head—to find that a hole the size of his thumb had been drilled through the side of the box a few inches above the bottom, wonderfully convenient for his eye.

The gait of the horse or horses was unspeakably slow. Through the hole Tom could see nobody. Neither could he hear much: the customary street sounds, the cries of peddlers, bump of barrows, bickering of housewives, all were absent—an eerie effect.

The street, from what he could see of it, was deserted, the shops closed. The wagon turned into another street, and that showed the same.

This must have been a considerable distance from the scene of the escape, for Tom's ears could catch no echo of the hue and cry. The only sound he did hear was a sad, crusty rustling just above his head, a sound that might have been caused by the swishing of very heavy, very dirty silk.

At last a man came within Tom's limited ken. He wore a smock, and obviously was a foreigner, an insignificant workman. He gawped at the wagon; and for one terrible instant—until he realized that this was impossible—Tom Savage thought that he had been seen. Then the man, a dull clod, crossed himself, took off his cap, and held this over his heart while he stood at attention to permit the wagon to pass.

And Tom, for the first time, knew that he was in a coffin.

The wagon was a hearse, that rustling a catafalque!

He began to laugh. He couldn't help it. He had behaved well

in public, but it was no more than natural that his tight nerves should twang back upon him when he was alone.

"Sh-sh," came a whisper. "Easy, 'Arry! A corpse ought to keep quiet!"

Tom obeyed, though with an effort. Never before had his risibilities been so violently tickled. This was delicious!

Truly, though, the need for silence was becoming marked. After the clod, there were others. Shutters were being taken down. Waterboys clattered past. The familiar "What d'ye lack?" rang out.

There were soldiers, too. More than once Tom heard them asking questions. But they never bothered the funeral wagon. Brutes though they might be, they respected mourning cloth.

Tom had no way of knowing how long that trip was. The pace was lugubriously slow, so that each minute crawled past like a wounded hare, and he could not hear church bells.

It might have been noon, even a little after, when the wagon turned off the cobbles, sogged its way through mud for a while, between walls so close that they scraped the sides, and came to a halt.

By that time it was raining. Tom could hear the patter on the lid.

A door was dragged open. There was the rattle of a chain. The wagon lurched ahead. The door was closed, the coffin opened.

"Damn me, Harry, it's done! Step right out, sir!"

He rose, excruciatingly stiff. His head swam.

There were no windows, but despite the time of day, there were many candles. He was close to these men now, looking right down at them.

"Thank you," he said crisply, and he leapt to the floor.

"Who—who the devil are you?"

Tom started to brush his breeches and his coat. He did this because he feared that his hands were trembling. Yet the seeming insouciance had its effect upon the rough men who surrounded him, men paralyzed by amazement and traditionally awed by fine manners. In a moment, at this rate, he might venture to address them. Meanwhile, fastidious, keeping up the spell, he brushed.

"That isn't Harry Tewkes!"

He looked up. The girl with the purple eyes stood in a doorway, a candle in her hand. The other hand slowly rose to a mouth that had fallen open in fright, while the eyes grew larger.

Thomas Savage made a leg.

"Ma'am, if you will permit me to explain—"

She gasped, and ran away, sobbing.

Tom faced the others. He spread his hands.

"Gentlemen, I assure you that I am not and never have been Captain Tewkes, and I've spent most of my time these past two weeks saying so. I am sorry to disappoint you. But I do wish to thank you from the bottom of my heart, and at the same time to congratulate you on—"

They weren't listening. No doubt their own nerves for some time had been taut. No doubt the release was heady. They asked no questions, for they would have listened to no answers anyway. Brown Coat snorted like a buffalo and charged, both fists swinging. The others followed.

Tom never had a chance. Almost from the beginning, caught across the right ear by one of Brown Coat's mighty buffets, he was dizzy. He found himself on his knees. He tried to get up, striving at the same time to cover his head with his arms. Then he was fully down, and they were kicking him. It didn't hurt much, it happened so quickly. The kicks might have been that many pokes with a mop. This was his last thought before a great roaring blackness engulfed him.

5 *ONLY ONE WAY IS OPEN*

THE RETURN TO CONSCIOUSNESS WAS NOT ABRUPT BUT FUZZY. HE found himself on his knees. The place was not so dark but that, looking back, he could see the way he had crawled, for it was marked with blood.

He collapsed, panting, and lay motionless for a while.

Pain came slowly, as did resentment; but though the one was acute, the other, which would remain, outstung it.

Thomas Savage was a good-natured young man. Had he taken the trouble to frame in words his objection to fighting, he would probably have said that it took too much time. Any matter of animosity, even when not accompanied by actual combat, could keep a man away from his books. Tom simply wasn't interested.

Essentially a country boy, he had once been diverted by sports. He was a tolerably good fowler, an exceedingly good horseman. In Lincoln he had wrestled, both Cumberland style and catch-as-catch-can. He had even taken a few lessons in boxing from a passing-through pugilist named Croucher Givens, reputedly a protégé of the great Jack Broughton, using, of course, the "mufflers" or padded gloves; and, liking this, he would have continued it, had not Givens been chased out of town by an indignant husband. His fencing alone Tom had kept up. If not brilliant, he was a skilled, experienced swordsman, handling with equal ease the old-fashioned rapier, the current "court," or small sword, the back sword, broad sword, saber, and heavy, basket-hilted Schläger.

In all this he was easygoing. He never pressed. He scorned to strive for supremacy, and could lose with a laugh.

The beating he had just taken was different. It was more than merely humiliating: it was an insult.

They should have killed him. Doubtless they still meant to do so. Obstructing justice was itself a hanging offense, and they could not afford to let the false Harry Tewkes, who had seen them, go free. But the most debased butcher can sicken of kicking a man who doesn't stir or even groan. In a little while they would return and finish the job.

He moved about a bit, arms extended. He recovered his hat. He found no window. This building appeared to be made of rough, splintery boards, and it was airy, for the boards were not all touching, as his fingers told him. However, he had nothing with which to enlarge those cracks. Nor did any light shine through them.

It must have been night, then, and a dark night too. The only light in the stable came from around a door—the same doorway in which he had seen the girl. That door was closed now.

As the pain crept into his face, and all up and down his body his bruises began to throb; his head at least became clear. The ringing in his ears subsided, and he began to hear the patter of rain on the roof, and a bumble of voices from the other side of the door.

He found the outside doorway readily enough, the one through which the hearse had come, but its latch was caught by a padlock so large and strong that in the darkness, with no tool, and with the need for silence, he despaired of breaking it.

The floor was stone. He got up on the hearse again and with his hands examined the roof: it was discouragingly sturdy.

This left only the door from which the light and voices came. He listened, but could make out no separate words. He could only take comfort from the fact that the mumble did not sound like a spat but, rather, the casual talk of men who, say, play cards.

He took out his kerchief and wiped, not his face, where the blood was drying, but his hands, which had been sweaty. Very gently he tried the latch. It offered no resistance and made no noise.

He faced a bare hall suffused with light from a source not visible to him. This could have been the living quarters of the proprietor of the stable it adjoined. The voices, like the light, came from around a bend in the passageway.

Tom paused. Having come this far, he didn't know what to do next.

Then his ears caught a lower sound, from the right, where now for the first time he noticed another door.

It was the sound of a woman sobbing.

He wiped his hands again. He took a deep breath. He opened the door on the right and went in.

At the click of the latch she sat up. Undeniably, even in this light, her cheeks stained with tears, hair disheveled, eyes packed with fright, she was lovely. Tom spread his feet and put his fists on his hips, regarding her.

"Harry Tewkes is a lucky man," he murmured.

The room was narrow, and there was a window at the far end. Rain sloshed against this, the only sound, for Tom had closed the door, shutting off the blur of voices. No air stirred the flame of the candle on the table. The girl sat on a pallet, the coverlet of which was rumpled. The only other article of furniture was a chair on which reposed one of those leghorn bags women so often clutch in their laps on long journeys; it was open, its contents in disarray.

"I—I was afraid they would kill you," she whispered.

He nodded.

"I was afraid of the same thing," he said.

He must have made a gruesome sight, his face puffed, bruised, bloody. But he kept staring at her, with a boldness that was not usual in him. She dropped her eyes. She swallowed.

"And they will still do so, if I call them."

"I don't doubt it," he said.

He took a step toward her. All he meant to do was reach past her for something he saw in the leghorn bag, but she misread his purpose and shrank back.

"Stay there," she commanded.

He took another step.

She might have screamed, and this was what he feared, though he had been careful to measure the distance to the window. But she didn't scream. Instead she reached into the leghorn and drew out a pistol.

He stood looking down at it, smiling a bit. It was ludicrously small. The butt was carved Circassian walnut stippled with tiny silver stars. The barrel itself was steel, but the mountings were silver.

"Now, you know, I had not thought of that," he whispered. "But as long as *you* have—"

He moved toward her.

She pulled the trigger.

At the click, he reached down and took the thing out of her hand. He had seen that there wasn't a grain of powder in the flashpan.

She made no further resistance, and indeed seemed stupefied. He slipped an arm under her and lifted her from the pallet, and he kissed her long and greedily. She never stirred. She did not even close her eyes. When he released her, she still was staring at him.

"Who are you?" she whispered.

"An humble student of the classics who has been most bar-barously imposed upon, ma'am, but who means," he added, "to get his own back."

He went to the window and looked out. There was nothing to see. A few persons passed, heads down against the wind and rain.

"And—you?" he asked softly.

"My name is Molly Evans, if that means anything to you."

He shook his head.

"I never got about much in the underworld," he said. "Now—where is Harry Tewkes?"

"If I knew, do you think I would have taken all this trouble today, sirrah?"

"Aye, there's that. But—you do want him?"

"More than anything else in the world!"

He nodded. They were speaking in low voices, confidentially. It was as though they had known one another for a long time. She was now not afraid of Tom, who was thoughtful.

She might well have been afraid. Anybody might. For this was not the Tom Savage the people at home would have remembered. It was not even the Tom Savage of this morning. Had he coarsened? If so, it was simply a measure of defense, for this was a coarse world into which he'd been thrust.

"Well, I'll find him for you," he said at last.

He pocketed the pistol. He took a yellow cockade from the leghorn, and from that same bag, a purple silk handkerchief.

"How?" she asked. "How will you find him?"

"By *being* him. What have I got to lose? If I'm caught, I am a convicted felon anyway. I've got no other place to go, so I'll go down. I'll travel in the tracks of the master—until I overtake him."

"And then what?"

"God knows what will happen then," he said glumly.

And he climbed out of the window.

He walked for fully fifteen minutes before he found what he had been looking for. This was a sedan chair occupied by a not altogether sober man who, from its depths, cursed the wet, bedraggled carriers.

Tom Savage—the new Tom—did not hesitate. There were persons within call, and many of the windows were lighted, but he stepped coolly into a doorway, fastened the purple silk handkerchief across his face, drew and cocked the pistol, stepped out again.

25

"Run away," he told the chair men.

One obeyed instantly. The other, the forward one, at first was petrified with fright; but when Tom raised the pistol toward his very face, he bolted without a word.

The occupant of the chair had subsided. Tom went to the window, leaned on the sill, waggled the gun.

"And now, you old fool," he said, "will you give me your money or shall I take your life?"

6 EVERY MAN WHO HAS SEEN HER

HE BOUGHT A SWORD. HE BOUGHT A WIG. HE CONSULTED A CLERK at the College of Heralds. Then he went to Tunbridge Wells to think the whole thing over.

None of these moves was haphazard.

The rake he robbed must have spent a profitable evening at the card table, for his purse was heavy—and, *mirabile visu,* all in one place! It was the custom for travellers at night, even within the city, to split their portable possessions into many parts, stuffing some here, some there, excepting that a small set of coins would be left in the purse proper, to be handed over without remonstrance to a possible robber, who might, because of this, refrain from seeking further. The man in the sedan chair, drunk, had not taken this precaution. Neither had he sent linkboys ahead, or hired bodyguards. Nor had the chair men been cudgel-equipped ruffians of the sort who sometimes, for an extra fee, consented to carry home lucky gamesters. They had been his own servants, wearing livery, as Tom Savage saw.

Whatever the reason, Tom now had more ready cash than ever before in his life. There is nothing that a fugitive from justice stands in greater need of.

The sword was symbolic, an announcement of rank. In England as in France, Tom had noted, the wearer of a sword said to the rest of the world: "See me for what I am. Step aside." It

27

made no difference that the thing might be no more than a steel toothpick, an ornament, and that the man who had it strapped around his waist would be afraid to draw it. He wore a sword: he was deferred to.

The first thing that Tom Savage must achieve, if he hoped to keep out of the hands of the constables, was gentility. A sword was gentility.

His own blade he had sold at Newgate, as he'd sold his wig, in order to raise funds for his defense.

There was nothing unusual in this purchase. All armorers were used to the man who strode into the establishment and demanded to be sold a sword—any sword, the fancier the better. Every year scores of merchants "crossed the line," or deluded themselves into thinking that they did. To "sink the shop" and buy a "box in the country"—that is, to become gentle—was the aim of every tradesman who was not lost to sloth.

Tom Savage's case was different only in that he was selective. He didn't take the first silver-gilt weapon he was shown. He did not fail to draw each one he examined, and to the astonishment of the armorer, even make a few passes. What at last he settled upon—and paid an exorbitant price for—was exquisitely balanced, as fine a strip of Toledo as you could have found in the three kingdoms. It felt good at his hip.

The matter of the wig was much the same. A man without a sword might yet be a personage in his own world, but a man without a wig was a penniless wretch. Even the keeper at Newgate, surely no soft-heart, had taken pity on Tom when he saw him about to set forth wigless on his last ride, and had offered to lend him one of the prisoners' wigs he held as security against payment of their food fees, an offer Tom refused only after he saw how dirty the thing was, fearing that it might be lousy as well.

There was a brisk market in wigs. One was much the same as another, except as to size, for they had come to be nearly uniform of late, and it was seldom that a man could prove possession of his own. Bishops and barristers, as well as persons of high official position, still wore their large wigs, but for the average man, the peruke that fell in folds below the shoulders was a thing of the past. Nine out of ten wigs these days were readily interchangeable with their fellows. Combed, cleaned, re-lined, freshly powdered, the sack brushed and pressed, they could be sold again for new. Being small, too, they were easy to snatch. Nor were they dangerous to have in stock, as stolen watches were. Indeed, there was a new class of criminal—hair-nippers they were called—the members of which were as proud of their craft as were the pickpockets of theirs. Some of these artists were exceedingly tall and swift of foot, and they would simply grab a wig and run. Others, who might once have been what, on the highroad, were called "hookers," and might have operated through open farmhouse windows from the outside, or from behind hedges lifting clothes off a line, in London today fished from rooftops, where they were difficult of access, and from whence they could easily escape if an alarm was sounded. Finally, there were hair-nippers who used children. Such a one would walk a crowded street with a large wicker basket on his shoulder, as though carrying, say, vegetables. He'd bump a hat-less man whose wig looked expensive, at the same time hissing a signal to the boy or girl in the basket, who thereupon would pop up, snatch the wig, and disappear again—before anybody could see what had happened.

Therefore, it was in no way suspicious when a bareheaded Thomas Savage presented himself at a wigmaker's shop.

It was the same in the College of Heralds, where all sorts of cranks went with all sorts of queer requests, and where a seamed and juiceless man, a man unspeakably skinny, with-drawn from all mundane matters, living aloof in a special place, gazed down upon Tom Savage through steel-rimmed spectacles, with no more interest than he would have shown some insect.

Tom had in one pocket a gold snuffbox, in the other a dia-mond-studded watch, each decorated with the same device. These articles were an embarrassment to him; but it would have been senseless to steal only money, which was all he truly wanted, for it would never have suggested Harry Tewkes. Tom fully intended to pay back that choleric party in the sedan chair —when he had learned who the man was.

"It's a red lion standing on his hind legs against a white background, and there's a wide blue ribbon running straight across the middle."

"Argent, a lion rampant guardant gules, debruised by a fess azure," the juiceless one wearily intoned. "The arms of Henry Malsby, Earl of Carnborough."

"But Carnborough's in Paris! He's on some embassy there, trying to stave off war! I saw him myself, last week!"

"I believe that's true," dryly. "Perhaps you mis-described this device? If you will permit me to see it—"

"No, no! I told you aright! Only maybe—Excuse me."

He turned, slipping the watch from his pocket, but holding it close to him so that nobody else could see it. Then he put it back.

"There's something else," he announced. He took up quill and paper. "It's a thing like this—"

"Ah, a difference!"

"That makes a difference, does it?"

"It said it *was* a difference. Sometimes known as a brisure."

"I see."

"It is the sort of difference we call a label. It's emblazoned upon the escutcheon only by the oldest son and heir. In this case, that would be Henry Malsby, Lord Falk. *He's* in London. Five shillings, please."

"Cheap enough," said Tom as he paid, "for such an exalted pedigree."

The clerk made no comment on this.

Tom had his coat brushed and mended, his shoes shined, his face massaged and patched and powdered, so that he made a neat if unobtrusive picture when he went to Tunbridge Wells.

"Or could I show you a place nearer the Parade, my lord?"

"This will do very well, thankee. Here—"

"Your lordship will take the waters?"

Every male visitor who was not actually in rags was "your lordship" to the attendants at Tunbridge Wells.

"Um-m, perhaps."

Part of his reason for coming to the Wells was personal: he had heard so much about the place. The rest of the reason made more sense. Tunbridge was fashionable; and fashionable people, he had observed, do not look at one another's faces but at one another's clothes. Among so many rich and titled men, his would be an inconspicuous figure. The resort was off the well-patrolled London-Dover highway, which passed through Gravesend, Rochester, Sittingbourne, Canterbury. Harry the Horsepad was known to operate along the Great North Road and the roads that led out over Hounslow Heath. Nobody would dream of looking for him at Tunbridge Wells.

The life amused Tom. He took walks over the countryside. He visited a barber-surgeon for treatment of his face: "Never hunt on that damn' nag again," he explained gruffly. He strolled along the Parade, watching the watchers watch each other. He browsed among the news sheets in the coffee-houses. He listened . . . Most assiduously he listened.

The chief topic of conversation here, as at less exalted places, was Harry the Horsepad and his miraculous escape. The *valet de chambre*, the waiter who brought Tom his breakfast chocolate, the boots, were rather more than likely at any given time to be whistling, singing, or at least humming a newly-minted ballad that celebrated this event:

> Hark to the tale of Harry!
> Hark to the song I sing!

while at nearby tables their betters discussed it without pause.

A newer and related topic was the reward. This was not one offer, Tom overhead, but half a dozen—from the city of London itself, several coach companies, and the county councils of both Hertford and Buckingham. They added up to six thousand pounds, but every one was differently worded. As soon as Tom had been arrested, there was a perfect scrimmage of claimants—the three Bow Street runners who had done the actual nabbing, the magistrate who had sent them forth, the proprietor of the tavern in which Tom had been seized, the informer who had pointed him out to that proprietor, the jeweller's assistant who had identified the watch taken from Tom's pocket, the draper who had identified the handkerchief, the four robbery victims who had identified Tom himself, and sundry others. Since each had a separate lawyer, and the stakes were high, the squabble had reached dizzying heights—when the prisoner escaped. This made a great change. Each corporation that had made an offer reread that offer, and learned that it contained some manner of "to justice" clause. But—the prisoner had not been brought to justice. Or, more correctly, the sentence that justice had pronounced against him—death—had not been executed. Therefore, many solicitors averred, the reward offers, which in the eyes of the law were a sort of contract, remained inoperative, though not, of course, null. Others said no. Some of the claimants, with a sigh or a curse, dropped their claims. Others continued theirs. But no money had been paid out, despite this disgusting show of greed, this scramble, and it was not likely that any would be. The six thousand pounds' reward, learned lawyers had enunciated, still stood. And it was being advertised. There were notices in all the news sheets; there were handbills in all manner of public places: there was one posted on the wall of the taproom in the very hotel where Tom Savage stopped.

When Tom wasn't listening to talk along these lines, he pondered his own fate. Why had this happened to him—*him,* of all persons?

He had no enemies. It was unthinkable that his cousins had contrived to get him arrested. Even supposing them to be scoundrels, Thomas Savage, what with the remainder of his heritage, was of more value to them alive than dead. Moreover, how could they possibly have known that he resembled Harry Tewkes?

No, the mastermind must have been Tewkes himself. Tewkes

might have been laying plans for a disappearance; and when he saw a strange youth who resembled him, he might have jumped at the chance. It would be cold-blooded almost beyond belief, thus to doom some unknown stranger to humiliation and shameful death; but by all accounts Harry Tewkes *was* cold-blooded. Those robbery victims who took the stand to identify Tom as Harry the Horsepad might have been mistaken—or they might have been bribed. But the handkerchief and watch found in Tom's pockets were stolen property, and they had been placed there by somebody close to Harry Tewkes, conceivably by Tewkes himself.

At first Tom had been furious; then sick, discouraged; but now he laughed. He was at the beginning of a search, for it had been plain from the start that he could only clear himself by somehow finding and exposing Harry Tewkes, and this thought exhilarated him. The languid, pale young man with the scholar's stoop who strolled along the Parade each morning, or took the waters, smiling vaguely when he was addressed by servants or shopkeepers, avoiding others, sometimes snipping a pinch of snuff from Lord Falk's mull, sometimes shifting his tricorn from one arm to the other, in reality, inside, seethed with excitement.

What manner of man was this Harry the Horsepad? A rascal: that went without saying. But there are rascals and rascals, most of 'em stupid, which Harry Tewkes most certainly was not.

One thing at least was sure. Tewkes had shown Tom Savage no mercy, and Tom, when he caught the man, would show none to *him*. This was not a hunt for sport. This was for death.

It is at once provocative and dismaying for a man to learn that another man looks like him. If the other chances to be a notorious thief, it sets up a complicated train of thought. When they noticed him at all, the visitors to Tunbridge Wells took Tom for a remarkably meditative lad. Some of the females twittered that he had been crossed in love. The men, by and large, sniffed. Tom was mannered, and his mien was mild.

Some described him, in whispers, as "mysterious." After all, these canaries didn't have much to cheep about.

There is a hunter in each of us. Tom had been a fair fowler, but his position in Lincolnshire had not required him to join any chase. He could even feel sorry for a fox, and faintly disgusted with the pink-coated yoicks-yellers who from time to time desecrated the countryside. Yet now he found himself all but choked with desire to run a certain man to earth. A *man*, not a fox.

"Damn him!" slapping the table.

"My lord?"

"Oh . . . Will you bring more coffee, please?"

"Surely, my lord."

The way to get Harry Tewkes would be to go to his own lairs and hideaways. Your roadpad was by all accounts, off duty, a spendthrift. He threw away his loot. Sponges, whores, pimps, innkeepers, all who snapped up coins as soon as they were thrown down, clustered around him. It was thus that he was caught, nine times out of ten. But Tewkes did not seem to be one of this kind. He was astute. Brutal in his work, he could be subtle in his private life. For all the stories and ballads, nobody knew much about Harry the Horsepad.

Yet he must live *somewhere*. He must eat, drink, relieve his feelings. It stood to reason that when a group of men went to the trouble and risk of rescuing a convicted felon on his way to the scaffold, that felon at least had associates. You chance your neck, as those men had done, for love or for booty. It was not likely to be love. Harry Tewkes, wherever he was, held a secret. It must be a stupendous secret.

What was it?

Tom Savage bought a new coat, and counted his money.

He could loaf no longer. He must make up his mind. The weather was good, there was often sun; and he was well attended at Tunbridge Wells, for he tipped handsomely; and well fed and bedded. His face was better, his limbs strong. He must go to work. He sighed.

"Evans? La, Fletcher'll never get her here!"

"Seares?"

"Seares be damned, my love."

"Your language, sir!"

"I still say Lord Seares be damned. Why should she leave London when she crams the theater each night? My eyes, she's the finest Polly P. since Woffington climbed back into bed with her manager."

Tom Savage sipped sherry, pretending that he hadn't heard.

"Wallace," the lady sneaped, "it comes to me that you are in love with Molly Evans yourself!"

"Darling, it comes to me that every man who has ever seen her is."

Tom paid his chit and sauntered off. Even before this talk, he had been thinking of the woman in the gang, the one who snapped the pistol at him. He still had that small silver pistol.

Undoubtedly she was Tewkes's property. Why else should she have done a part in the great rescue? He remembered her eyes mostly, but also the delicate curve of her chin, the over-high but rich, round forehead she had—and her hands. "My name is Molly Evans, if that means anything to you." It hadn't then. It did now.

The way to a murderer is through his mistress. This was the oldest adage in the annals of man-seeking. Yet—women are unpredictable. At another time Thomas Savage would gladly have sought out Molly Evans. The way things were, he decided to hold that card at the back of his hand.

The air was balmy. The peacocks who strutted in their samite and fine silk, in their rose point, twittered and chattered of fashionable things. Tunbridge Wells did well for itself, a sedate place.

But Tom had work. He must find a man. He told his landlord that he was leaving.

"I regret that, my lord."

"Y'know, so do I!"

His plan so far had failed. He assumed that Harry Tewkes,

learning that the scene at Tyburn was not fulfilled, would curse —and hold up another coach. No such word came. Tewkes was lying low. He would create no clue.

"The quarterly's at ten, my lord. Or would you prefer to ride post?"

"What would a nag cost?"

"Two guineas, without the deposit. But—if your lordship will permit me, my house can stand the deposit. Of course I trust you."

"Of course," absently. "Thank you. Yes, I'll ride post."

Tunbridge Wells had been expensive. There was left in his purse, when he got up to London and turned the post horse in, exactly four pounds, nine and three. He bought some Danish snuff. Then (having decided upon a course of action) he bought two long, brass-barrelled pistols.

7 IN THE DARK OF THE NIGHT

THE COBBLES GLEAMED BALEFULLY. FOG STREAMERS WRITHED. Somewhere a mongrel, beguiled by the bleakness of the sky, bayed a moon that wasn't there. It was a night when almost anything might happen.

Moving in and out of the stables, each with a lighted lantern, the ostlers looked like galvanic, misshapen, hunched, malicious gnomes, toilers in some dread nether region, congregated, it could be, on the shore of the River Styx, though it must be admitted that the London-Bath coach they readied—bright, wet, polished ash, with a dark-brown leather top and steel-plated fittings—in no way suggested Charon's ferry; and the voices from the taproom were cheery enough, in all conscience, even if the words were not ones a lady should listen to.

The schedule called for the coach to reach Slough on the far side of Hounslow Heath, the west side, before sundown; but a series of unlooked-for mishaps had put off the start, and now it was clear that much of the night would be spent on the heath, a wasteland beloved of brigands. This prospect accounted for the air of hush about the Black Swan in Holborn (the men in the taproom were local). However, it did not faze the old woman with the brown mustache. *She* dipped her eagle's beak into her mug, afterward slamming the stein to the table and leaning back with the snort of a dragon.

"Gawd love us, lad, there's nothing to be afraid of! This man Tewkes? Awr, I'll bash his face in if he shows it!"

Tom chuckled.

"I'll wager you would too, granny."

He stared out the window at his side, his regard directed toward a horse. And what a horse! It was tall, strong, a stallion, glossily handsome in the light from the inn, motionless, an unrelieved shiny black, though in truth it had not been well curried. It would be fast. Tom Savage, who knew something about horses, knew that. Tom also believed that it had a great heart. He did not fall in love with it, but he felt pleasure well up within him when he looked at it, and felt some pain at the same time, for *this* was what he really needed.

He had the sword, the wig, the pistols, yes. He even had lead and powder for the pistols, and a bag to carry them in. But what was a highwayman without a horse? Clumsy, a tyro, Tom had not made arrangements for this. He had paid for his lodging of last night, as for his dinner of a little while ago. He could pay for the beer before him, having enough left to get him a seat in the Bath coach, at least as far as Slough. But he did not have enough, or anywhere near enough, to buy a horse. Nor, lacking the deposit, could he hire one.

Was Harry the Horsepad to degenerate into Harry the *Foot*pad? It was unthinkable. Footpads were the lowest of the low, and easily caught. Tom Savage's opening crime, the robbery of Lord Falk, had been prompted by desperation. To keep up such behavior would be shameful, foolish as well, what with the Fieldings and their announced policy of "quick report and hot pursuit" within the municipal limits. Such robberies, even when the yellow cockade and the purple mask were worn, even if the big brass pistols were used, would do nothing to stir the ire or provoke the curiosity of the real Harry Tewkes, causing him, perhaps, to show himself. Tewkes might never even hear of them. And Tewkes was the man in all this world that Tom Savage was thinking of. After all, Tom had no intention of embarking upon a road agent's career simply for the fun of it. He doubted, indeed, if there *was* any fun in it. The meeting with the old woman from Bath, the woman with the brown mustache, had been fortuitous.

She was small, swart, scrawny, all knobs. Now she laid a hand, a talon, rather, on his arm, leaning close. Her fingernails were fecaloid, her breath acrid; but there was a twinkle in her eye.

"Awr, come along, lad," she urged. " 'Tis a drear ride in the night, and I need company."

"There will be others."

"And who? Fat arses, all of 'em. Bags of wind. Lookee, lad, if you'll come along with us I'll keep you entertained."

"That I don't doubt!"

"I'll tell you the story of how I got rid of my husband."

"Which one?"

A hulking, dark, beetle-browed newcomer to the innyard was saddling the black stallion, cursing it as he did so, sometimes angrily slapping a flank. He pulled the girth cruelly tight. Before he mounted, he yanked the reins so hard—and for no reason—that the beast's mouth must have been badly torn.

"What're young fellows made of these days, eh? that they're afraid of tobymen on the heath? Lookee, 'twill be plain safe. See that man out there? That's Black Nat, the pugilist. He'll ride along with us, and he'll poke into every bush before we come to it."

"Oh?" said Tom. "Black Nat, eh?"

"The coaching company hires him."

"I see." Tom finished his beer, beckoning to the drawer for the chit. "You know, granny, now that you've pointed out that it's perfectly safe, I do believe I'll risk it."

The ride was indescribably dull, hour after hour of rumble, mile after mile of bump. The hooves squodged in the mud, and the wheels, squealing, dribbled the gluelike stuff from the rims. It was cold in the coach, yet the air was close, smelling of human flesh, of dirt.

"These people," Tom Savage thought, "should be glad to be held up. It will break the monotony."

There were six of them. The talk at first was all about where to hide various valuables, and particularly coins, and Tom was deferred to several times, his advice being asked. Gravely he approved each hiding place, and gravely he assured his fellow passengers, again and again, that all he kept in his own purse—and he would open it to show them—were two copper pennies. The implication was that these coins were for show purposes, while many more were artfully concealed upon his person. The truth was that they were all he had.

The old woman from Bath, the woman with the brown mustache, was as good as her word, and her narrative of how she'd got rid of her husband Tom found uproariously funny, though the other four passengers, somewhat shocked by the woman's language, did not laugh. But in time this ended, and the old woman, weary, bleary, let her head rest on Tom Savage's shoulder, and from this position soon began to snore. It was a wheezy sound, that snore, filling the coach. The others too slept, or tried to sleep.

Tom, jouncing, sat looking out of a window. There was little to see—the dark suburbs, now and then a skulking gang of ruffians, and mud—but the behavior of Black Nat interested him.

The guard stayed close to the coach as long as it was in the city, but once the open country had been reached, he rode ahead, seeming to pay little attention to his charge.

Hounslow Heath might have been designed for highwaymen. It was dark, rocky, splotched by thickets and hummocks, stippled with small groves or stands of trees. At a glance, desert-flat; in fact, it soon was seen to be rolling, so that the horizon never was far away: a well-mounted horseman could have appeared or disappeared very swiftly. There was no moon to-night. The road, parsimoniously marked with milestones, in places could scarcely be made out.

Nevertheless Black Nat did not appear apprehensive as he

rode into thicket after thicket. He was casual, scornful. He did not draw his pistols, and his hanger remained scabbarded by his side. He searched the thickets in a perfunctory manner, for he must have believed that his mere presence would dispel all danger.

At the village of Hounslow itself, on the eastern edge of the heath, they dropped a bag of mail but did not stop. The inn was dark, its proprietor no doubt having assumed that the coach would not travel at night.

"Might at least've given us a chance to go to the jakes," a passenger, half-asleep, mumbled.

This is what gave Tom Savage his plan of action.

He endured the drabness of the heath for a long time, perhaps an hour, saying nothing, moving but little. He did work loose from under the seat the bag that contained his pistols, a flask of powder, lead, a bullet mould; but he didn't open this, only sat with it resting quietly in his lap.

The old woman from Bath snored on. The wheels made a sucking sound.

At last, Tom reached out of the window and rapped the driver's elbow. There was nobody up there with the driver, only luggage. Black Nat had just finished inspecting a thicket a few hundred feet ahead.

The driver stopped, grunting.

"All right. But be quick about it."

"I'll be quick," said Tom Savage, disengaging himself from the old woman from Bath.

She blubbered something, and her snores ceased. She half opened her eyes.

"Where are you—oh!"

"Yes," he said.

"Well, don't jar me, or I'll have to go too. And it's cold out there."

Tom nipped into the thicket, having noticed that Black Nat, who had heard the coach stop, was riding slowly back to it.

Tom took off his hat and mounted the yellow cockade. He

fastened the purple silk handkerchief over his face. He took out the pistols. He thrust one beneath his waistcoat, and as he stepped back into the road, he raised and cocked the other, pointing it at Black Nat.

"You! Get off the horse!"

He opened the door of the coach. He drew and cocked the second pistol.

"All of you! Come out and be robbed!"

Then to the old woman from Bath, in a undertone meant to soothe: "Never mind, granny. Remember what Seneca said: *'Non decipitur qui scit se decipi.'* "

She cried: "Well, I'll be buggered!"

8 RIDE FAST, RIDE FARTHER!

HE WAS TO LEARN THAT HIS FEARS WERE WELL FOUNDED. HIGH-way robbery in England in the year 1755 *was* dull—for the highwayman.

At the same time, it was dangerous. It racked the nerves.

He came to see why the pattern for a highwayman was un-varying. The fool spent a few weeks on the road, then a few days in London, where he lived riotously. If not peached upon, as more often than not he was, he then spent a few more weeks on the road, living a life likely to erode the hardiest. Then, again, he scurried for the fleshpots. Sooner or later it was there, in London, that the highwayman was caught, as all thieves are caught. Thus Jack Sheppard had had his Edgware Bess, Jonathan Wild his Anne Cook, and in the play, Captain Macheath his Lucy Lockit, not to mention a tavernful of bawds, each with deceit in her soul, each a would-be Delilah.

Harry Tewkes: did he have his Molly Evans? Or was he the one, and the only one, with power to keep to himself?

But, *could* a highwayman keep to himself? On the road, yes. Yet it was not possible to stay on the road all the time, no matter how good the pickings. You can't eat a gold watch. You can't throw a bracelet across your shoulders and keep off the rain.

Harry Tewkes had been known as a grabber. For all his flamboyance, he never, with a gallant bow, gave back some trinket when a woman wept. He never gave back anything, as he never overlooked anything. Tom, though he strove to live up to this glittering name, could not go along with an absent master in the matter of gauds, nor in that of brutality either. Tom saw no reason to punch a helpless man's mouth or twist his arm, in order to gain a name. He never forced a ring off a woman's finger. Indeed, he tried to look the other way when any victim, male or female, strove to hide some piece of jewelry. This was not always easy to do, and in spite of himself, Tom began to accumulate these articles. He didn't like it. Money was one thing; money was impersonal. Its value was fixed. But jewelry, though sometimes no more than show, often had attached to it memories more valuable than its worth. It was bad enough to be stealing cash; he didn't wish to steal sentimental reflections as well. He felt like a snake whenever, in the course of work, he was obliged to lift some piece of ornamentation.

What to do with these things? If he was seized and searched, any one of them would hang him. To throw them away would have been unnatural—and dishonest. It would have gone against the grain. They were lovely in themselves, and it was not right that they should end in a duckpond.

He might *give* them away, a bit by a bit, among the drawers, waiters, valets, chambermaids, at the inns that collectively constituted his "home" these days, asking, in return, information about other transients—whether they carried guns, where they hid their coins, what time in the morning they would leave, what road they planned to travel. The world knew that this was the way the common highwayman operated. But Harry Tewkes had not been a common highwayman. Even if Tom had been willing to admit others into his secret, revealing his identity to persons of low life and unknown antecedents, how could he trust them? Rewards totalling more than six thousand pounds had been posted for Harry Tewkes, dead or alive, as Tom was reminded a dozen times a day, seeing the posters at every crossroads, in every taproom and the entrance hall of every inn. Would a person who, with a twenty-shilling necklace could be bribed into spying for an outlaw, boggle at betrayal when a prize like that was dangled before his eyes?

So, along with the paper he kept in his purse—a paper intelligible only to him—which kept count of the coaches he had held up and the passengers, Tom retained the *bijouterie* in his wallet, which every night grew heavier. Grimly he told himself that in time it, like the money he had taken, would all go back to its owners—if the law didn't get him first.

In this, then, he departed from the pattern set by his enemy. In most other matters he conformed to that pattern—a good one. He did not scorn the appurtenances of his trade—the cockade, the purple mask; while the brass pistols, though awkward to carry about, and unsafe when loaded, by their very size and brightness struck awe into the heart of the beholder. Tom did not invest in a flowing cape such as Harry by tradition wore, for with summer coming, this would have been outlandish; but he did have a black stallion. This was by chance, not design. Though he listened attentively that first night on Hounslow Heath, he had not heard Black Nat give the beast a name. Perhaps Nat, no lover of horseflesh, didn't *know* the name, had not asked it. Tom picked Erebus. The black horse proved to be powerful and fast, delighting his new owner. Not until several night later did Tom learn, from taproom chatter, that Harry the Horsepad was reputed always to ride a crow-black stallion—called Erebus!

It was convenient, this coincidence. It was also, when he thought it over, somewhat eerie. Tom Savage was not a superstitious man, but he couldn't help wondering if something more than chance was at work here.

Where *was* Harry Tewkes? Why didn't he show himself? He had been challenged, and stingingly. Wouldn't he reappear?

The Latin tags were Tom's own contribution to the Tewkes *mythos*, an amusing if not significant one. It was an unexpected one as well. Tom was not a man to lapse into another language in the hope that his hearer would be impressed. He had learned the dead tongues almost as early, and knew them almost as well, as his native English, and much better than he would ever know French. Had he cared to, no doubt he could have thought in either Greek or Latin.

That night of his first coach robbery he had, in a moment of playfulness toward the old woman from Bath, quoted Seneca. At least, he had *thought* it was Seneca; he had *said* it was. The effect, as he learned the very next day by means of an overheard conversation—he himself seldom entered into casual off-duty talk with anybody—was another facet uncovered in the legend of Harry the Horsepad, who, previously called the black sheep of an earl, now was accepted as a mad professor, a renegade from Oxford. Since it so obviously made people happy, Tom tried to remember, every time he held up a coach, to quote a little Ovid here, a bit of Horace there. "I never asked for this part, but since I have it I'll play it in my own way," he had told the keeper at Newgate. It was like that now. He had his public, come-willy, come-nilly. Dutiful despite himself, he gave it what it asked.

The English might have been disgusted with an everyday academic snob. An academic snob who happened also to be a highwayman delighted them.

The work was arduous. He had to be out in all sorts of weather, and he had to keep moving. Always his eyes had to be open, his senses alert, which in itself wore a man down; but his muscles, too, ached, and at first he suffered from saddle sores. The strain of being forever on the watch for law officers told, not in his hands as might have been the case with many men, but in his eyes, which throbbed and reddened more than they ever had when he had burned midnight oil at the Sorbonne. He would not start at a sudden sound, but his eyes twitched.

It would tell soon, he knew, on his stomach, too, until now a sturdy one. He couldn't even eat in peace. He was careful, of course, to sit with his back to the wall and one eye on the door. Many inns served beer in pewter steins with large glass bases, a survival of the days of the cavaliers, who might have to spring to their feet, drawing at an instant, and who wished to watch the tavern door even as they drank. Tom Savage was told this quaint tale and thought it might even be true, but his own experiments showed him the glass-bottomed steins were ineffective. No matter how careful he was, there was always an instant of blindness—an instant he could not afford. The glass misted. Fortunately he was not overfond of beer, anyway, preferring a light dry wine. He could always look over the top of a wine-glass. But he made it a rule to smile and murmur "How picturesque!" when a waiter told him the purpose of those glass-bottomed steins.

His speech with servants was friendly but guarded, and he stayed away from other travellers, at the same time striving not to seem standoffish, lest this too bring attention upon him. He might smile vaguely when addressed, but his answers, when he answered at all, were brief.

His work was dangerous, though not in the sense that a layman might have supposed. Nine times out of ten the act itself, the holdup, was absurdly easy. After the waiting, it was even a relief. A harsh command and those pistols were all that was needed. The women, by and large, took it better than their male companions, and often used to shrill at him, slanging him; now and then one tried to flirt with him. The men seldom even cursed. Tom would make them march back and forth before the horses. He could tell, in this way, when a man had coins concealed in his boots. It was amazing how many of them had.

No, the danger came at other times. It lay in his all-but-uncontrollable desire to rush up to a stranger, anybody, and talk, confess. He was so lonesome that he feared he might go mad.

In Lincoln it would have struck them as odd that Tom Savage had ever felt lonesome. Tom, who always had his nose in a book, they remembered as a self-sufficient lad, uninterested in the world around him. Others might have thought of him that way in Oxford too, and in Paris.

But to be by oneself in the midst of fellow students, and to be by oneself in the midst of potential enemies who wonder who you are—these are quite different. The divine Homer, Thucydides, Herodotus, Plato, were incomparable companions. But only in remembrance! Though he might quote them by the hour, riding alone, Tom no longer felt their presence when he couldn't scan their words. He simply didn't have time to read. Besides, he could not have concentrated. His eyes hurt.

This is why he pined; and the days, and even more the nights, were unconscionably long.

"May I fill your glass, sir?"

"Thank you. Won't you join me for a moment?"

The landlord consented, sitting opposite. This was near Ipswich, in Suffolk, a vicinity Tom Savage had not previously visited. Nevertheless, he faced the door.

It was customary in the better inns at mealtime for the host to pick out single men and offer to make talk with them. It was customary too, when this offer was accepted, to buy the host a drink. Tom was reserved on these occasions, though polite, for the managers of inns in England, he quickly perceived, were honest, earnest men. They were on the side of the law, and being shrewd judges of character, were best avoided by such as he.

A man whom it pains to smile, say the Chinese, should not open a shop. Even the popular name of your inn proprietor, "boniface," suggested this. But beaming could be overdone. For the most part, the boniface was a calculator with an even temper and a long memory; but some, too successful, were so filled with their own majesty that they couldn't have summoned a smile for anybody lower than a duke; while others smirked altogether too much.

This man tonight in Ipswich was one of the last. New in the profession, Tom Savage surmised.

Tom raised a ceremonious glass.

"Confusion to all roadpads," he murmured.

"By God, sir, now I'll gladly drink to that!"

A little later Tom said: "It's a curious thing, mine host. I have lived in France much of my adult life, and I can't help noticing that here in my own England we have wonderful inns."

"The best in the world," smugly.

"Doubtless. And so *safe*! Highwaymen roam the land, but they must sleep somewhere. They must get their information about coach movements somewhere. But—where? You never see one at an inn."

"Are you quite sure that you'd know one if you *did* see him, your honor?"

""Um . . . There's something in that."

"And as for English inns being safe, why, that's the law."

"Oh?"

"We are responsible for our guests, and their goods too. We proprietors. Let somebody steal from you, sir, *as long as you are under this roof,* and I have to pay it out of my own purse."

"Is that so? I hadn't known that."

"So you can see why we're careful about whom we hire."

"Yes. But once a traveller has left—"

"Oh, then he's on his own. What happens to him after that is the sheriff's affair, not mine. When they're robbed they can sue the county. And they will!"

"The county has to pay, eh?"

"Unless the crime has been committed on a Sunday. The theory is that folks who travel on Sundays deserve what they get."

Tom sat up, interested.

"Then there's a record kept of how much is stolen?"

"Of *more* than was stolen, most times. A man loses five pounds, he puts in he lost eight. That's why so many claims are thrown out. And *that's* why the coach companies themselves get sued, so they've got to take out insurance to cover their investment. But it's all a matter of record, yes."

"I see."

This made Tom Savage feel better. He was keeping tabs on

his own robberies, which were neither as many, nor anywhere near as profitable, as popular rumor painted them; but he would be glad to have figures to check against when the time for repayment came.

"All the same," the proprietor went on, "I can't help thinking that men like Harry Tewkes are bad for business."

"Yes. Um, I could see where they would be. But," as though by afterthought, "you're not worried about Harry the Horsepad out here? I understood he only rode north and west of London?"

The boniface harrumphed, leaning close.

"I don't look to scare you, sir, but I have reason to believe that Harry Tewkes is in this inn, right this minute."

"*Eh?*"

"There's a tall black horse in the stables, a stallion. Brought there this afternoon. The ostlers ain't sure who owns it. But somebody will call for it in the morning, and he'll be nabbed."

"You recognize—a horse?"

"*I* didn't, no. But there was a coachman went through an hour and a half ago, and *he* did. He used to drive on the London-Bath run, and he swears this is the very horse Harry Tewkes stole from a bullyboy three weeks ago out on Hounslow Heath. This driver will be ready to identify him next time he comes to Ipswich, day after tomorrow. Meanwhile, we'll hold onto him."

"I see. Well, good luck."

Tom finished dinner and went to the stables.

"Saddle me, lad. Sorry to bother you at an hour like this, but I'd visit a friend who lives up the London road."

"Certainly, sir. Let's see . . . Which was yours, again?"

"This one," said Tom, touching a dark brown mare.

At the far end of the stalls he could see Erebus; but he turned away quickly.

"Certainly, sir. Half a mo'."

Tom Savage did not ride to the home of any friend. He did

not have any friend. He rode instead, right for London. And he rode all night.

It was time to get rid of those trinkets. It was time, too, to have a long, searching talk with the actress known as Molly Evans.

9 STEP RIGHT UP AND GET MARRIED!

HAVING DINED ON KIDNEY PIE, TURNIPS, AND SPITCHCOCKED EELS, plus a memorable hock, he sallied forth to see the city. There would be two hours before the coming of darkness, a full three before the rise of the curtain at what was officially known as the Queen's Theatre, more generally, the Haymarket.

Tom Savage did not know London intimately, and didn't think he liked it; but tonight, well fed, well turned out, he was happy. He had spent four days in this great sprawling city five years ago, while on his way from Oxford to Paris. His second look had been no more than that many hours, delayed as it was by the rough Channel and interrupted so cruelly by his arrest.

His opinion of London, thus far, was unflattering. He saw it as a sea of reaching arms, convulsive palms, greedy eyes. London whined. It was filled with men who whispered in doorways, looking sideways at you as you passed, and with women who leered from under lowered blinds. The prices were outrageous. Everybody was trying to get what he could, by whatever means, as quickly as possible. Londoners might snigger, and most assuredly they might sneer, but you seldom heard there a good, clean, loud, healthy laugh. A giggle, yes; but rarely a guffaw. London was not a carefree place. It was dirty, and it was loud; mean-tempered, too. Worst of all, it appeared to distrust the whole world, itself included. You should beware turning your back upon anybody in London. You should never put anything down, unless you kept a hand over it. Why, even the street-walkers dragged their heels, slouching, and their solicitations held no hope of joy, but sounded instead like the wheedling of a leper with a can. In Paris, Tom had noted, the streetwalkers looked as though they loved their work. In London, they looked as though they'd been driven to it.

Nevertheless, he was light of heart when he set forth that afternoon. His coat was brushed, his wig freshly powdered, and his sword, like his boots, had been polished. Life, just at that moment, was his oyster. He had left in his bedchamber not only a wallet heavy with bracelets and brooches and watches and rings, but also the huge brass pistols, veritable cannons, that he had come to think of as symbolic of his profession, a hated one. In addition, he was wearing a satin embroidered waistcoat he had purchased soon after his arrival in the city. There is nothing like an embroidered waistcoat to raise a man's spirit.

So it is not to be wondered at that his step was gay. He was as far as ever from learning the whereabouts of the true Harry Tewkes. But he hummed a light air, strutting, making his sword stick high behind him.

In one lower pocket of the waistcoat was a small silver pistol. In the other was a ticket of admission to the Queen's Theatre for tonight's performance of *The Beggar's Opera*. It was a ticket of admission to disillusionment as well, he believed. This he'd welcome. He had been thinking too much about Molly Evans' lovely face. He required a clear mind for the problem at hand. This was no time for infatuation with anybody, least of all a play-actress, the doxie of a thief. He had been carried away by the circumstances in which he'd previously seen her. If he was to do business with her, he must first learn to think of her hard-headedly, not like a romantic fool. Tonight would do the trick. When he saw her, her face painted, wriggling back and forth across a stage while she pretended to be unaware

53

of the whistles of the lascivious, striving to fill the role in which Tom Savage had once seen the incomparable if aging Peg Woffington—*then* he would be in a better emotional condition to make a deal.

For *The Beggar's Opera*—not an opera at all in the Italian sense of the word, but a farce with street ditties—would not be new to Thomas Savage, who had seen it in this same theater five years before. Indeed, was it new to anybody? Since its first presentation, when Lavinia Fenton as the original Polly had captured the heart and, soon afterward, the hand of the Duke of Bolton, it had been revived time after time. Every leading lady yearned to be Polly Peachum, as every leading man dreamed of himself as Hamlet. *The Beggar's Opera* always filled the house, though it had been done by companies of amateurs, dwarfs, Negroes. Everybody whistled it, everybody quoted it. Scenes from it were painted on porcelain and on ladies' fine fans. Tom Savage could not see why. The topical quips that had convulsed Londoners a quarter-century ago, and especially the quarrel between Peachum and Lockit—supposed to be almost a word-for-word transcription of a spat between Walpole and Lord Townshend—today were meaningless. Tom had gone to see not the play itself but Peg Woffington, called the most beautiful woman in the history of the English stage. He had fallen in love with her, as any young man might. Molly Evans, so skinny and small, so pale, could only be preposterous if she tried to follow in those footsteps. Tom looked forward avidly to a crashing disappointment.

He did not fear recognition. He had learned something of the way men identify, or fail to identify, their fellows. Not one in a hundred, unless he had been specially trained, could pick out the same face twice from among others. He might *think* that he could; it might well be that all four of those men who, in the Old Bailey, had solemnly sworn that the prisoner in the dock was the one who had robbed them, sincerely believed that. Three times, at inns north of London, Tom Savage had stared at persons to whom he'd been wont to bow a few weeks earlier on the Parade at Tunbridge Wells. Never had there been a flicker of recognition. Yet if it had been *suggested* to those persons that they knew Tom, doubtless they would concur. Thousands had looked, *hard, eagerly,* upon him, all unwigged too, when he was being taken from Newgate toward Tyburn Hill. It was likely that he was strolling past some of those persons at this very minute. Did they cry out? No. For who would expect to see Harry the Horsepad in the heart of London?

When people in London looked at you, he reasoned, it was not to make out who you were but merely to estimate how much they might get from you. He was untroubled. If he did not go to Newgate, it was only because he had no wish to see that place again. He did go to the Fleet—but for a different reason.

At the time of Tom's first visit to London, the environs of this most celebrated of debtors' prisons—the "liberty," as it was called, where trusties could go, reporting back to the prison proper only at night—had been one of the sights no visitor would miss. There were sure to be at least a few clergymen confined to the Fleet, and these were understandably concerned, as were all their fellow prisoners, with getting out. That took money. Sermons would bring them no silver; but marriages might. They were still priests of the Established Church, even though in jail for debt. Touts and bullyboys got hold of such clergymen—or it might have been the other way around—and soon "chapels" sprang up in nearby taverns. There were even signs: Cheap Wedlock, Bargain Marriages, Be Joined Here. The touts made speeches, barking hesitant couples in. They grabbed them, pushed them. You could be united for ten shillings, for five—damn it, for a bottle of gin! This was a rowdy neighborhood.

While a large part of the crowd might be made up of sight-seers, the morbidly curious, there were always others who wavered. Some only watched, but many went in. At one time, Tom had been told, those who controlled this business boasted that they were marrying between four and five hundred couples a month. That meant lucre.

Not all of the marriages were legal. For an extra fee, the clergyman would sometimes refrain from recording the ceremony, so that the "husband," after a few nights or a few weeks, could safely decamp.

Another class of female had profited. The law said that a married woman could not be imprisoned for debt: her husband, even though he couldn't be found, was responsible for her obligations. When, then, a widow or maiden was threatened with jail, she could hie herself to the marriage mill of Fleet Market and, for a trifling sum, perhaps the price of two drinks, command the services of a bridegroom called in from a street corner. Of course the "groom" gave a false name, and the marriage contract would then—for another small extra fee—be predated. And the woman could tell her accusers that she had been married all the while. Her husband had left her. Could she help that? One man, a casual acquaintance, told Tom Savage that he'd been married more than thirty times in this fashion, five times in one afternoon alone. He had never mentioned this to his wife, he added.

But things were different in the neighborhood of the Fleet now. There were no Marriages Cheap signs, no importunate touts. Nobody jostled vacillating couples into sawdust-strewn groggeries where "church" decorations had been reared. No trembling, hiccupping, red-eyed priests peered timorously but hopefully into the street. No coarse-mouthed louts accosted every unattached woman, asking her if she sought a husband— on paper.

A single loafer loafed there, and he looked disgusted.

"Damn me," cried Tom, "where's everybody gone to?"

"Your worship?"

"The marriage mill!"

"Oh. That's ended. Last year. You must've been away?"

"I was. How did it end?"

"A law. Them bastards in Parliament. They call it a Candle-Seed Marriage law. Something like that."

"Clandestine Marriages Law?"

"Aye. That's it. The bastards. A marriage can't be legal now, not unless it takes place in a real church. Takin' the food right out of our mouths, the bastards."

"And the liquor too, eh?"

"Aye. You call that fair, sir? Was we bashing anybody's face? Fact is, there's many a man, and many a woman too, what blessed us for what we done. Aye, got down on their knees and blessed us!"

"I can believe it."

"And the padres too. How many of them d'ye suppose we set free from this place?" He jerked a contemptuous head to mark the prison behind him. "Why, at one time there they was getting out faster'n new ones could come in. We had to pay 'em less, so's to keep 'em longer. We couldn't let our public down, now could we?"

"Of course not."

"And they spoil it all with this bloody Candle-Seed Act. The bastards. Makes me thirsty just to think on it . . . Oh! Thankee, your worship! Thankee very much! . . . I will, I'll do that, I'll drink to your great good health, Gawd bless ye!"

That was one disappointment, if a minor one. At least it had served to pass an hour at dusk. When a little later, after dark, he settled into a seat in the Queen's Theatre, and the music died, and the men with the long snuffers were moving from sconce to sconce, and the curtain started to go up—then, Tom Savage told himself with a chuckle, he was about to be *truly* disappointed.

He was never more mistaken in his life.

10 *SING THEIR HEARTS AWAY*

THE SONGS IN THE BEGGAR'S OPERA HAD NOT BEEN WRITTEN FOR it, but were merely populars airs of the time, most of them still hummed and whistled—"O Jenny, O Jenny," "Lillibullero," "Over the Hills and Far Away," and suchlike. They were homey in their lilt, and whenever one of the first three performers sang, he was accompanied by his hearers, who hummed or whistled, or else rhythmically slapped their hands upon their knees. Each of these, too, had been greeted at his entrance with cheers and whistles. They were old friends. The audience was fond of them.

It was not like this when Molly Evans came on.

Then the house was hushed. Each man, and many of the women as well, gave her all they had—silence—a tribute much more touching than thunderous applause. When she had finished her first aria—

> Virgins are like the fair flower in its lustre,
> Which in the garden enamels the ground;

—the applause, though frenzied, was brief, chopped off, as though they feared to miss a single word of the speech that would follow.

In truth, Molly Evans didn't have a great voice, or even a very good one. Melodious enough in the middle register, it became reedy and uncertain as it rose. Nor was it strong: it would not have filled the hall, save for that jealously maintained silence. She would be hooted off the stage in Paris, where they took their music seriously.

Or would she? Perhaps what she had, whatever it was, held a universal appeal. Perhaps she would have been adored wherever she went, even if her audience did not understand the language.

She was lovely in apricot and green, a pert lace cap on her head, her panniered hips daintily swinging as she moved about; but she was no Peg Woffington. From where he sat, Tom Savage could not make out the brilliance of her finest feature, those large, soft, amethystine eyes. The face looked even more sharply triangular than it had when he first saw it in that Lincoln's Inn Fields window. On the other hand, the hair now was glorious, a glowing rich brown, wavy, soft, touched at times with specklets of red, as though the light of a fireplace played upon it.

She made them all love her. What more could any actress ask?

It must have been her *helplessness*. Small—though every inch a woman, no gangling girl!—she had about her an air of unfathomable sadness. It was impossible not to feel sorry for her, not to wish to protect her. She didn't play up to this; she did not shed a tear that wasn't called for in the part; but simply by *being, existing*, she was femininity entoiled, and every man's heart went out.

A competent, even a gifted actress, she knew the nature of the hold she had, and she didn't overdo it. Indeed, there was no call for her to blubber. Only let her pull down the corners of her mouth a mite as she prepared to sing—

> Can love be controll'd by advice?
> Will Cupid our mothers obey?

—and she had every man on her side. The audience was predominantly male. When the parents raged and stormed at her for having secretly married the highwayman, Captain Macheath, they were not hissed—

that would have been too intimate—but they were soundlessly, passionately hated.

It was at this agonizing instant of the play that Tom Savage's right-hand neighbor, a lumbrous, lugubrious, guts-rumbling, overdressed milord who had arrived late and sat on the aisle, elected to stretch his legs. One of his knees butted Tom Savage, who was in no mood to be jarred, howsoever slightly. With exasperated impatience, Tom, never taking his gaze from Molly Evans, knocked the knee back as he might have brushed away a fly.

"See here, sir, that happens to be my limb!"

"Then why was it trying to climb into my lap?"

Not for a flicker had Tom turned his head. He heard a bearlike grunt, and sensed rather than saw that the other was about to say something further. He slapped a finger to his mouth.

"*Sh-sh-sh,* you oaf!"

There was a scuffle, a clatter of shoes, and the overfed one stamped up the aisle, puffing like a porpoise the while. This was all to the good, it would have been generally agreed among Tom Savage and his male neighbors, for the ineffable Molly was about to launch into the song that so plaintively ends:

> But he so teaz'd me,
> And he so pleas'd me,
> What I did you must have done.

At the end of the act they not only clapped, they shouted. The others took their usual bows, but Molly Evans was called before the lowered curtain, alone, six different times. She curtsied seriously, meekly, and with an untiring grace.

Tom's hands were so sore that they tingled when at last he stumbled past the empty seat on his right, and stepped into the aisle.

Though he had meant to make his way to the green room at the end of the performance, he had not planned to go into the foyer between acts. Once again, there was but the slimmest chance that someone would recognize him; but fashionable assemblages made him fidget, and he did not like to be stared at through a quizzing glass. Yet he was much too excited to sit still.

"And *I* have kissed her!" he kept whispering in wonderment.

The foyer was jammed, and everybody walked around and around, each pretending to see no one but his own companion, though in truth their eyes darted indefatigibly, and they kept exchanging, in undertones, snippets of gossip. In this exalted company Tom Savage was neither the brightest nor yet the lowliest. This was as he wished it. He was unribboned, un-ruffled, and he wore no lace; but his apparel, if plain, was good, and he took snuff with a disdainful air.

"And *I* have kissed her!"

Quick as light came an afterthought, black and bitter: "So has Harry Tewkes—and more!"

He looked up sharply, as though pricked. The couples still marched around. When they were turned his way they looked past him. He had not until now thought of searching their blank faces, for he'd assumed that none would be familiar; but he caught himself with a curious, utterly unreasonable convic-tion that he was being watched.

He looked this way and that. He recognized no one; and no one, at least while Tom was looking, stared at him. Yet he still had that feeling—and it made him uneasy.

The bell rang. Couples began to drift back into the audi-torium.

It came to Tom Savage that there was one, at least, whom he might do well to seek here. If Harry Tewkes ever came out of hiding in order to see his beloved at her best, while himself lost in a crowd, here was the place. It was altogether possible that he was in the audience. Tom, of course, could not scrutinize every face.

His shoulder was touched. Edgy as a racehorse, he whirled around.

This young man he was sure he had never before seen. He was tall, and every inch the fop, wearing mulberry silk over a gold-threaded waistcoat. When he talked, it was in a fashionably nasal drawl. Nevertheless, there was no fat upon him, nothing loose, and for all his affected languor, his frosty blue eyes shone hard as adamant.

"Your name, sir?"

"Who the devil wants to know?"

"La, sir, 'tis no more than a mannerly precaution, in the event that a letter should be sent to you."

"What letter?"

"But perhaps we have no need to be so formal, since clearly you prefer bluntness. Very well then. A little while ago, sir, you put an affront upon my uncle, who was sitting next to you."

"Oh . . . the fat one?"

"Lord Sutton weighs less than fourteen stone."

"What of it? What's that got to do with me?"

"My uncle suffers from a foot trouble. He is in no physical condition to, uh, to resent as he'd wish to do the treatment you accorded him."

"Nonsense. All I did was snap back when he prodded me with his knee."

"You cast an affront upon him, and in the presence of a large number of persons."

"None of them," Tom said earnestly, "was listening to *us*."

He glanced in desperation across the foyer, now all but empty. He could see attendants in the auditorium going along the walls with candle-snuffers.

"You have not answered my first question," the tall, elegant young man pointed out.

"Very well. My name is Thomas Savage."

"Esquire, I assume?"

Tom swallowed. Unexpectedly that question hit him in a tender spot. He no longer owned any land. No longer, properly, could he sign himself "Esquire." The thought unsettled him.

"Of course," he lied.

"And your seat, sir?"

"Let it suffice that for the hour I am putting up at the Bull in Half Moon Street. And now if you'll permit me—"

"See here, sir. I take it that you are prepared to give my uncle the satisfaction he so properly demands, through me. But—why should we drag in our friends? I happen to be sober, and I dare say you are too. We have our swords, the park's not far away, it's a moonlit night. Why don't we—"

"And miss the second act?" Tom cried. "Man, you must be mad!"

He made the briefest bow allowed by etiquette, and hurried back to his seat.

The curtain went up.

But Polly Peachum does not appear in that first short scene of Act Two, as Tom in his haste had forgotten. He was straightening himself, scarcely heeding the persons on the stage, when there was a shadow, as of something enormous, and a very large man took the seat on Tom's right, the aisle seat. Just for a moment Tom was glad. He would, in this scene, have an opportunity to apologize to the crusty old codger he'd offended, and so spare everybody trouble on the morrow. He turned.

But it wasn't the overfed Lord Sutton. It was a much larger and less aristocratic figure.

"Oh," said Tom.

"Yes," said Brown Coat. "You and me are going to have a lot to talk about, mister."

11 *ON WITH THE PLAY!*

Depicted on the stage was a tavern near Newgate, a district with which Tom and Brown Coat were familiar. The actors, however, were strangers. Dressed in bright colors, some with eye patches, they sat amid cards and bottles while they hammered the table, minced their lines, scowled, and, in short, behaved like the storybook criminals they were.

It was not like this with the man whose bulk overflowed the seat beside Tom Savage. He was by no means as picturesque as the mummers—Jemmy Twitcher, Mat-o'-the-Mint, Cross-finger'd Jack, and the rest of the gang the other side of the footlights—but he was real. Moreover, he had a fist as hard as any rock: Tom knew that! His name no doubt would prove plain, scarcely calculated to adorn a *dramatis personae,* yet he had no need to growl and grind his teeth, posing as a rogue. He *was* a rogue. Within the sight of hundreds, he had bodily lifted a felon from the hangman's cart, bringing about the most sensational escape in the history of Tyburn Tree.

"What are you doing here?" whispered Tom.

"Looking for *him.* And you?"

"Looking at *her.*"

Brown Coat chuckled.

"That's all she's likely to let you do—look at her—and across the top of them candle-boxes too."

64

"How so? Doesn't she receive in the green room?"

"Not her. Not any more. She has some special contract with the management that says she don't have to receive. And you can't blame her! She's the sweetie of the season. She's being done. Every shrivelled-up old rakehell that wants to stay in fashion toddles around back there with his arms full of jewelry. But he's got two hands too, and he wants to use 'em. Naturally Miss Evans don't like that."

"Naturally. Every gaud has a string on it, no doubt."

"Mister, it's got as many strings as a violin. And anyway, she don't need jewelry, so long as she has Lord Seares."

Tom had heard of this nobleman before. Where? At Tunbridge?

Now there entered, with a flourish, Captain Macheath, Polly Peachum's beloved—sash, sneer, jackboots. He strutted and stamped about up there, the greatest highwayman in that world of make-believe, while a few yards distant, the understudy for the greatest highwayman of the real world fingered his chin, glumly eyeing the man.

"Does Seares know about Harry Tewkes?"

Brown Coat shrugged.

"What they do in bed," he muttered, "don't concern me."

"Why, if she's hooked herself a lord," pursued Tom, "should she be so eager to get Tewkes back?

His companion shrugged again.

"Women," he pointed out, "are a peculiar sex."

It hurt Thomas Savage. He asked himself what in hell he expected a stage actress to do: wasn't she entitled to try to better her station in life, just like anyone else? All the same, it hurt. For some time he was silent, morosely watching Macheath, who soon would kiss her.

"About Tewkes," Brown Coat pursued. "I don't take it that Lord Seares do know about him, no. I can't be sure, but it seems likely Tewkes might come to see the play some night, being still balmy about Miss Evans. He wouldn't dare show himself in the green room—"

"I would!"

"—but he could mix with the crowd out here. But if Seares did know about him, don't you reckon Seares would have that same thought I had when I came here, and he'd speak to somebody in Bow Street, and this theatre would be packed with runners?"

"How do you know it isn't?"

"Mister, it's my business to know a runner when I sees one. And they ain't here tonight, I can tell you that."

"Just what *else* is your business, by the way?"

They talked quietly, in undertones, out of the corners of their mouths, all the while looking at the stage. They might have been any two men who were not deeply interested in what was going on before them, yet had no wish to disturb their neighbors.

"I do a little of everything," Brown Coat answered affably. "I prig, in a push. I spung. Sometimes I even nim. I receive. If I'm offered enough I'll bash a man on the head. But I'm not a file."

"No?"

"No. Never had the training. That takes a lot of training."

"I see. But what is your connection with Harry Tewkes?"

"Mister, that's something I'd like to take up later—when I have the rest of the gang with me."

"You feel you need backing?"

"It ain't that. It's because I want them to hear what I say. They're touchy these days, after what Harry did to us."

"And what did Harry do to you, man?"

"Well, just as we was all arranged to—"

"Sh-sh-sh!"

For Molly Evans had come upon the stage.

This time she wore yellow trimmed with pink, and when she had finished "No power on earth can e'er divide the knot that sacred Love hath ty'd," there was not a dry eye in the house. Even Brown Coat, who for a set sum would bash in a man's head, sniffled.

"Gor, she's lolly," he mumbled.

However, his recovery was quick, and after a while—they were to sit this entr'acte out—Tom became aware that he was speaking.

"—another one of 'em. He'd give all his teeth, even the good ones, if he was so much as allowed to even *meet* her."

"Who's this?"

"Lord Sutton."

"Oh—Fatty?"

"Aye. The one whose seat I got right now. What ever did you say to him?"

"I've forgotten."

"That nephew of his challenge you to a duel?"

"Um, yes."

"You better apologize."

"I intend to. If I can only remember what it was I said."

"From what I hear, that lad's one of the best swordsmen in the kingdom, even when he's drunk, which he usually is."

Stiffly, "That was not why I planned to apologize."

"Of course."

"Now see here—What the devil's your name anyway?"

"Palmer, your worship. Pottsy Palmer they calls me."

"Well, listen, Palmer. You say that Miss Evans wouldn't receive me if I sent my name in to her?"

"No, I didn't say that. I said your name would never *get* in to her. Leastways that's what I meant to say."

"But how will you—Does Miss Evans know you're out here?"

"It was her suggested it. She saw Tewkes here the other night. Spotted him in the audience. But she couldn't stop singing. And then he was gone."

Tom Savage exhaled feelingly. One of his largest worries had been relieved; Harry Tewkes at least had not fled the country.

"Well then, suppose you do see him? How could you let her know?"

"We have a signal. Only for that. Of course I won't tell you what it is."

"Damn it, man, I didn't ask you! Nor will I! But if you can give that signal when you sight Tewkes, why couldn't you give it when you sight me? It comes to much the same thing, doesn't it?"

"Well—"

"I want him just as badly as you do, and she does, though I guess it's for a different reason. And if I see him first—"

"What will you do if you see him first, mister?"

"Kill him."

"No, no! You mustn't do that!"

"Why?"

"I—I'll tell you later. With the other boys. After the play."

The candle-snuffers were going back and forth. The curtain began to rise.

"We've got a reason, believe me, your worship."

"It'd better be a damned good one," said Thomas Savage. "Now shut up. Here she comes."

12 *FROM OUT OF THE JUNGLE—*

A CUP OF CHOCOLATE ON HIS KNEE, HIS HEAD PROPPED WITH pillows, Tom Savage studied the wainscoting of his fine big bedchamber, and reflected upon what a lucky fellow he was, after all. Your traveller in England in the year 1755, once he had come to temporary rest, lived, Tom supposed, as well as any unroyal person on this earth.

London seethed outside, never so noisy as now, in mid-morning; but the sounds came to Tom, as if strained through linen, distorted.

It was at woodwork that he *looked,* but what he *saw* was a ring of ugly hard faces, four pairs of eyes.

For he had met the gang.

It had been his first thought, on quitting the Haymarket the previous night in the company of Pottsy Palmer, to propose that this encounter take place on his own ground—that is, here at the Bull. But he had changed his mind. Instead, Palmer took Tom to *them.* And when he saw them, Tom knew that this was just as well.

First the two had come here to the Bull, for Palmer, though burly, put up a respectable front. They'd had a drink of brandy.

It was while he poured this, his back to his guest, that Tom heard a low appreciative whistle. He turned to find that Palmer had come upon and casually opened his, Tom's, wallet, a large canvas sack filled with jewelry.

Tom cursed himself for carelessness. He must do something about that wallet. Suppose some servant of the inn had thus carelessly come upon it?

"That will do," he said, closing the thing.

"You've got some beauties there, mister. Some real beauties."

"Doubtless."

"They say you took four thousand pounds' worth, this past month."

"They say all sorts of things."

"Well, even what I seen just now. . . You'd better let me handle those for you, mister."

"No."

"You won't get a better price anywhere in town."

"No."

Palmer said nothing more; but when he sat down to write a note to be sent to the theater—for the man, astoundingly, was literate—his eyes had a faraway look.

The note might or might not result on the morrow in some form of acknowledgment, he told Tom.

After that they had gone to a small gin shop in Alsatia Street, near the Bloody Bowl, and there, in a back room, a sort of private drinking compartment, Tom met the balance of the gang.

They were an unexciting quartet—shabby, surly, oblique with their glances. Nothing could have been less like the flamboyant figures dreamed up by the late Mr. Gay. Not one of these men had a patch over his eye. None showed his teeth or fisted the table. And they were too busy staying unhanged to sing.

They were sly and at the same time furtive, like foxes, seldom glimpsed, often felt. Like foxes too, they trusted nobody. Life was a bitter struggle, mercy an emotion they never could know. In the same room with Pottsy Palmer, who clearly was their master, they were ignorant men and small. But they weren't contemptible! Raised in the jungle that was London, each had the ferocity, as each had the cunning, of a beast of prey. When, as occasionally happened, Tom Savage did catch for an instant the full gaze of one of these men, he shuddered in genuine fright. They would kill him as coldly as they'd step on a cockroach: this he knew. But just now they needed him, as he needed them, and the discussion, while scarcely cordial, never was edged with violence.

Neither was it marked by any hemming and hawing. These cutthroats were not circuitous. They knew what they wanted of Tom Savage, who knew what he wanted of them, and nobody wriggled or tried to sidle away when the cards had been put on the table.

It quickly came out that these five men, professional thieves and kidnappers, doomed to dangle some day from five gibbets if ever five men were, in fact once *had* trusted somebody.

Harry Tewkes, his successor dourly reflected, must have been a marvelously persuasive man to get around such scoundrels. Yet undoubtedly he'd done so. Tom did not ask for details, but it would appear that Tewkes had talked them into combining their loot with his—and both parties had been holding an uncommonly large supply of stolen jewelry, waiting for a war between receivers to hike up prices—on the belief that he, Tewkes, could realize a much larger sum in cash for it than either side could have done separately. It seemed Tewkes had connections, high up—among people who could afford to pay. Some of them even might be across the water. Tom didn't ask what persuasion he had used to put over this plan, but anyway, the rogues had pooled their takings and turned the total over to the glib Mr. Tewkes, who thereupon vanished.

They knew—who better?—the falsity of that old saw about honor among thieves. Yet, whether in a moment of bedazzlement brought about by his great name as a road agent, or by his honeyed tongue, or both, they had trusted Harry Tewkes. That's all that mattered to them here.

There was more than money involved, though Tom gathered that there was much money. They had their pride. In the world in which they lived, nether world though it be, prestige counted for everything. Once the word got out that they had been flim-flammed, their careers, both individually and as a group, would be at an end.

Their first feeling was professional, their second personal. They must get the money back, and this meant getting Harry Tewkes back—alive. Tewkes must be taken, and taken by one of themselves, not by the King's men, nor by any sheriff or constable, nor by Bow Street runners. It would be necessary to question him carefully, and no doubt forcefully. Once he'd let his secret go, then he might be done in. But not until then! He must not be killed out of hand! They made this very clear to Tom Savage, who nodded in sympathy.

When they had heard of the arrest of Harry Tewkes, as they believed, they at first supposed that there had been a slip. This could happen to the best of operators. Harry the Horsepad, then, would be hanged, no doubt of it. All the lawyers in the world couldn't have saved him. The reason no member of the gang had gone to Newgate for a visit was that they feared they would be followed from the prison by Bow Street runners, who, it could be assumed, were at least as interested in Tewkes's loot as in Tewkes himself. It would be like Harry the Horsepad to take his secret to the grave, damning their eyes. They knew this. They knew, too, that they couldn't question him as they would have wished in the presence of jailers, or at least within their hearing.

What they had done, with the aid of a rented house, shovels, a bribed funeral manager, and a woman of the stage—Tom inferred that Molly Evans had gone to them, not they to her—was to rescue the prisoner on the very road to the gallows.

"And a masterful plan it was, too! And masterfully executed!"

"Thankee, sir."

About the barbarity of the attack that followed, they had felt, the previous night in Alsatia Street, diffident. While not going so far as to beg his pardon, they'd shown sheepish.

Tom had waved this aside. He was no man to hold a grudge.

Immediately they learned their mistake they had started to lay plans for the unearthing of the real Tewkes; but except that Molly Evans had glimpsed him in the Queen's Theatre night before last, there had been no word. They had known vaguely, as she had, that Harry Tewkes, with an eye to retirement, had recently invested in a house in the country, but what sort of house or what part of the country none of them knew.

They had, of course, followed the reports of Tom Savage these past three weeks with the greatest of interest, never entirely sure but that Tewkes had resumed operations after all. They had checked each robbery with Tom last night, from time to time uttering reluctant grunts of approval. They had agreed with him that, until some better clue could be found, the second and simulated Harry Tewkes should continue, and in as sensational a manner as could be, for this might taunt the real one out of his lair. They had promised to get him another black horse.

"But don't pay too much for it," Tom had warned.

"Stones, man, d'ye think we have to *buy* our horses? D'ye think we're that low that we can't prig a prancer no more?" This had been Pottsy Palmer, who turned to the smallest of the group. "Joe, you see to it, first thing in the morning. And take it around to the gentleman's inn. A black one, mind you!"

What they had chiefly sought to learn was whether the arrest of Tom Savage was chance or design. He had assured them that he didn't know, but he'd pointed out that Harry Tewkes could not possibly have anticipated his, Tom's, appearance in London.

It seemed certain that Tewkes, seeing this young man, had thought fast. That he'd been prepared for such an event seemed equally certain. He could not otherwise have disappeared so efficiently.

To reach and further question those four travelers who had taken the witness stand to identify Tom as Captain Tewkes might, at this stage of the game, prove impossible. It should not be difficult, however, to track down the pickpocket who had planted the monogrammed handkerchief and the gold watch

73

on Tom Savage's person. That Tewkes had hired an outsider for this was in itself a suspicious circumstance. Excepting Joe, the prigger of prancers, and Pottsy Palmer, who had sadly confessed to Tom that he lacked the training to practice this particular branch of the criminal art, they were all expert pickpockets themselves. Why hadn't Tewkes used one of them?

"Where was you when the blokes from the beak napped you?"

"In a gin shop near Covent Garden. But I'd just got there. Barely'd sat down. It couldn't have happened in that place."

"Anybody jostle you on the way?"

"Not that I know of."

"Was you fried?"

"Eh?"

"Swacked, oiled, ossified."

"Oh. No, I don't think so. I'd had half a bottle of claret and a couple of brandies, that's all."

"Where was you before you went to this gin shop?"

"In a large place right inside the market rail itself. On the west side, near the church there. Low ceiling. Crowded. A big picture of a nun and a monk over the fireplace, who were—well—"

"Tom King's?"

"That's the name."

They had nodded. They knew Tom King's place, an expensive one much frequented by fashionable visitors and the merely morbid. King himself, who had gone to Eton and to King's College, Cambridge, was dead, but the business remained in the hands of his widow.

"You go to the jakes when you was there?"

"Yes, I did. Just before I left. It was crowded."

"It always is."

It had been at last agreed, and without bickering, that Joe should steal the horse and deliver it to Tom, who should ride Hounslow Heath and the Great North Road once more in an attempt to entice the hidden Tewkes out into the open, while Pottsy Palmer went each night to the Queen's Theatre, keeping a watch there, and the rest of the gang conducted a sharp and perhaps even explosive interrogation of all pickpockets who might have been in the vicinity of Covent Garden the night of Tom Savage's arrest.

With this the conference had broken up.

Now Tom, putting aside his cup, frowned petulantly at the wainscoting and strove to bring his mind away from the comfort stall at King's to a much more pleasant subject—Molly Evans.

He was beginning to make headway in this when the valet knocked, announcing a caller, the Honorable Ned Blane, and the door was opened, and in walked the tall young man of the previous night.

13 *AM I MY UNCLE'S KEEPER?*

HE WAS RESPLENDENT IN SCARLET AND SILVER, BUT HE WALKED
with a curiously stilted uprightness, and his eyes this morning
were not frosty but glassy. The truth is, the man was drunk.

He planted himself in the middle of the room like a flagpole.

"I am come to see if we should exchange communications,
sir?"

Tom got off the bed, night robe and all, and made a bow.

"Nay, I see no reason for such formality, sir. I behaved
abominably last night, and to a man of more years than mine
and of higher station. The only excuse I can plead for my con-
duct is that I was carried away by the charms of that actress
woman."

"Well, damn it, you showed good taste in that, anyway!"

"I am prepared, believe me, to apologize to your uncle by
mail, by messenger, in person, any way at all."

The other slapped Tom's shoulder, then flumped down upon
the bed, all stiffness gone.

"Good! So we'll not have to fight after all? Damn me, man,
I'm glad of that!"

"Won't you join me in a cup of chocolate, sir?"

"No, no! Give me brandy. What about you?"

Tom shook his head, but got out the bottle.

"Too early for me."

"You have business today?"

"Um, yes."

The Honorable Ned Blane swayed where he sat—and this was an hour before noon—yet his words were not slurred. Determinedly the fop, doggedly flippant, he was conscientious about his fashionable chitchat. It was difficult for Tom. Nevertheless they did talk. Or Blane did, as Tom got dressed.

"Beautiful . . . beautiful woman. . . . Only wish I could afford to fall in love with her myself. But my life's my uncle's. He's rich. I must toady to him. I must resent things for him, the silly old goat. But—*he's* for her, y'know."

"Oh?"

"Aye. That's what he was doing at the theater last night. That's why he's there every night. To slobber at the sight of her. To drool. Ha! He hasn't got closer, I can tell you!"

"The lady's, uh, inaccessible?"

"Damned near, I take it. Seares perhaps. I can't think of any other who can even get into her presence. Ah, ah, Savage, if I could only present my uncle to her . . ."

There was some silence. Tom swallowed, for he was finding this part of the talk distasteful. But he maintained a smile.

"Why, what's so hard about that?"

"Damn me, I don't know! An actress! A stage woman! Who the devil is *she* to hold herself so damned almighty aloof, eh? Savage, confound your gizzard, I ask you *that!*"

Tom shrugged, sipping chocolate.

"It could, of course," he mildly pointed out, "be her own business?"

The Honorable Ned Blane belched, shaking his head.

"It could not. She's an issue. She—she's a *political thing,* d'ye see, Savage?"

"No."

Sunlight seeped through the curtains, tentatively, as though unsure of itself. The street cries increased. "What d'ye lack? . . . Brooms, green brooms! . . . Water for your house, sirs, ma'ams! . . ." Downstairs the taproom was filling, and a snatch of song rose:

Hark to the tale of Harry!
Hark to the song I sing!

"Prestige, Savage. That's what it is."

That's what it was too in Whitefriars, Tom thought. That's what it was among the pimps and prostitutes and the pickpockets, as among members of Parliament. Prestige. Yes.

He rides the roads on Erebus,
His rapier brandished high—

"And my uncle's an ambitious man. He has gone as far as his money will take him. Now he leans on me. But he could break me, Savage."

"You're getting drunk."

"*Getting* drunk? Don't be a dolt! I tell you my uncle could snap up my estate, such as it is. He could leave me without one farthing to rub against another. And he would. But that he needs me."

"To challenge men for him?"

"He enjoys that. The swagger. Only with him it's vicarious." He swallowed some brandy. "I hope I pronounced that word aright?"

"You did very well."

Blane put down his glass, shaking his head when Tom made a polite reach for the bottle.

"No, no, I've other chores. He keeps me busy, I can tell you. But—*she*'d clear things, if I could only arrange a meeting."

He hawked and spat into a lace handkerchief.

"I don't suppose—well, see here, *you* wouldn't be able to arrange such a meeting, would you, Savage?"

"Come, come," Tom laughed. "I don't even live in London. I have nothing to do with the stage."

"Of course. Yes. Forgive me, old friend. And—thank you for the brandy. You must come and swallow some with me some time."

"I'd admire to do that," Tom said warmly.

"Good. We'll arrange it. And now—"

There was a knock at the door, and the valet called that Mr. Savage had another visitor.

Tom called: "Who the devil is that?"

"Your worship, it's a—"

The door was opened; and Molly Evans stood there.

She wore a bottle-green cloak, black slippers, a tiny black tricorne tipped low over her forehead. She looked like a slim boy.

"Oh," said Tom.

"Oh, oh," said the Honorable Ned Blane.

Tom stepped past him and took the girl's elbow, and leaning low, he scolded her.

"You mustn't come to a man's chamber alone! God's word, you're a lady!"

"No, I'm not a lady," she answered. "I'm an actress."

"But—"

"Can you get rid of him?"

"He was just leaving," said Tom, and threw an arm across Ned Blane's shoulders, leading him through the doorway.

Blane giggled. He nudged Tom with an elbow.

"Ah, you dog! You dog! We'll talk of this later."

"No doubt," said Tom. "Now—mind those stairs. They're steep."

"Ah, ah, you dog!"

Tom Savage turned back into the bedroom, and he closed the door behind him and threw the latch. He exhaled.

"So?" he said.

14 *WHEN IN DOUBT, BOW!*

LIGHT AS A SAILBOAT SHE MOVED ACROSS THE ROOM, NODDING approval at what she saw. Yet there was nothing saucy about her. Rather, she was grave, pulling off her gloves as she walked; and when at last she turned to face him where he stood with his back against the door, there was no smile on her face.

She studied him with much the same expression as she had studied the panelling, and she appeared to find him, like it, satisfactory. She gave a small nod.

"You have done well for yourself, Sir Student. Highway robbery agrees with you."

He bowed, as much to cover his confusion as to acknowledge the compliment, if compliment it could be called. For he was bewildered.

The other time he had faced this woman, three weeks ago, she had been armed with a pistol and had sat within calling distance of a pack of paid bullies, while he, Tom Savage, had been bloodied, bruised, beaten, with a face that must have looked like chopped raw beef; weakened besides by the stay in that noisome cell in Newgate. On that occasion she shrank, and he was bold. This morning the meeting was in his own bed-chamber, where in the absence of other company she had no call to be; and he was rested, fed, politely dressed. Yet she was the cool one here, while he for a time was tongue-tied.

So he made a leg, in keeping with the adage: "If in doubt, bow."

Upright again, however, he managed to speak.

"The name is Thomas Savage, ma'am, and I was at the Queen's Theatre last night, and lord, what a performance!"

"Thank you," she said quietly.

For a moment they were silent, and simply gazed at each other. He made no movement toward a chair, his manners having failed him.

"Do I really look like Harry Tewkes?" he said at last.

"Hardly a bit, no. For one thing, you are younger. And handsomer."

"Thank you."

"Tewkes is no Adonis, though he does have a certain—well, *force* in his face."

"I should imagine so."

"But at a slight distance, yes. You hold yourself the same way —that set of the shoulders. Your eyes are the same, your chin. And the build: you must weigh within a few ounces. But at close range you wouldn't fool anybody."

"I never meant to fool anybody."

"True."

"Yet in Lincoln's Inn Fields you were within a few feet of me."

"Please to remember the conditions. I was overwrought. La, I was frightened half to death!"

"You didn't look it."

"And consider the part imagination plays. I *assumed* that Harry Tewkes would be in that cart. So I did not really look at you."

"Ah."

"If you'd been a foot taller or a foot shorter, or if you had been very thin or very fat, or very dark—"

"Anyway, you played *your* role to perfection. It was perhaps the best in all your professional career, ma'am."

"It's the one I would most like to forget." She seemed to

speak bitterly, and at his grin and lifted eyebrow, collected her-self to put an apologetic hand on his arm. "I should not have said that—forgive me! After all, I saved the life of an innocent man that morning. Where was you going, Master Savage, before all this happened?"

"I had supposed I was on my way to America."

"America!"

"They tell me there are no theaters there. Only forests and swamps and red Indians."

She nodded absently. As she seemed of no mind to leave, he got her a chair.

"Will you have a cup of chocolate with me, ma'am?"

It was the custom for men of fashion, especially the younger, unmarried ones, to breakfast with friends. So in response to Tom's wake-up ring the *valet de chambre* had brought a pot of chocolate and no fewer than four cups and saucers.

Now, as the lady sipped, she asked with a nod toward the door, "That was Lord Sutton's nephew, wasn't it?"

"Yes. He's keen to meet you. For milord."

"Please don't let him."

"I'll not. Though I make no doubt that you could protect yourself if I did."

"I'd hardly have reached my present position if I couldn't."

"Yes. I remember that when I became too pushing, the other time we met, ma'am, you pulled out a pistol and pointed it at me."

She flushed, looking down.

"I—I was nervous."

He gave her a grin, then rose.

"I've meant to return it to you," he said, "but I have been occupied out in the country, as you must have heard."

"Yes."

"Permit me to restore it to you now, ma'am."

He brought forth the pistol, a minnow alongside his brass-barrelled whales. He had become fond of it, and now he rubbed his fingers over it.

"Isn't that dangerous?"

He sat down beside her.

"Not if you're careful to keep the striker low and don't let it bang against another piece of metal, anything that might make a spark. You keep this little cap down on the flashpan, like this. Then, even if some powder works its way up through the touch-hole while you're travelling—maybe the thing is turned upside down in your bag, say—it still can't go off, even if it's jarred. Truth is, that powder's got stiff in there now. I'd better draw the charge for you. Look—"

It gave him something to do with his hands, so that he did not have to look at her; but he was aware that she was looking at him, as with pliers from his own kit he worked out the wad and the ball. He knocked the powder into a waxed-paper container.

"See, that's about the amount you should use for a weapon like this. Put in more and there's a chance it will blow up. Put in much less and it would hardly shoot the chunk out of the barrel."

"I see."

"I'll leave you several of these little containers. They're handy to have. Then even if you're nervous you won't get the wrong amount of powder in. It makes a sort of cartridge. And afterward you can crumple the paper up and use it as wadding."

"Master Savage, you will ride out tonight again?" she asked slowly.

"Um, yes. I believe so. If Joe brings me a mount in time."

"I never knew any of the gang, really. I dealt only with Palmer. Do you—Have you any address in the country, sir? In case we should need you?"

"Well, I shouldn't care to go on holding up people if I could be of use here. Nothing in the west, no. But the Adam and Eve, at the upper end of the Tottenham Court Road where it becomes the turnpike—that might reach me. The boniface is a friend of mine."

"The Adam and Eve—" She laid her hand gently on Tom

Savage's right forearm. He did not dare look up. His mouth felt dry; blood thudded at his temples.

"Master Savage, I want you to do something for me. Or rather for—for a friend of mine."

He wetted his lips, angry, still not looking up. So she would play him for a fool, tickling him as though he was a kitten, coaxing him, wheedling him?

"Harry Tewkes? I have already promised not to kill him if I see him first. You needn't trouble yourself there."

"No, I didn't mean Harry Tewkes. I meant Lord Seares."

He rose, yanking his arm away. He tossed the pistol into her lap.

"Isn't it enough that I spare Tewkes, the man who would have sent me to a felon's grave? Must I play the lackey to *all* of your lovers?"

The pistol clattered on the floor as she sprang to her feet. She slapped him twice, hard, one time with each hand.

"I knew that most men were fools, but must they be nasty-minded as well?" She swept past him, chin high. "Good morning, sir."

She was out of the door, which she left ajar, being too good an actress to slam it.

Tom Savage stooped, scooped up the pistol, and ran into the hall. He was in time to hear the street door clap shut.

"Wasn't that Harry Tewkes's doxie, just now?"

Here was Joe, who stood in the shadows of the hall: he had been about to knock when the door was flung open.

"Yes," said Tom Savage. "Yes, that's who it was."

"Your horse is waiting. Saddle and all. But it could help if you rode right out of London, soon, begging your worship's pardon. They'll be searching for that nag."

"Um . . . I will."

"And Pottsy said to tell you you'd best leave that wallet behind."

"No."

"We'd give you a good price. Better'n you can get anywhere

else. Well, the *only* one you can get right now, here. Pottsy sees to that."

"Fancies himself as another Jonathan Wild, does he? Well, you know where *he* wound up!"

"Pottsy says—"

"Pottsy can go to the devil. But here's something for you, Joe. For your trouble."

"A silver pistol! Gor, that's worth all of— Say, you sure you don't want this, mister?"

"I'm sure of it. Now I must be off."

"Say, thanks. Which way will you be heading, your worship?"

"Hounslow."

15 *AGAINST A GORGEOUS SUNSET*

THE CREAKING OF THE COACH COULD BE HEARD LONG BEFORE THE
vehicle itself came into sight, the slow squeal of leather against
wood, the thunk of horses' hooves, the soggy slop of mud on the
wheels.

From the thicket where he waited, Tom Savage had seen the
coach make a dip into Dog's Hollow—an exceedingly shallow
hollow, but deep enough to hide it from his sight—and thereupon, as though by some Oriental trick, vanish. He had been
listening for these very sounds, which now came nearer . . . and
nearer . . .

He got out the brass-barrelled pistols.

A nasturtium sunset, oranged at the rim, had made the world
a sea of blood. Soon it would be dark. No doubt night already
had gulped Dog Hollow, where the coach slogged its lumbrous
way. Tom remembered the rhyme:

When Hounslow Heath is all afire,

Then Hounslow's roads are naught but mire.

Seldom, he reflected wryly, were they anything else anyway.

He frowned. Hating his work, he caught himself filled with
a cold contempt for every coach, driver, passenger, guard. He
was waxing over-cocky. It needed only one small slip; and *this*
time, caught red-handed, he most assuredly would hang. It was
a ridiculous and humiliating way to make a living.

There was more than this to his touchiness. There was more than mere physical discomfort too, and fatigue, though it was true that he'd spent the previous night in saddle, and was hungry and dirty, his throat dry, his eyes athrob. With the vehemence that always marks self-castigation, he was telling himself that he had behaved badly in Half Moon Street. What concern of his was it how many lovers Miss Evans allowed herself? To look at her, any man could see that she could have as many as she wished. And wasn't it a part of her professional tradition? Weren't stage women classically libidinous? "I'm not a lady," she had told him tartly. "I'm an actress." What's more, she was a damned *good* actress, as Tom had cause to know.

She had saved his life; and he repaid her with insults. What if she did seek some service for her protector? Who was he, Thomas Savage, to withhold it? If only as a matter of policy, if only in order to do everything possible toward catching the true Harry Tewkes, he should place himself at Molly Evans's beck and call—within reason, of course.

Besides all this, there was his personal feeling. If she was not a lady, surely he had been no gentleman, there in the Bull. Tom was not a man to put on airs. He was middle class, and knew it, and would never pose as a personage of *ton*. Yet he had his code. No popinjay, neither did he care to be taken for a boor.

Whatever else he owed Molly Evans, he did owe her an apology.

But he couldn't go back to London when he had less than six shillings in his purse.

He should have more than that, very soon, after he had held up the occupants of the coach he could hear approaching.

He looked back toward the village of Hounslow, where the two great roads from the west met, and where just now, at the inn, servants were lighting candles, causing windows to blink into view like so many fireflies.

For his purpose, conditions were perfect. This was the way he preferred it. Once the coach from London had climbed out of Dog Hollow, its driver and passengers would see those lights, and would nod, complacent, sure that the most perilous part of the passage was over. Like the horses, they would be tired. They would also be careless. They'd pat again the places where they had hidden their valuables. They'd begin to get bags and boxes down from the rack.

Then, like a giant, like an ogre of old, weirdly black against the glory of a setting sun, there would spring the figure of Harry the Horsepad, complete with cockade, purple mask, and those two long pistols.

The rest would be easy.

Nevertheless he frowned.

Suddenly he lifted his head—not at a new noise but at the absence of any, which can be even more jarring. Thus, when a clock ceases to tick in an otherwise quiet house, the effect on the ear is as crashing as gongs. And now Tom no longer heard a squeal of leather, or the slopping of mud from the coach in Dog Hollow.

To the south there was a mumble of thunder, and some breeze stirred. A smell of rain was in the air. It would be a wet night. A burst of song came from the cluster of lights at the edge of the village, those lights that pricked out the inn.

> If buttercups buzz'd after the bee,
> If boats were on land, church on sea,
> If ponies rode men, and if grass ate the cows—

But from Dog Hollow—nothing.

Surely this near to Hounslow itself—and though he could not see the village from down there, the driver must know every foot of the way—there would be no pause for the purpose of letting passengers relieve themselves?

Had a linchpin fallen out?

Or a horse thrown a shoe?

A wild, a mad thought came: could there be another highwayman, unknown to Tom as Tom was unknown to him, lurking on the near slope of Dog Hollow? Was the London coach at this moment being held up?

What an indignity that would be! He scarcely knew whether to laugh or to curse.

He was not long in suspense. Almost as soon as they had ceased, the coach-sounds started again.

What had happened he was never to learn, nor did he care. Conceivably the driver, dead-tired, had fallen asleep on the box, and the horses, sensing the lack of direction, had stopped to whuffle for grass. The driver, in that event, would surely be awakened by indignant, impatient travellers.

Whatever the reason, the coach could be heard coming closer . . . and closer . . .

The black mare stirred restlessly under him, and Tom reprimanded her with his knees, sighing to remember Erebus, who had been the soul of docility. He checked mask and hat. He placed the reins over the pommel. He cocked the pistols.

Three minutes later he was yelling: *"You, driver! Climb down and open the door!"*

*   *   *   *

He slept on the ground that night, for a few hours. He was lucky in that it didn't rain after all.

He had escaped east, the direction of London, but he kept that course for only a few miles past Dog Hollow, after which he turned somewhat north, right out upon the dreariest part of the heath—and it was full night by then, too.

Tom did not favor the Great North Road as a hunting ground. Finchley Common had its advantages, but it was no Hounslow Heath. Though the inns were good, the coach passengers, by and large, were North-of-England men and Scots, who were unlikely to carry many coins. Besides, the Great North Road was too flat, and not well wooded.

Yet it was toward the end of the Tottenham Court Road that he headed when he woke; and that afternoon, splattered, drooping with weariness, as was also the beast that bore him, he dismounted in the courtyard of the Adam and Eve.

"You sag, my friend."

"Truly, Master Welch. It's been a many mile."

"Here, boy! Take Mister Savage's mount! And treat it well!"

John Welch was a good advertisement for his inn, being fat, jolly of appearance, genial, as a boniface should be; but in secret he was a serious-minded man who would have liked to talk by the hour with Tom Savage, philosophy being his chosen subject. Twice before they had discussed philosophy, in which this erudite young man, Savage, seemed steeped. But John Welch knew at a glance that they wouldn't do that tonight.

"Dinner, your worship? 'Tis just now coming on."

"In my room."

"I understand. But—a glass with me first, eh? That's good for you, whilst the chambermaid lays out the linen."

"Fairly spoken, mine host! Come along—"

The dining hall at the Adam and Eve was large, but at this hour it was less than half filled. From what already seemed an old habit, though it had been but recently formed, Tom Savage, when he entered such a room, searched out the two back corners, the corners from which a view of the entrance could best be commanded.

Today they were both occupied.

In one sat Molly Evans. In the other sat the old woman from Bath, the woman with the brown mustache.

16 *OVER A BIRD AND A BOTTLE*

HE TURNED AROUND, AND WITHOUT ANY BREAK IN HIS STRIDE, without taking his hand from the host's shoulder, walked out again.

If he'd been seen, if an alarm was raised, he was lost; for the ostler already had led away his horse, a spent steed at best, and this was open country.

But since all was silent behind him, he exhaled.

Who would have looked for the Wife of Bath here? Tom's contempt for would-be identifiers knew exceptions; and she was one of them. For more than an hour they had sat across from one another in Holborn, drinking beer while they waited for the coach to be made up. Then they'd ridden, side by side, across a good part of Hounslow Heath. *She* wouldn't forget! She might even have cashed in on her knowledge. Right now, she might be visiting a series of inns along the Great North Road in the hope of getting a glimpse of him. She could be in the pay of the sheriff, or of the coach people, or even of the brokers at Lloyd's coffee-house in Lombard Street, who had been paying out fabulous sums in insurance because of the exploits of Harry the Horsepad.

John Welch in the course of his calling had become used to eccentricity, to unaccountable exits and entrances. He had, however, esteemed this Mr. Savage an eminently level-headed young man, well versed in the classics and having some interesting if unconventional views on predestination. Now he gawped.

"Forgive me, my friend," Tom muttered. "Dizziness . . ."

"A touch of brandy—"

"Not right here, please. All those people confuse me. We—we'll have that drink later, eh? When things are quiet. When there's not all this cackle."

"As your worship pleases," a bit stiffly.

"And meanwhile would you be good enough to send a bird and a bottle up to me? Your best claret. The kind we shared last time. And—Welch?"

"Yes?"

Tom, with a backward jerk of his head, dropped his voice.

"There's a woman at each of the corner tables in there. Which is the one on the left?"

The boniface popped his eyes. With an infallible memory for faces he had no need to open the door and peer again into his own dining hall: he knew where everybody was.

"Why, I didn't learn her name. Should I ask her?"

"No. How long has she been here?"

"Half an hour. She came by the Barnet diligence."

"Is she alone?"

"Why, she appears to be. I haven't noticed anybody speak to her."

"And will she leave when the diligence starts south?"

"Well, she hasn't engaged a sleeping chamber."

"Ah."

"If you'll forgive a proud proprietor, Mr. Savage, it's at the woman in the *other* corner that you should have looked."

"Oh, yes. Molly Evans. But I didn't notice: is she alone?"

"She is with my lord Seares. He's very close to Mr. Pitt."

That's probably not all he's close to, from time to time, was Tom's black thought; but he said nothing, only nodded.

"When the other woman's gone, you might tell Miss Evans that I am here."

"Do you wish to see her?"

"That depends upon her. Just say that I have a room. But—not until that woman with the mustache has departed, d'ye understand?"

"I understand, your honor."

He was comfortable, as always at an English inn, but he was as restless as a recently caged animal. He in part undressed, and he washed, and when he sat down to drink the wine and pick at the fowl that had meanwhile been brought, he noticed that his hands were trembling. He cursed. A little while ago perilously over-confident, now he had been reduced to a state of funk by nothing more than the sight of a bewhiskered crone who probably was here only by chance—who might be in the process of being shoved from relative to relative—without the slightest thought of Harry the Horsepad.

It was a good example of what this life, the life of the road, could do to a once high-spirited and healthy young man. Now he was starting at shadows, ready to leap if a mouse squeaked.

When he heard the coach brought into the yard he went to a window, and from under a lowered shade he watched the Wife of Bath climb into it. He did not return to his meal until the Barnet diligence was out of sight.

A few minutes later there was a rap on the door. Tom, thinking that it was the valet, called "Come in," and Molly Evans entered.

She was flushed, her mouth a little open, as though she had dashed up the stairs. She came to a sudden, birdlike stop only a few feet past the threshold, as though not sure what her reception might be.

"You got my message," said Tom, and went around the table. "Ma'am, forgive me," he whispered with real contrition, taking her hands. "I behaved like a bumpkin."

"Oh, no . . ."

"My years in France, ma'am, were not spent at the court. But they weren't spent in the gutter either. There's no excuse for it."

"No, it was only natural for you to think—that. Everybody does. And I don't care. But I didn't want you to."

"I—I lost my temper."

"I'm afraid I lost mine too."

"Tut, my dear," spoke a voice behind her, "a woman who has already lost her reputation can't afford to lose her temper as well."

Lord Seares came into the room.

He was elegant in black and silver. He was young, slim, erect, easy of carriage, and though his head was somewhat horsy, handsome in a rugged, angular way—disconcerting Tom Savage, who had pictured him as a fat, leering roué.

Seares bowed, and not mockingly. He raised his eyebrows as he advanced into the room, as though asking Tom's permission. That he was a man of affairs, large affairs, was clear at a glance; but he wasn't a whit pompous. He studied Tom frankly, if shrewdly.

"There is no need for the lady to protest, Mr. Savage. I'll do it for her. Perhaps that will make it easier to believe, our sex being," and he coughed, "what it is."

"What the devil are you talking about?"

"Only that I seek to offer you a certain employment that will be of the highest importance to the future of our country. I am not making an oration, Mr. Savage. I mean this."

"Go on."

"The work will involve a certain amount of danger. But I am told that you are surrounded by danger. You live danger—"

"That still doesn't mean I like it."

Lord Seares' frown crossed his countenance only for an instant. "I want it first clearly fixed in your mind that I am not Miss Evans's lover, as she is not my mistress."

"La, my lord, that's hardly gallant," Molly murmured. "You made it sound so—so *smug*."

"Forgive me, my dear. That you'd make a toothsome tidbit for somebody's table I would be the last to dispute. But not for mine."

He said this so bluntly, and in so manly a manner, that Tom never doubted the truth of it. Yet Tom, if immensely relieved,

94

was at the same time angry. He had expended a great deal of terrible fear on something that never was there, and when the strain slacked off, he felt rage at those who had fooled him.

"Damn it," he cried, "why, everybody says—"

"What everybody says and what's truth, Mr. Savage, are seldom the same thing. You must be man-of-the-world enough to know that."

"But every actress's got to have her protector!"

"Yes," Molly Evans put in. "It's convention. It's expected of us. If an actress doesn't flaunt a protector they tell all sorts of tales about her—how she practices disgusting vices—Fah! I am only shielding myself when I ask Lord Seares to stand for the story."

"May I add that Lady Seares perfectly comprehends the situation, and accepts it. She and I are most happily married."

"When he came to me—" Molly started.

"I did indeed. I was glad to offer her my 'protectorship' without any demand."

"Prestige?" asked Tom.

"There is a certain amount of that involved. But it was not what I had in mind. Politics, Mr. Savage, is much more than mere Parliamentary debate."

"So I've been told."

"There are certain services that a woman in Miss Evans's position, a reigning beauty, a distinguished ornament to the English stage, is able to perform. And I can assure you that these services are in no way lewd. May we sit down, Mr. Savage?"

"By all means."

He found them chairs. He shouted for more glasses.

"Now," he said, seated.

Molly was silent, her hands in her lap, looking down, though surely she listened to every word. Lord Seares praised the claret, but said little else while the valet was in the room. After the valet had gone, Seares sat eyeing the door for a moment, then rose and strode to it, and flung it open. There was no one in the hall. Seares looked up and down, then closed the door and threw the latch. He hung his tricorn over the lock, so that the keyhole was covered.

"Would it be impolite to suggest that your lordship has missed his métier?" said Tom. "You might have won laurels alongside of Miss Evans here—up on the stage."

Seares was not an easy man to ruffle.

"I concede that it could seem melodramatic, Mr. Savage. But wait until you hear what I am about to ask you to do."

"Have some more wine," said Tom.

He returned to the dismemberment of his bird.

For a little while it was quiet in the bedchamber. The only sounds were those that drifted up from the dining room or in by the window from the courtyard. Somewhere a fly buzzed. Tom went on eating.

"I need hardly say, Mr. Savage, that if you undertake this—this adventure, you will be well paid. A hundred guineas?"

Still chewing, Tom waved this aside. The holdup near Hounslow the previous afternoon had been highly successful, and he was no longer worried about cash.

"More than merely money, too. Miss Evans has acquainted me with your predicament, and while I know that your first object is to lay hands on Harry Tewkes, and I can sympathize with that, nonetheless you must see that there will be trouble—bound to be—and it doesn't hurt to have a friend at court. If you was to co-operate here, Mr. Savage, I can promise you that my chief and myself will do everything within our power to make things easier for you with the law."

"Now," said Tom, putting down his knife, "you talk a language I understand."

"I'm glad of that, sir."

"Your chief, I take it, is Mr. Pitt?"

"Aye—William Pitt, the hope of the people, the Great Commoner. D'ye know, Mr. Savage, that we are on the brink of war with France? We're actually fighting, on sea. There will be a formal declaration soon. And unless Mr. Pitt becomes the King's first minister the country will be smashed—*smashed*, I tell you!"

He was passionately in earnest, pounding the arms of his chair. William Pitt, Tom had heard, often affected men this way. Intelligent men, too. There were those who hated him, for his tongue was sharp, his audacity astounding, and, as Croucher Givens would have put it, he never pulled a punch; but no one denied that he was the most able man in English public life. The pool was presently not well stocked, true, and if the Great Commoner showed a whale it might have been largely because he swam among minnows; but no matter; the simple fact remained that he was the only English statesman worthy of the name, and the only one capable of guiding his nation through a war.

"I can believe it," Tom said dryly. "Especially after all I have heard about the way Newcastle runs the Government. But from what I hear, too, Mr. Pitt could step into power any time he wished. Isn't that so?"

"Not entirely. For one thing, the King hates him."

"Oh, the King!"

"He still has great power. And he will never forgive Mr. Pitt for trying to block subsidies to Hanover. But there are other reasons. Mr. Pitt may yet become first minister in time to save this country from humiliation and disgrace. We can pray for that. But—"

"But what?"

"The possibility of a scandal."

"Scandal?" Tom, who had gone back to his bird, again put his knife down. He shook a puzzled head. "God's eyes, man, what scandal could ruin a politician? I don't seek to belittle your hobby, my lord, but—after all—what scandal *could?*" He spread his hands. "Corruption? But Pitt's poor. And the man he seeks to supplant is by all accounts the greatest hander-out of bribes in English history."

"He is."

"Venality? After Walpole, after Newcastle? Why, the people will stand for anything. His private life? In this day and age? Man, he could be drunk every morning, he could sire the nation's largest crop of bastards, and nobody would think the worse of him. They might even like him more!"

"It could be something else."

"What else."

Seares glanced at Molly Evans, but she did not stir. He cleared his throat.

"First, permit me to review the qualifications of my patron. You said that Mr. Pitt is poor. And he is. The only thing his family could afford to buy him was a cornetcy in Cobham's horse, for twelve hundred pounds. And Mr. Walpole snatched that away from him because he refused to make his vote available."

"All this I know, my lord. Everybody knows it."

"Mr. Savage, you mentioned corruption in the Commons. And I'll concede this. For everybody knows about *it*, too. But there is one member of the House who has not sold his vote, though he's been offered a mighty high price, I can tell you!"

"And that is your Mr. Pitt?"

"That is William Pitt. Don't you see, sir, it's just because there *is* so much corruption that he stands out! That's why the people love him. And in them lies his strength. He doesn't control the Commons. He never can, vote for vote, as long as those votes are sold in a shop like so many firkins of butter. Why, Newcastle controls millions! But Newcastle does not control the confidence of the people. I may seem to talk wildly, Mr. Savage, for a person of my rank. But I am not blind. And I do know my politics."

"I see what you're getting at. In your friend's very freakishness lies his strength. The crowd is as excited to see a politician who's honest as it would be to see a horse with feathers."

"Precisely. Mr. Pitt has been called the greatest orator since Demosthenes. But it isn't the orator that the people know. How could they? They're not allowed inside the House, and the proceedings are never published. No, what *they* see is the Paymaster of the Forces who refused to put the public funds out at interest for the benefit of his own pocket and refused to take gifts from

Continental princes when he disbursed money to their hired troops, as every other paymaster had done. No wonder he's poor! And they love him for it."

"And if this well-publicized honesty were impugned— *Optima corrupta pessima,* eh?"

"Your pardon, sir?"

"Yours, my lord. I was but talking to myself, which is damned bad manners. But let's be more outspoken. I can't imagine why you are trusting me like this—"

"Miss Evans said I might."

"Um . . . Well, let's have it forth. There is some paper you want stolen? I see I've hit upon it. Good. Now, will you assure me that if this is done, no harm will come to England as a result?"

Seares rose, fervent, intense.

"Mr. Savage, I give you my solemn word that if this is done nobody will lose, either in cash or in honor, and England cannot help but be benefited."

"But—why me? London swarms with thieves of more experience."

"Your peculiar talents, uh, fit you for this."

"So it's to be a road crime? And this—well, letter?"

"There is a letter, yes. And I'll show you samples of the handwriting, so that you'll know you are getting the right one. And there is also a page torn from a marriage registry. It would take too long to tell you how I know that this man has these two papers, but I do know it. And you must get them. Strip him naked, if need be, on the road from Scotland."

"Very well. Strip him naked. But I am not yet clear why you find anything difficult in this assignment."

"That's because you don't know who the messenger is."

"Well, who is he? And what's he doing in Scotland? And why should the King accept his word if he wouldn't accept somebody else's?"

"He has been in Scotland inspecting army installations. For

he happens to be the captain-general of all His Majesty's land forces."

"Oh."

"And the King would believe him, if backed by those papers, because he is the King's brother."

"I see. Billy the Butcher, eh?"

"The messenger I refer to, Mr. Savage, is His Royal Highness William Augustus, Duke of Cumberland."

Tom rose and went around the table and stood over Molly Evans. It was impossible not to delight in the curve of that slim neck, the creaminess of the skin, the riotous ringlets.

"Ma'am," he said, "my life lies in your hands. Lord Seares says this is a crisis. But I heed you first, ma'am, and him second. What shall I do?"

After a while she replied, in a whisper, "As you think best."

This wasn't good enough. Tom wanted her to look up.

"If I take him right, he offers me the King's pardon for doing the King's business. And though it's a bit on the shady side, it sounds, somehow, useful to the country. May I take it that your pardon, ma'am, would go with the King's?"

Although she still made no promise, she looked at him, then, with a smile in her eyes. Seares cleared his throat, shifting in his chair.

"You have heard my offer, Mr. Savage. What do you say?"

"I say," Tom replied slowly, "that I'd better send down for another bottle—this really is good claret, you know—and you can tell me more about the road from Scotland."

17 *ATTACK FROM BEHIND*

IT WAS LATE AFTERNOON AND THE SHADOWS STRETCHED LIKE sleepy risers, while the tips of trees were smeared with a red that had not yet reached the ground, when Tom Savage began to load the pistols.

This was his favorite time for a robbery. He liked it better than moonlight. At this hour he could count upon a certain natural laxness among the victims-to-be. Who could stay tense while the sun was low? As day died, so for a little while did caution.

He squatted at the edge of a wood. This was a couple of hundred feet from the road, but he believed that he could ride out quickly enough to surprise a passer, and the ground was level here, so that he could see to right and to left, south and north respectively, for a considerable distance. It was the north he was interested in. If anyone came from the south, or if any but the royal party came from the north, he would simply nip into the wood and permit them to pass. With this in mind, he had tethered the horse, still saddled, just inside the shadows of the trees. It was a new horse for him, light brown in color. It was tired, for Tom had been riding steadily all day, on two occasions cutting ahead of the royal coach, then permitting it to pass without a challenge.

It had been his observation—from a distance, to be sure—

that Cumberland, whether from boredom or a desire for semi-privacy, often rode ahead of his coach, accompanied by a mere handful of men. Those men might have been officially assigned bodyguards, but more likely they were officers with whom the captain-general wished to hold talk away from the servants. A soldier himself, he perhaps preferred to ride, keeping the coach, as became his position, for entrance into any town. Sometimes this group was several miles in front of the main party, at other times only a few hundred yards ahead. When it was done, the deed would have to be done quickly. How long does it take to undress a duke?

The horse of a different color was not the only change. He no longer mounted the yellow cockade, and he had in readiness a mask that was white, not purple. For this particular crime would not be committed by Harry the Horsepad.

Only the pistols were the same, and they would *feel* different when they were loaded. It was the first time that he had loaded them.

Many a de-pursed traveller in that part of England in the year 1755 would have choked with chagrin to learn this; but Tom knew what he was about. Though the pistols were for more than appearance, their appearance was the most important part of them. Their heavy butts were fishtail-shaped, so that in an emergency the pistols could be reversed and used as cudgels. However, he would never dare to do this if they were loaded. They were very heavy anyway, what with their long brass barrels; but loaded, they would be heavier still, for each was large-bored and required a huge ball, which in turn called for a great deal of powder. It was all Tom could do to get on and off an unfamiliar horse while keeping the empty pistols reasonably well in line. He didn't believe that it would be possible—and he was convinced that it would not be advisable—when they were full. Those were crucial moments: when he dismounted and when he mounted again. Popular report—he had overheard this at inns—asserted that Harry the Horsepad never put foot into stirrup, but could leap to the ground and vault back into saddle again with a mere flick of the knees, and presumably of the buttocks as well. This was a part of the legend that was being reared around him, and Tom Savage knew that it simply wasn't true.

Another objection to shooting was that, unlike today, he customarily robbed within call of a village or inn. A shot, while it would not be likely to bring a rescue party, could inspire peekers, who later might help describe the tobyman.

In the best of circumstances pistols were tricky. They could explode at a jog; on the other hand, if it rained or even if the air was damp, or if there was wind to blow the powder out of the pan, or for any one of twenty other reasons, the pistols might not go off at all. On the whole, Tom had preferred them empty as long as this was not known to the travellers.

But there was no rain this afternoon; neither was there a breath of breeze; and the captain-general of His Majesty's land forces, the victor of Culloden, the redoubtable Cumberland, would not be a man easy to scare. So Tom loaded his weapons.

This took some time, but he had all the materials, and in the absence of any stir of air he worked rapidly with scales, a mould, cutters, a ramrod, a scoop, tweezers, wadding, tamps, rags, needle.

Twice, with the jerky alertness of a deer, he lifted his head, holding his breath, to listen. So often these days he was like that. Jumpy. He hated himself for it.

The first time, he thought he heard a sound in the wood behind him, and he swivelled his head, his eyes narrowing. The shadows were thick in there, but he could see none that stirred, save where his mount, on a long tether, snuffled wearily among the leaves and acorns. Nerves? It was likely. Who would prowl in a small isolated wood like this, at dusk, four or five miles from any village?

The second time, he thought he heard a clack of hooves to the north. His chin up, his back straight, he listened for long moments; but there was nothing more.

Nerves or no nerves, how far he had come from the unworldly student of less than two months ago! Then he had looked forward, if without gusto, to the New World and a new life. Now he looked forward to nothing more than the next quarter-hour. Then he'd been a dreamer. Now he was a beast of the jungle, at once hunter and hunted, like those steel-eyed members of Pottsy Palmer's gang. When he took to the road he had not anticipated this. He didn't like it. His stomach wambled. Once when a coach driver, sitting stark upright at Tom's command, had, a moment later, edged toward a blunderbuss in the dickey-seat at his side, Tom had thought wildly: "Let him do it! Let him kill me!" and only at the last instant, shaking and sweating like one who has been yanked back from the verge of a precipice, did he command the man to climb down.

At the most, he had planned to hold up only two or three vehicles. Knights of the road, Tom had heard, were vain. It seemed incredible that Harry Tewkes would not sally forth to assert his pre-eminence, to show up this usurper. Yet nothing of the sort had happened. And here was Tom Savage, an habitual highwayman, confronting traveller after traveller, consorting with pickpockets, doing an actress a favor . . .

True, he'd been approached, sought out, by the confidant of one who might soon be the first minister of England. He believed in Lord Seares, and sincerely hoped that he would be helping his country—even saving it from ruin, as Seares had insisted—if he prevented that piece of paper from reaching Windsor. Yet he did not delude himself. It was only in part patriotism that had prompted him to take on the task. There had been also, undeniably, the appeal of Mistress Molly Evans, singer, discredited adventuress, who would stoop to any indignity in order to get her lover back, and who had solicited him as a cat's-paw.

He was no longer independent. He'd been engaged—like a bravo, a bullyboy—to fight another man's battle.

Sighing, he put the tools away, closed the case, and rested

the pistols upon it, side by side. They were loaded now but neither primed nor cocked. He started to rise.

It was then that, unmistakably, he heard a step behind him.

Half up, knees bent, he twisted.

He caught the fleetest glimpse of the man who sprang out of the wood, for almost immediately he was punched over the right ear, and he spun away, stumbling so that it was all he could do to keep his feet.

The other charged, arms swinging. Tom, stunned, dizzy, barely had time to lean backward from the waist, as Croucher Givens had taught him, and to raise his own arms, fists clenched, palms in.

He blocked one blow with his left elbow, ducked a rounder, and without giving ground, jabbed twice to the face with his left, corkscrewing it. His fist met stubbled skin, a soft mouth. There was a grunt of amazement. The fist came back wet with blood. The other man attacked again. Carefully, though quickly, feet spread wide, heels firm on the ground, his guard high, Tom retreated.

He could see of the other man that he was large and that he held himself in the classical boxing position—knees bent, fists high, elbows out. Tom sensed rather than saw that the fellow was roughly dressed. Of the countenance he could make out nothing, for he himself looked toward the sunset, which meant that his opponent's face was in shadow.

Tom should have stayed still, or else retreated yet further, in order to give his head a chance to clear. But he was outraged. And when he saw the other, perhaps startled by the expert way in which his rush had been met, lower his guard like a man overcome by puzzlement—then Tom, impetuous, leapt forward.

He swung from low and far back—a long, high right overhand. It was meant for the space between the eyes. It found nothing at all. Tom, gasping, felt as if the earth had been pulled out from underneath him like a rug. As he started to fall forward, he struck and swiftly toppled over an outthrust thigh. At the same time, he was slugged in the back of the head, which caused him to pitch forward the faster.

Cursing, furious with himself, as soon as he struck the ground he started to roll.

He knew what had happened. He'd let himself be caught in a flying-mare, one of the most difficult throws to execute—it called for perfect timing—but one of the easiest to avoid, if you saw it coming.

The other man twirled like a dancer, and would have thrown himself full-length upon the prostrate Tom Savage—but Tom, having rolled, no longer was there. Tom was several yards away.

Still, Tom was flat on his back, and his opponent was poised and ready, so that he could have jumped on Tom's belly with both feet. He was about to do this, when—their positions now being reversed so that the man from the wood faced the sunset —Tom let out a yell.

"Croucher!"

"Eh?"

Ponderous but wary, like a bear, suspecting a trick, this man let down his heels, though he kept his fists high.

"Croucher Givens, don't you remember me? Tom Savage, in Lincoln, four-five years ago."

"Gawd help us, it *is*! I know that voice! I would've knowed your face but I wasn't thinking—"

"Come, help me up, Croucher."

"Right, sir. There we are! And may I ask, sir, what are you doing here?"

Tom brushed his coat.

Affably he said, "Let me put it this way, Croucher: what the devil are *you* doing here? You look seedy. And fat, for you."

"Aye." The pugilist knuckle-rapped his chest. "Too much gin. It tells on ye."

"You haven't answered my question."

Andrew ("Croucher") Givens was more than willing to do so. A gregarious man, he had been waiting alone in this wood for almost five hours, and he was lonesome, and would have talked about anything to anybody. Besides, he was genuinely fond of Master Savage, one of his best pupils in the old days.

Five years ago, Croucher said, beginning far back as was his wont, he had been close to the great Jack Broughton and had worked for him as a sparring partner, trainer, and instructor at the famous academy in Tottenham Court Road, where the master, between ring fights, taught the rudiments of his art to dandies in search of a thrill. The work was easy, the glory great, and there had been a heap of money to be made.

Then had come the fight with Jack Slack, an obscure butcher. The champion, the man who had studied under Figg, who had knocked out of time such valiants as George Taylor, Tom Pipes, George Gretting, Stevenson the Coachman, and many another, was a ten-to-one favorite. Croucher was in his corner. Broughton was forty-six years old, and the challenger was scarcely more than a boy, but what of that? When they met, on that raw April morning in 1750, there was a great deal of money at stake, including every shilling that Croucher Givens could scrape up.

It was as though the world had stopped, Croucher said, when Slack whipped the champion. Blinded by a lucky punch, Broughton had really showed his bottom—that is, his great courage and staying power—when, unable even to see Slack, he had felt his way around the ring, again and again being knocked down. Men wept. Givens admitted he himself had wept. But there was no doubt about the outcome of that fight.

" 'Twas a scandal, sir," Croucher now told Tom. "There was them said Jack Broughton did a dive—for money. They lie! I tell you I know him as well as any man alive, and he really couldn't see. 'I'll kill him if I catch him, Croucher,' he'd say each time we carried him back to the scratch. But then—he'd go down again. That wasn't no dive, Master Savage! But they closed Jack's school. They even passed an ordinance against boxing anywhere in Middlesex County."

"I know all this," said Tom, all the while watching the road that led north. "Get on with your story."

Cocky still, believing that the "scandal" would blow over, Croucher had quit a place where he could no longer make a living, and had sought some smaller city in which to exploit his talent. That was how he had come to Lincoln, which, however, he'd been obliged to quit after a while because of an entanglement with a tradesman's wife.

Contrary to his expectations, Croucher said, the ban on boxing in the capital had continued month after month, year after year, Jack Broughton's celebrated academy remaining closed.

"It's politics, that's all it is, sir! Everything's politics these days!"

"Yes, yes. Get on with it."

Yesterday, though, Givens had learned that the ex-champion had been permitted to open another academy, somewhat smaller but by that token more exclusive, in the Haymarket. And Givens would have headed back for London—but for one thing. He had no money. He had just been thrown out of employment as a stableman in the nearby village. Overdrinking had done it.

"I'm slow. But I could train down again. But I'd have to have some decent clothes."

"You seemed fast enough to me, just now. You saw me from behind, and decided to jump me, eh?"

"Ah, ah, Master Savage, you should never have left yourself open like that!"

"I know it—now."

Tom had caught a glint of gilded coach on a rise of ground far to the north. Nearer, he could hear hoofbeats. Three men? Four? He couldn't be sure. He seized his companion's sleeve.

"See here, Croucher—"

"All I need is a coat. I could *walk* the whole way to Lunnon, and I would, if I could only—"

"You have no horse?"

"If I had a horse I'd sell it and buy a coat and a wig. Jack'd take me back, once I got there looking all right."

"Pistols?"

"I wish I did. I was plannin' to scare 'em just with my fists."

"Um . . . Don't you know that with men like Harry the Horsepad riding around loose, there aren't many travellers who go forth these days without a gun of some sort?"

"I suppose so. Look here, Master Savage, comin' to think of it, *you* ain't answered *my* question yet, and I asked *mine* first. What are *you* doing here?"

The hoofbeats were nearer. Soon the riders would come into sight.

Tom nodded toward the pistols, which he now picked up.

"What d'ye think I'm doing here?" he replied.

He found the horse, strapped the pistol box back on the crupper, untethered the beast, checked her harness, and mounted.

"Listen, Croucher. There's a party coming, and they have money. I could use some help. I'll split half-and-half with you. Is it a go?"

"But I don't know much about—"

"You don't have to know anything. Just do as I say. If I say knock a man down, why, knock him down."

"*That* I can do!"

"And don't call me Master Savage. Call me Colonel or something, but not Savage. And I'll call you Jim, right?"

"Right."

Tom was fumbling in one of the saddlebags, in search of masks. His usual purple mask fell out, and the bright yellow cockade followed this to the ground. Givens picked these up, studying them with a frown.

"What's these?"

"Nothing," said Tom, and took them away and stuffed them back into the saddlebag. "Here, put this over your face."

He fastened on his own mask. Between the leaves at the edge of the wood he saw three horsemen surmount a rise to the north, possibly a quarter-mile away. The one in the middle was stocky, and the setting sun blazed on a decoration that hung at his breast. That would be his St. George.

"You know, Croucher," Tom said in an even voice, "that we will hang if we're caught?"

"I—I know that."

"Good. Now, don't come until I call, and then come at a run."

He checked his mask. He rapped the pistols against the pommel, causing a little powder to work up out of the touch-holes and into the pans. He cocked the strikers.

"Here we go—"

He put spurs to his horse and galloped for the highway.

"*Halt!*"

18 "I SHALL REMEMBER YOU"

ALL THREE WORE REGIMENTALS, GLITTERING, BEFROGGED, BRIGHT, with crisp small plumes in their hats; and each too was astride a military mount, high-stepping, a gallant sight to see.

Two, leatherskinned, lank, might have been English. The third, the middle one, most emphatically was not. He was short and thick, heavy, though there was no loose flesh on him, and he sat in saddle well. This man had about his neck a collar of gold links holding large enamel plaques, each brightly flowered, each reading HONI SOIT QUI MAL Y PENSE, and from this —the thing that had caught Tom Savage's eye from far away— hung a splendid St. George, done in diamonds and rubies, the dragon itself being emerald. In the setting sun seeming to pulsate, it was a thing of breath-taking beauty.

Not so the face above it. If, as it is said, Nature abhors a straight line, then Nature must have abhorred this man, whose head seemed in all truth square, resting, apparently without neck, upon a square frame. Though it could be guessed that beneath the wig the hair was blond, like his companions he had a complexion darkened and toughened by many a sun and rain, and perhaps for this reason his straight cruel mouth showed without lips, while the eyes, as blue as ice, and no warmer, stared as though from cavernous blank sockets like the eye-sockets of some gruesome *memento mori,* some skull bleached by the years.

"By God, gentlemen," he said, "I believe we are being held up."

He spoke with a thick German accent, and his mouth appeared not to move. He sounded, and he looked, like what he was—a brute whose brutality was the talk of Europe. It was not for nothing that he was nicknamed Billy the Butcher. If ever there had been any chivalry in modern warfare—a debatable thesis—this ogre had done his best to drive it out. Tom Savage was no Jacobite; and he was too young to have been shocked by the horrors that followed Culloden, when the clans were smashed systematically, mercilessly, their wounded warriors one by one cornered and killed. He was ready to grant that the Stuarts had outlived their usefulness, if ever they had any, and that it was better to pay lip service to a crowned pail of lard from the Continent than to tolerate a British king who took orders direct from Versailles—or from Rome. Tom never waxed maudlin over his Madeira, sighing for the King Across the Water. He had no wish to see the Young Pretender land once again on these shores. At the same time, when he contemplated the ruling house imported from Germany, he, like so many of his fellow countrymen, sometimes could not hold back a sigh. The Stuarts at least had been gentlemen.

"Damn it," one of the officers cried, "do you know who this *is?*"

"Yes," said Tom. "Now keep your hand away from that pistol."

Like a tumbler, like one who walks a rope, Tom Savage had need to concentrate upon his task to the exclusion of every other thing, lest he break his neck. Already he had so trained himself that, without the flick of an eyelash, he could *sense* what was going on behind him, all the while staring straight ahead. Unyielding eyes above the mask, he had learned, were almost as effective as the pistols in making victims obey. Tom indeed conducted his holdups largely by feel, and his feel was exceedingly sensitive. Distraction was something he could not afford.

Nevertheless here, at this critical juncture, he was distracted. He had little regard for the duke's attendants, both of whom watched him closely, holding themselves in readiness to draw their swords, conscious that they must not play a craven's part. Tom knew this, but he did nothing about it. Ordinarily he would have called them to attention with one short negligent waggle of a gun. He did not waggle those guns today. They might go off. Besides, he was fascinated by the man in the middle.

For ugliness *does* fascinate. When the duke spoke, his voice, unexpectedly, was rather squeaky, though clear. His looks were such as to make your skin shrink away.

"No, Stoles, Grady," he said, mildly enough. "Your lives are worth too much. Don't draw. And toss the knave your purses."

This the two did, the bagged coins clicking on the ground. The first purses usually were puny; Tom had to scowl and threaten, and sometimes search, for the real ones. But these were fat. No doubt the two officers had never supposed they'd be held up while in such exalted company.

Tom paid no heed to the purses, which lay in the dust of the road.

"I myself don't carry one," the duke went on. "It follows, with the coach. One of my secretaries. Would you care to ride back for it?"

Tom's attention had shifted from the face to the glorious gaud beneath it. HONI SOIT QUI MAL Y PENSE: evil to him who evil thinks. And there was the jewelled St. George, symbol of purity, spearing the emerald dragon. The Order of the Garter—the oldest and noblest in all Christendom. This German beast wore it as a peasant might wear a kerchief knotted about his neck, whereon from time to time to wipe his face.

The duke's reference to the coach sharply brought Tom back to the present scene.

"Dismount," he said curtly.

"Oh, now, see here! If you—"

"I said dismount! All three of you!"

Out of a corner of his mouth, but without moving his head, he shouted: "*Jim!*"

The three climbed down. At Tom's command they turned their backs to him.

For a moment he feared that the Croucher had lost courage and would not quit the wood. But soon he came, running. His head was low, his mask in place. It was obvious that he was frightened.

"Jim, unbuckle those swords from behind . . . That's it . . . Now thrust them back of the girth straps and lead those horses away."

Very carefully, while the Croucher did this, Tom Savage dismounted. Speed was needed, and in the event that his assistant did give way to panic, Tom wished to be ready to continue the search himself. Yet he shuddered at the thought of passing his hands over the thick, solid body of the Duke of Cumberland, probing here, prising there. It would be like handling a snake.

"That middle one, Jim. Take his coat off."

Again the officers started, scarcely able to stand such an indignity, and again the duke, in a low voice, in words not audible to Tom, soothed them, counselling submission. But the duke did call one request over his shoulder:

"You will let me unfasten the Garter, Master Highwayman? This lout might damage the clasp."

"I don't want your geegaw," contemptuously. "Jim, just take the coat. And toss it here."

This was easily searched, yielding nothing. The pockets were ornamental—and empty. It was a military coat, and thus not encrusted with embroidery. Tom's hand had told him within half a minute that there was nothing hidden in it.

"Now the waistcoat. Then the boots."

Here was a harder job. The waistcoat was plain—not a patch to Tom's own—but of course it buttoned up the front, and there were many buttons, so that Croucher Givens for the first time was obliged to go before the victims. Despite the mask he kept his head averted most of the time, but when, as he was unbuttoning the garment, he fumbled badly, the duke with an exclamation of impatience took the task, literally, out of his hands. It was then that Croucher Givens, as though he had recognized the voice, looked up. And he went pale as death, and staggered, and all but swooned.

Looking back then, pop-eyed, like a man who has seen a ghost, he ran to where Tom, a pistol in his left hand, with his right went over the confiscated coat yet again.

"Master—Master Tom, d'ye—"

"Sh-sh!"

"I mean, Colonel. D'ye know who that *is?*"

"I do. Now get back to work."

"That—that there's *the King's brother!*"

Croucher Givens was a Cockney, born within sound of Bow Bells, and the average one of this kind, it is said, dearly loves a lord. It could be added that he adores a duke. The Croucher, on this occasion, for fully a minute and a half was helpless. He might have been struck by lightning. He could scarcely quiver; sweat rolled off him; his lips were working, though he said nothing.

But—how had he known?

Then the answer came to Tom Savage. Of course! His Royal Highness William Augustus, Duke of Cumberland, had long been pleased to lend his smile to all the so-called manly sports, the bloodier the better. His was a familiar figure at prize fights, and until the Broughton-Slack upset of five years ago, a contest that had cost His Highness ten thousands pounds, he had been known as a patron of Jack Broughton. He was reputed to have lent Broughton the money with which to build the amphitheater in Tottenham Court Road. He must often have visited the academy, where young Andrew ("the Croucher") Givens worked.

Why had not Tom Savage thought of that beforehand? He was getting careless. One little slip—

"I can't take *his* clothes orf, sir!"

"Why not? He's a man, isn't he?"

"He—he's a *dook!*"

From beyond the rise, not far away, Tom could hear the clop of hooves, the creak of a carriage.

It was a time for emphatic measures. Tom tapped the end of a brass barrel against Givens' chest.

"Listen: you'll go over and strip that man, or as sure as our Lord was crucified I'll blow you to pieces."

It was not necessary to go much further. The waistcoat, once off, provided that which Tom sought. He knew it the instant his fingers felt it, sewed into the lining near the right breast. He had to tear that lining to get it out. It was a flat, black-leather pocket-wallet, and it contained a page of a marriage registry, also a letter in a hand that had been painstakingly described to Tom. He nodded, pocketing these things. It had been his belief, all along, that Cumberland would keep them concealed upon his own person.

The creaking of the coach was louder now, and so was the sound of hooves.

Tom looked up. The duke had turned, disobeying orders, and he was looking at Tom Savage in an altogether different way, now that he had seen Tom pocket those papers. His head a little to one side, feet spread wide, fists on hips, he nodded knowingly.

Though Cumberland was the one who was but half dressed —his shirttails hung free, and the Croucher had taken his boots off—it was Tom Savage who felt naked before that penetrating stare. Despite the mask, Tom shivered.

"I shall remember you," Cumberland said.

Tom dropped the tersest of bows, a mere bob.

"Your highness is welcome to any memories he may have."

"I'll be there," the duke pursued. "When they turn you off, I'll be in the crowd."

"I'll throw you a kiss," Tom promised, "Jim! Come along!"

They rode two of the seized steeds, leading the others. There

116

was little enough to choose among them, for they were all tired. It was for this reason that Tom and Andrew ("the Croucher") Givens made immediately for the wood.

They were about to enter this wood when the first of the horsemen appeared above the rise, and there were shouts; the hoofbeats were suddenly accelerated. A moment later they heard a shot. But by that time they were within the shadows of the wood.

19 *GAZE, YOU FOOLS!*

THE CORPSE HUNG WITHOUT ANY SORT OF MOTION, SEEMING LESS A pendulous article than something arrested in rigidity, forever paralyzed, a stalactite on the ceiling of a low, grisly sky. Tendrils of mist dandled it, or else broke against it, to roll back, baffled, as though by a post or tree.

It didn't stink much; for though this was June, summer was late and the morning was cool.

No breath of air stirred; but in truth it would have needed a gale to swing that cadaver, so weighted with metal was it. It was suspended from the gibbet by means of a chain, and additional chains enwrapped it, while the head was protected by a cube of steel mesh, meant to keep off kites. The thing bore little resemblance to the human person it once had been.

Tom said, with a wave of his hand: "There, but for the grace of God—"

Croucher Givens stared at the loathsome exhibit, and swallowed hard.

"Fair gives a man the mulligrubs."

A felon was hanged from a gallows, a body from a gibbet, *in terrorem*. Such clods as could not afford to get to the city for the former event, a benevolent government gratified with the latter. Not every hanged man was so exposed—only the stubborn ones, the ones who refused to confess. Most of them cracked, for by

118

and large they feared this final indignity more than they feared death itself. It was the hope of every convicted criminal that he would have a decent burial. His coffin was his last and most prized possession, and to show the world that he had one, he would carry it in the cart with him from Newgate to the place of execution, or else arrange to have it on display at Tyburn Tree itself, where it might await his arrival.

Those who were subjected to gibbeting were not kept in the capital, but scattered. In part this was for reasons of health—the flies, the pollution. In part it was because the government wished its message to extend as far as possible, especially along the well-travelled roads, where the sight might be viewed by the largest number of persons.

But there was the additional reason that relatives and friends of the deceased could cut the corpse down at night, to bury it come-willy, come-nilly, even though in unconsecrated ground. Hence the chain, rather than a rope. Hence the linked armor in which the remains were sheathed, causing that corpse to resemble a medieval knight rather than a pauper who had stolen, say, twenty or thirty shillings.

Kin or comrades had been known to chop down the gibbet itself when they learned that they could not unfasten the body, and to haul the whole affair away. This was why the upright was driven so far into the ground and, as in the case of the one Tom Savage and his friend came upon this bleak morning, banked with rocks and wrapped high with metal. As a final precaution, a border of spikes had been fastened into it, to discourage climbing.

So it was that long after he had expiated his sins, that fool—or what was left of him—dangled as an Example.

"Disgusting," Tom murmured.

The Croucher was awed. Agog, he gaped at the monstrosity. He trembled, sweat beading his face.

"I hope they never do that to me."

"They will," Tom said cheerfully. "Let's rest, eh?"

They were weary. The brown nag had given out; Croucher

Givens was no horseman; and they had agreed, after several hours of aimless floundering, that it would be better to go it afoot than to risk being overtaken riding horses from the royal party—which horses, or at least their harness, could readily be identified. The countryside was in arms. Tom's hope that the holdup would not be reported, the duke not electing to make himself look a fool, had been dashed. If they didn't get to London soon they were lost. And they could hardly stand on their feet.

"Gawd," was the Croucher's comment, "we *would* meet this!"

Tom was more practical.

"We're at a road," he pointed out. "It must be the road from Wickford. Listen—"

A coach approached. The pace was not spanking, but it was fairly fast. This vehicle had but lately started from some inn. The hour might have been five, or a little after.

"Back of the gibbet," Tom ordered.

"I don't like to get so near that thing."

"Better near it than—*it!*"

The Wickford stage had two horses, a driver, five passengers. It gleamed with early morning moisture. It stopped at the gibbet; and the passengers, grinning nervously, tumbled out.

"Ghouls," Tom muttered.

"What?"

"Shut up."

As the sky lightened, the mist thinned, though wisps of it still wandered past the thing that hung from the gibbet. This fascinated the passengers, who gawped as though they confronted some significant national monument—as indeed, in a sense, they did.

Had any of those passengers found the courage to walk *around* this display he would have come upon two dirty, dusty men.

Tom got a pistol out.

"They ought to be ashamed of themselves."

"Why?"

"How far d'ye suppose we are from a village? A mile? Two, three miles? They usually put these things far out."

"Master Savage, what is it you're thinking of?"

"Fix your mask," Tom said. "We're going to London."

When he stepped around the mound of stones, flabbergasting the coach party, he had the air of a man who knew what he was doing. He was Harry the Horsepad, complete. He waved a weapon.

"My *capias ad computandum*," he drawled, for he had remembered that he must be a professor again. Then, harshly: "Turn your backs and raise your hands, damn you!"

"Their purses?" the Croucher asked, emerging.

"Curse their purses! We haven't time. We've trudged too long, and now we'll ride. Get up there, Jim! Get up and drive!"

"But—"

"The horses are fresh. Be Jehu, son of Nimshi! We're going to town!"

The little group of six men, mussed, confused, looked uncommonly silly in the dawn, Tom Savage reflected as he waved them good-by. After that he made himself comfortable on the cushions, and drew from his pocket the thin black-leather wallet containing two pieces of paper.

"If they get back there in time," said the Croucher, "if they send soldiers—"

"Keep driving, fast," Tom answered. "We'll make it."

There were soldiers, yes; all England's military forces were being put into a condition of alarm and alert; but no soldiers came from the road behind. Twice they passed squads— dragoons, not good riders. The Croucher, inspired, waved his whip; and the dragoons waved back.

"Good," said Tom Savage, as he spread the page from a marriage registry across his knee. For the sun was up now, and he could read.

20 *HOME IS THE BRUISER*

BROUGHTON HAD BEEN A BOATMAN ON THE RIVER, AND A MORE boisterous, blasphemous set than the Thames boatmen it would be hard to find. Yet Broughton exuded good nature. A fist fighter should scowl. Jack Broughton had an easy warm smile.

"Any friend of Croucher's is a friend of mine," he said as he and Tom shook hands.

"Croucher used to give me lessons, up in Lincoln."

"You like to spar, Mr. Savage? Perhaps you'd have a set-to with me?"

"Not now, no, thank you just the same. I've been travelling and I'm tired. But I would admire to look over your establishment."

"Of course!"

Givens, brave in a new coat and wig, was a new man here in the Tottenham Court Road. Driving the coach into town he had been flustered; and for some time after they abandoned the vehicle in a street where it would readily be found and identified—near the stable where Tom had abandoned the brown mare from Ipswich the previous week—he remained, as they sauntered away, twitchy, jumpy. But now he had steadied, and could laugh again, and did. Eager, walking on his toes, he longed to get among his fellow pugilists, and to swap stories, perhaps punches as well. Once he had introduced Tom to Jack

122

Broughton, he edged away to seek out cronies. Thus it was that the ex-champion himself conducted Tom on a tour of the academy. Tall, broad, in his fifties, toothy with a greeting, Broughton never hesitated; there was something boyish about him. Though he strove to be modest, the pride that he felt in his place thrilled in his voice. Tom liked him for it.

"Not a palace, you understand—"

"I have never cared for palaces."

"I would not know that. I've never been in one."

"Bless you, Mr. Broughton, neither have I."

The building might have been put up for its present purpose, though the proprietor told Tom that it was once a stable. It had been extensively done over, and was clean and bright. In the basement were dressing rooms, loafing rooms, rubbing tables, tubs of water. The ground floor consisted of one large, square, high-ceiled chamber. The windows were very high, so that few of the street sounds filtered in, though there was light in all weather. A small entrance hall was crowded with hard-faced men who smirked upon each exiter but sternly examined each applicant for admission: Tom deduced that pugilism still was against the law in London, a circumstance that undoubtedly made it the more attractive to the gilded youths who gathered at Broughton's. In the middle of the chamber was a wooden stage surrounded by posts and ropes in simulation of those at a proper fight site on turf. This "ring," as it was called—though it was square—measured twenty-four feet on each side, that being the size specified by the great Broughton, Tom's present host, who himself had framed a code for pugilism, the only one the sport had known. On this stage, inside the "ring," a dozen half-dressed young men were making arrangements for another bout. One of these was the Honorable Ned Blane, who waved to Tom.

These premises did not in any way constitute a theater, as Tom was told the former place in the Tottenham Court Road had been. There would not have been room for a large betting crowd, nor was there any manner of balcony or gallery. What spectators there might be would of course stand, as though they were attending a true prize fight out-of-doors. There were few benches, or even stools, and what there were were heaped with clothing and equipment.

Along the back wall, however, extended a row of wooden compartments or lockers that in no way suggested prize fighting. There might have been thirty of these, each a cube about the size of a hat box. They were painted with different colors, apparently in accordance with the fancy of those who rented them, and many had initials on their doors, or else heraldic devices of some sort—chevronels, cinquefoils, franches, saltiers, etc. It was plain from his mien as he conducted Tom Savage to this place that here was the great Broughton's pet particular pride.

Using a master-key, he opened several of these compartments, and Tom peered in.

"Oh, I see. The mufflers. The pillows."

"I prefer to call them 'boxing gloves,' " Jack Broughton said.

Tom stifled a smile. After all, the man who had invented them, popularizing the sport, was surely entitled to name the things. If the great Broughton preferred that pretentious "boxing gloves," who was he, Tom Savage, to sneer?

"You've seen them before?" Broughton asked, obviously dashed.

"Croucher Givens had a set in Lincoln."

"Oh, yes. Then you were obliged to use the same gloves all his other students used?"

Tom had found this no discomfort; but he said nothing.

"Most of the gentlemen who come here prefer to maintain their own, and I have boys who keep them in condition."

"Wipe off the sweat and blood and spit, you mean?"

"Well, yes. If you are truly interested in some lessons, Mr. Savage, I would recommend that method. Though of course I have house gloves as well."

"I think I might look at some. The new ones, I mean."

He bought a pair, and rented a locker. Though he had plenty

of money, he did not make the mistake of offering to pay out of pocket, immediately. He'd be billed in due time. This was a gentlemen's club.

"Uh, any device on the door, Mr. Savage?"

Gules, a mask sable, ensigned with a hangman's noose proper: that might serve the purpose? But he shook his head.

"No, no device. Just my initials."

There were many calls on Jack Broughton's time, and Tom said that he would delay him no longer, though he thanked him for his kindness, and promised to appear the following morning for a lesson. Again they shook hands, grinning at each other, and Tom took his departure.

He went to the stage door of the nearby Queen's Theatre, a portal he'd already rapped today. He got the same answer. *The Beggar's Opera* had closed, and Mistress Evans was resting out in the country somewhere. No, the doorkeeper didn't know where.

Tom hailed a chair and went to visit the gang.

They were expecting him. Soon after his arrival in Half Moon Street, and immediately after his first visit to the Queen's Theatre, he had sent a card to tell them that he'd appear.

They were mean men. Black and bitter as gall their thoughts must have been; and they sat in a circle and stared at Tom, saying nothing.

He ignored them to concentrate on Pottsy Palmer.

Success was going to Pottsy's head. He wore expensive clothes. His fingers gleamed with rings. There was rose point at his throat, and the heels of his shoes were red. Always physically arrogant, a man who had never met anybody he couldn't knock down, now, in addition, he had the assurance that goes with cash.

"You had no luck at the theater?"

Palmer shrugged.

"No. I went there as long as that play was on, and then she didn't send me any more money to go, so I didn't go any more."

"Where is she?"

"How should I know? Out in the country somewhere."

There was a pause. They were in the back room of the little gin shop in Alsatia Street, a place the gang virtually owned.

"*You* haven't caught sight of him, have you?"

"No," Tom said. "But what about that other possibility? What about the pickpocket who planted those stolen articles on me?"

"Oh, we've found him."

"You *have*?"

Trembling with excitement, Tom was on his feet. He leaned across the table.

"Tell me, then. Who is he?"

Palmer did not stir. His eyes, ice-blue under craggy brown brows, appraised Tom.

"First of all, mister, you've got certain watches—"

"Damn you, I'll not bargain!"

For one wild instant Tom thought of telling them that he was never going to sell the loot from the road—that somehow he would see that it all got back to is rightful owners. But he abstained. The gang simply wouldn't have understood. They'd have taken it for granted that any such silly statement was meant to hide something else.

So he spoke, instead, in a language that they *would* understand. He whipped out his sword.

"Now—*tell me*!"

He was the only one in that room who had a sword, and they must have seen from the way he held it that he knew how to use it. They could have rushed him, swinging snatched-up stools, and by sheer weight of numbers hammered him to the floor, though it was certain that at least a few of them would be hurt if not killed in the process. They must have assumed that he didn't have the wallet of loot with him. He would hardly have dared to bring it to a place like this. Nor could they be expected to know that he carried something far more valuable than watches and gold snuffboxes—a certain piece of paper that

126

made him, at that moment, the most valuable man in England.

What they saw was the sword—and the look on Tom Savage's face. They didn't move, only watched their leader for a clue.

Palmer was no fool. Hate and fear flared in the ice-blue eyes, like a spark that fails to reach the tinder, and then were gone; and the man somehow managed a smile—a smile made of suet.

"Now let's not have high words, your worship. We're all in this together. Remember that."

Tom said: "Where is he?"

Palmer nodded toward a member of the gang, a crow of a man, rust-colored, with small, dark, sour eyes, and lips intwisted as though he had a mouthful of verjuice.

"Arty here knows about it. Tell him, Arty."

"A spung-lifter named Mellish. A clean-pull cove, one of the best in the business—only sometimes he drinks too much. He just happened to be in Tom King's that night, looking around for somebody to rob, when Tewkes came up to him and pointed out you."

"You're sure of this?"

"Got it from three men he told it to himself. They wouldn't lie to me. Besides, what did Ase Mellish have to lose? He didn't have to *take something from* somebody's pocket, there in that jakes. What he was paid for was to *put something into* that pocket. Naturally he jumped at the chance—for half a crown."

"Would he testify to this effect?" Tom asked. "Would he sign me a deposition—an affidavit?"

"If'n you paid him he would. Ase Mellish'd sign his own mother's death warrant for a bottle of gin."

Tom had started out. He turned, sheathing.

"Where can I find this man Mellish? Where is he now?"

"Newgate."

21 *THE ENEMY OF MY ENEMY*

AN OLD SAYING HAS IT THAT THE ENEMY OF MY ENEMY IS MY friend. So it was with Tom Savage and the followers of Pottsy Palmer, the two parties having nothing in common save a desire to lay hands on Harry the Horsepad—the gang seeking his money, Tom his life.

For Tom Savage was utterly earnest in his determination to kill Tewkes. It was not a matter of personal vengeance; Tom didn't hate the man who had stepped without ceremony into his life, caused him to be jailed and all but hanged, and sent him out on the highway as a desperado. Rather, Tom applauded Tewkes for his quick thinking, his planning in advance, his adroitness in hoodwinking the Palmer gangsters, and his persistence in staying under cover, even when, as it were, fingers were snapped beneath his very nose. It was deeper than that. For Harry Tewkes, in Tom's way of thinking, by now was more than a man: he was the very spirit of evil.

Tom was not superstitious in the ordinary sense. Harpax and Marchosias, Modo and Hobbididance, he simply shrugged off: they were for children. He would, without a qualm, pare his nails on a Friday; he but chuckled when a black cat crossed his path; and when he gamed, which was seldom, he had not the slightest objection to winning the first cast at hazard, the first rubber at whist. Neither was he a mystic. Plato's cave-shadows

128

always seemed to Tom a little silly. Oh, he had read Plotinus, Aquinas, Spinoza, as well as William of Occam, Duns Scotus, Matthew of Aquasparta, and St. Bonaventura, but he found them fuzzy, and preferred either to go all the way back to Aristotle, or else seek his philosophy among the nearer and clearer writers—Locke, Berkeley, David Hume—who, though they might be less exalted, made more sense.

Yet here he was, steeping himself in a mystical stew. He could not deny that he had come to think of Harry Tewkes as something supernatural—an extension of his own self, an *alter ego*, a splitting-off of the bad part of him that the good part had always refused to see. Old-time Puritans believed that deeds of otherwise unaccountable bestiality or sacrilege were the result not of obsession but of possession. The Devil did not come from inside you but from outside. He was a very real, manlike being, equipped with horns and a forked, flashing, long tail. He would seize upon you when you were weak or not watching, and like a succubus cohabit abominably with you while you were all unaware of his presence, unless he was chased away by violent measures. Tom was not so naïf as all this. Yet some of the feeling clung to him now in his uneasiness.

His *practical* mind, by no means asleep, told him that Harry Tewkes was a retired criminal who, if not actually dead, from Tom's point of view was as good as dead. Tewkes had gone into hiding. He was hurting nobody. Why not let him alone? Tom's luck in escaping the gallows had been astounding. Why should he stir up more trouble? This was what his *practical* mind said. At the same time, he was shaken by the admittedly illogical conviction that Harry Tewkes was a predestined foe, one who must be sought out at all costs, and eliminated, before peace of the heart could return. Though he was posted in a thousand places throughout the land, and a huge reward had been put on his head, Tom still walked free. No hand was clapped upon his shoulder, no beak specifically pursued him. He had a bagful of the very best kind of money—bright, yellow gold. What was there to prevent him from crossing to France and resuming his old life? Or—under another name of course—going to the New World and starting a fresh one?

He couldn't. He didn't understand it, but he couldn't. There was something within him that forbade it, so long as Harry Tewkes remained alive. Indeed Tom went further, and against all dictates of reason, he inclined to the belief of the Puritans that only by extreme and even noisy violence can the Prince of Darkness be exorcised.

The enemy of my enemy . . .

Molly Evans did not fit into that category. Lord Seares certainly didn't. Seares had one thought and one only—his career, which was inextricably tied to that of his patron. When Tom sent in his name he was promptly received, his hand was shaken, and Seares himself closed the door behind the porter.

"You—you were successful?"

Tom frowned. He was in no hurry. Hurry, forsooth, was the bane of his existence here in London, where everybody scampered, as everybody yelled. Unlike his friend the Croucher, who expanded upon entrance into the capital, who—it could be taken—was never genuinely happy when he was anywhere else, Tom Savage did not like London. Now he was short, out of sorts.

"Where's Miss Evans?"

"Gone to the country. Kent. For a rest."

"What part of Kent?"

"I am really not supposed to divulge that. She seeks utter quiet. Now, did you—"

"I asked, what part of Kent?"

Lord Seares sighed. He wrote something on a piece of paper, and twirled this across the table to Tom.

"Did you—meet His Royal Highness?"

"Yes," absently.

Tom examined the paper, nodded, folded it, put it away.

"How did he—respond?"

"He resented it."

Even Seares grinned at this; but before he could speak again, Tom cut in.

"Look here: You didn't tell me the other day what your real relationship to Molly Evans is. All your talk about 'protectorships' and 'services' she performs didn't fool me. She was there then. She isn't here now. Suppose you tell me."

Seares nodded, unabashed.

"You could say that she works for me. She gathers certain snippets of information and I piece them together. She is never forced into anything. She takes what she hears, and passes it on."

"That is, she's a political spy."

Seares shrugged.

"I supposed it could be called that. Now, did you—"

"She helps you to do the dirty work for—*him*?"

He nodded toward a door at the far end of the room, a door from behind which came a voice. It was not an ordinary voice. It was no doubt the best-known voice in the world just at that time—the clear, measured, passionate baritone of William Pitt. Tom assumed that he was talking to a visitor, but from the boom it could have been to the House of Commons. Yet even muffled by a door it was a sound to hold any man spellbound.

"If you wish to put it that way. She's asked to do nothing shameful, of course. Moreover, she is in complete accord with Mr. Pitt's principles, and believes that she is doing no more than her patriotic duty in this."

"I thought he was above all that?"

"He is. But there are forces in politics, Mr. Savage, that simply can't be controlled by the finest intellect, by the highest integrity. They need, uh, constant curbing."

"I see."

"Offsetting."

"Yes."

"I don't want to make a speech, Mr. Savage, but—"

"I don't want you to."

"—would you think it rude if I returned to our original talk, which had to do with—"

"Why did the opera close?"

"It didn't close; it only suspended. I told you. Because Miss Evans needed a rest."

"She looked in good health to me."

"She did to me too. But she knows best. There was nothing abrupt about it. She made the arrangements with her manager, and she would already have been out of London three days ago if she hadn't gone to the Adam and Eve in the hope of catching sight of you."

"For you?"

"For me, yes. I wished to meet you—for reasons you are cognizant of, Mr. Savage. And *now*—"

"All right."

Tom flipped out the flat black wallet and tossed it upon the table. Lord Seares's avidity was touching. He fairly pounced upon the thing, and when with trembling fingers he had assured himself that its original contents were intact, he looked up at Tom Savage with tears in his eyes. Yet he was cool enough in usual circumstances, this Seares, and one who viewed the world with amused contempt, as though through a quizzing glass. Only in matters pertaining to Mr. Pitt did he show high anxiety.

"You are—vastly to be thanked, Mr. Savage."

Tom waved this aside.

Seares pulled out a drawer, a money box.

"I think a hundred guineas was the sum we agreed upon? But if you feel you should be paid more—"

"No, no! I have not named a price—yet. I'll do that later."

Seares looked at him for a long minute, like a gambler who sizes up a fresh contestant, fearing a trick. At last he put the box away.

"Do you mind, then, if I leave you for a moment?"

"Why not?" Tom nodded toward the inner door. There was no sound from that room now. "He must have prorogued Parliament. He ought to be alone."

Soon the inner door was swung again, and Lord Seares re-appeared in it, looking at Tom.

"Would you like to meet Mr. Pitt, sir?"

Tom did not hesitate. He had heard about the pomposity of this man, yet through all his adult life he had held Mr. Pitt in the highest esteem. He rose with alacrity.

"Delighted!"

Of that interview—if it could be called an interview—Tom Savage afterward remembered little. The truth is, he paid almost no heed to what the Great Commoner said, being absorbed in the study of the way he said it. Tom himself did not have a chance to speak, which was just as well. Every third word held at least four syllables, and it would have been a hard task to follow along anyway. It was better to enjoy the view.

The member from Aldborough could have worn a toga without being ridiculous. He was still in his late forties, though he sagged a little, and his face was unhealthily pale. He was tall, only a little flabby, and had a magnificent hawklike Roman nose, piercing dark-gray eyes. He would have made a great Lear, being somewhat too old for Hamlet. His hands, as he waved them, were long and white, and exceedingly delicate. And his voice, if loud, was musical.

"So you see?" he said suddenly, and for the first time was silent.

"I—I see."

"And now, if you'll forgive me—"

"Certainly, sir. I've been honored." He bowed. "Your servant."

"Your servant, sir."

But as Tom was on his way to the door of Seares's chamber, the great man spoke sharply behind him: "Uh, Savage—"

"Sir?" turning.

Mr. Pitt glanced over Tom's shoulder, as though to assure himself that his secretary was out of earshot. He leaned across the table; he put one of those lovely pale hands on Tom's left shoulder, and gave it a firm squeeze.

"Thank you," he whispered.

In the outer doorway, facing an empty hall, Lord Seares frowned as though at a departed shadow.

"You've met Ned Blane?" he asked. "Yes, of course. He challenged you at *The Beggar's Opera*, in the first interval, week before last. Said you'd offended his uncle."

Now it was Tom who frowned. Sometimes it gave him a creepy feeling, this London, a vast whispering gallery where everybody knew everything about everybody else.

"That affair was patched up. Why? Did you think that that was Blane, just now?"

"I'm sure it was. I am familiar with his dodge. Now he knows that you've been here."

"What if he does?"

"Only that he'll mark you for a Pitt man. And he himself, of course, is a Newcastle man—or his uncle is, which comes to the same thing." He shook his head. "Make no mistake about Ned Blane, Mr. Savage. He's not a popinjay. He is a desperate young man, badly in debt, and dependent upon his uncle, who is hand-in-glove with the Duke. Nineteen times out of twenty when Ned Blane challenges, the affair is patched up, as it was with you. But the twentieth time he kills."

"Isn't duelling against the law?"

"Why, yes, it is. But—didn't I say that Blane's uncle was an intimate of the Duke of Newcastle? Ned not only never comes to trial—he's never even been haled before a magistrate. He knows that too, each time he goes to the field. Mind you: I don't say that Ned Blane is stalking you! It may be no more than idle curiosity. He does have a great deal of time. But—I'd watch him, all the same."

They bowed.

"Your servant, sir."

"Your servant."

"Uh, Mr. Savage—" The secretary's tone was almost exactly that of his master, albeit less imperious. "One thing more—"

"Yes?"

"Did you, uh, did you read that paper yourself, Mr. Savage?"

Tom looked at him with no expression.

"My lord," he said at last, "I'm human."

Suddenly he chuckled. He jerked a thumb toward the inner door.

"And d'ye know," he cried, "by God, so is *he*!"

22 *CATCHER OF CRIMINALS*

THERE WAS AN ODOR OF SQUASHED LICE. THREE SIDES OF THE room were lined wih benches on which sat, hip against hip, the blowsiest set of sluts and rascals it had ever been Tom Savage's lot to look upon. None, he noted, was a member of Pottsy Palmer's gang, an underworld elite corps. These were silent but hardly still, for they fidgeted, scratching themselves, turning hats around in their dirty hands, putting elbows on knees, taking elbows away, shuffling their feet.

At the doorway, leading to a dim, narrow, long hall, which in turn led to Bow Street, was a clump of runners. *They* did not twist and turn, but stood like so many statues, arms akimbo, staring balefully at each newcomer, who quailed before them. Captaining these nimrods was the high constable of Holborn, a stocky man with a tun for a chest, legs almost unbelievably bowed, flat eyes, and fists the size and approximately the color of Westphalian hams.

The center of the room was occupied by a table at which three waspish clerks worked, bent over. Their pens made a prodigious scratching, and they acted like martyrs, men shamelessly put upon by all manner of pests. When approached—as sometimes, timorously, they were—they would hiss "Sh-sh-sh!" to indicate that their work was of surpassing importance, and they wouldn't look up.

The fourth side of the room was furnished, if stingily, with a podium and table. It was a plain place—no papers, no inkpot. On the wall behind the empty chair hung a portrait of His Gracious Majesty George II. It was not a very good portrait, and the frame wasn't clean.

Toward this table, as soon as he entered from the hall, the chief magistrate of Westminster, organizer of the Bow Street Flying Squad, loving brother of the late gentleman-novelist Henry Fielding, and in his own right beyond all question the greatest catcher of criminals in the history of the land, started to make his way. It would be a long way, as he no doubt knew, for there were many who sought to intercept him.

The pen-pushers sprang to their feet, and the runners stiffened to attention. The judge nodded genially at them, calling the chief constable by name.

"Good morning, Welch. The usual, I take it?"

"The usual, your honor."

John Fielding was rather short, rather dumpy. He had a quick, sure step, a low but crisp voice, and his clothes, though good, were curiously colorless: his mulberry coat was turned over with Mechlin at the cuffs, and the waistcoat buttons were crystal, yet somehow these weren't gay, brave. He wore a magistrate's full-bottomed periwig, and since atop that his standard-sized tricorn would have looked ludicrous, he carried the tricorn under his left arm. In his right hand he held a small whippy switch, a whisk he moved back and forth as though to shoo flies. His neck was thick, and his chin was firm, outjutting, but the sensitive small mouth and the thin, sensitive nose hinted of understanding and intelligence. No part of the eyes showed, these being covered by a black silk bandage fastened behind his head. For the man was blind.

He did not turn his head from side to side when he entered the room, as any other man might have done, yet each person who addressed him—and they were many, all petitioners, all whining—he faced directly. Most of them he cut short. But every one he addressed by name.

It was said of John Fielding that he knew three thousand thieves by their voices. This might have been an exaggeration.

Halfway to his bench he stopped short. It was as though he had scented something. Tom Savage, watching him, shuddered.

Then the man turned—all of him turning, like a soldier— and marched without hesitation to Tom. He stopped a few feet from Tom, as decisively as though somebody had put out a hand and touched him on the chest.

"But we have a stranger with us this morning, yes?"

Tom was frightened. It was like being accosted by a ghost. Yet the man's accents were quiet, the face below the bandage mild and even kindly.

"How—how did you know I was here?"

Fielding shrugged, ever so slightly. Exclamations of astonishment were an old story to him.

"Other senses are sharpened," he said dryly.

"Yes, of course. I'm sorry, sir."

"What would a gentleman be doing in this place? You think to learn how the other half lives, eh?"

"No, sir. It's information I'm after. Lord Seares ventured that you might be in a position to help."

Seares had said no such thing, but Tom was learning that noble names, in London, are keys calculated to open many a door.

Fielding, though not visibly impressed, nodded.

"Anything I can do—"

"Last week, sir, you jailed a man named Ase Mellish."

"That's true. Ase has been before me many times. Too many times. I should have let them hang him. But I hadn't the heart. So I accepted his plea that the watch he was trying to steal was worth less than twenty shillings, the neck price, though in fact I could tell from the feel of it that it was worth far more. Six months was the sentence. But I doubt that he'll last that long. Why do you ask?"

"What makes you think he won't last that long, sir?"

138

"Two things. Gin and the enemies he's made. Ase waxes talkative when under the influence. Careless, too. That's why he missed the pull the other night. If he had any sense he'd cease to pick pockets. But he hasn't any sense. No criminals have."

"These enemies—some of them are in Newgate with him?"

"Too many of them. And Ase helped send 'em there. And they know it. Sooner or later they'll put it to him, if he doesn't drink himself to death first."

"I wonder if I could see this man Mellish? To talk to. It's personal."

"You're not a lawyer. I can tell from your voice."

"No, sir, not a lawyer. As I said, it's personal."

Mr. Fielding was several inches shorter than Tom, and no doubt he was responding to the direction of Tom's voice when he lifted his face a little; but the effect was to give the lie to that black silk bandage, and Tom was weirdly convinced that he was being *looked at*, dispassionately *studied*.

"I take it, Mr.— uh—"

"Savage."

"—Mr. Savage, I take it that you are not acquainted with Newgate Prison?"

"Well . . ."

"No permission from me or anybody else is needed to visit prisoners during the regular visiting hours. But I should not advise you to go then. You can't hear yourself think."

"A private interview—"

"Once again no let-pass is needed. What you want, Mr. Savage, is a coin. Half a crown should do the trick. This is known as garnish. It's against regulations, of course, so don't say that I told you."

Tom had an almost overwhelming desire to run out of the room. He swallowed hard. He still felt that he was being physically *examined* by this blind man, his lineaments etched on a memory that was like a sheet of steel. Fervently, wildly, he wished he hadn't come. All bravado had gone out of him.

"Nevertheless, Mr. Savage, I shall be glad to give you a note to the chief turnkey. If you'll just come to me after the session—"

"Oh, no! I—I couldn't dream of putting you to all that trouble. You've been too kind already. Now if you'll excuse me—"

He bolted.

From the doorway, jostled by some late arrivals, and turned half around, he looked back. John Fielding had not moved, except to turn toward him, toward the doorway—fully around, like a soldier. He was staring—if a blind man can be said to stare—right at Tom.

It took a ten-minute set-to with the great Jack Broughton himself, and a rub-down—Croucher Givens still was celebrating his return and was in no shape to work—to quiet Tom's shaken nerves. While he lay on the rubbing table, he sent his boots out to be polished, his wig to be re-powdered.

His head still sang and his ribs ached—though he and the great one had used "boxing gloves"—when an hour later he presented himself at the main entrance of Newgate.

God, how that place stank!

Yet the Lodge, into which he was ushered, and which ordinarily was the lounging place for such debtors as could afford beer, brandy, and tobacco, if every bit as malodorous as he remembered it to have been, surely was less noisy. The few drinkers were silent and looked askance at Tom. Moreover, when the doorkeeper had accepted sixpence to call the chief turnkey, and had passed out into the Press Yard, Tom noticed through the opened door that this yard, usually the scene of the greatest bustle in all the vast sprawling prison, today was still. Indeed, there was an ominous hush over Newgate.

Tom had scant regard for the intelligence of those who staffed Newgate, from the governor down; and he had no fear of recognition. They did not customarily look beyond the coat; and his coat was a good one, as his purse was full. In addition, nobody would dream that a convicted felon who had so sensationally escaped would of his own free will return to Newgate.

140

The very audacity of the tactic, paradoxically, made it safe. But he didn't care for the quietude. It made him uneasy.

John Fielding had underestimated the chief turnkey's greed. Three shillings rather than half a crown was the garnish he demanded before he would even hear the name of the prisoner Tom wished to see. When he had pocketed this, and Tom had asked for Ase Mellish, the chief turnkey shook his head.

The drinkers, who were listening, looked at one another and leaned forward.

"He's not seeing nobody," said the chief turnkey.

"Why not?"

"He's had too much of a certain bottle."

"Damn it, man, put him in a separate cell then, where he can't get any—I'll pay for it—and I'll come back when he's slept it off."

"Mister, this is one he ain't going to sleep off."

The debtors did not snicker, as they customarily would have done at such a sally, a turnkey's wit, like that of a judge on the bench, being invariably funny. Instead, they looked frightened.

"What are you talking about?"

"I said Mellish'd had too much of a certain bottle. And it was broke before he got it—in his neck."

"Good God! Is he badly hurt?"

"Mister, he died ten minutes ago."

23 DOMINOES WITH THE COLONEL

HE WAS THE MAN AT THE NEXT TABLE. THAT WAS HIS CHOSEN role, the part he had played in London, on the road, at Tunbridge Wells. Never a garrulous companion, except when stirred on some such topic as predestination, in his student days Tom had not been much of a listener either—immersed as he was likely to be in a book or in his own thoughts or dreams. Today, with his life possibly depending upon overheard conversations, he paid more attention to his fellow men; and in truth he was learning that great profit can be found in keeping one's mouth shut and one's ears open.

It was but natural that he should go back to the Wells. After his previous visit to Newgate—a longer and far more painful visit—it had been his overpowering desire to get out into the country, to gulp good air. So it proved to be the second time. Though he'd loitered in the Lodge for less than ten minutes, he felt polluted, tainted. Grass that was green and the swaying branches of trees, in this slumbrous time of early summer, were to be had in Kent.

Besides, Molly Evans was staying at Green Bells, somewhere in Kent.

If so celebrated a singer was vacationing anywhere near the Wells, it would soon become cackled about. Tom already had learned that the visitors to Tunbridge Wells were not taciturn.

He rode down from London on a hired horse that was not black. Having made a before-dawn start, he was several miles short of the spa itself when two men rode out of a stand of trees, each with his right hand extended. The morning was still misty, and despite the unlikeliness of the hour, Tom thought of robbers, and his hand went into his saddlebag in search of a pistol. But immediately he laughed at himself, at the men too.

They were agents of innkeepers at Tunbridge Wells, come out on the London road in order to catch travelers before they reached the resort and to edify them with descriptions of this hostelry and another one, depending upon who had hired them this morning. From their presence, as from the breath-catching prices they quoted, Tom knew that this must be the height of the season at Tunbridge Wells. He would pay more, and he would not have the choice of quarters he'd enjoyed at the time of his previous visit.

Nevertheless he was well taken care of. There was not as much milording, and every place was more crowded—some of the water-takers looking to Tom's censorious eye a trifle common, with a touch of the *arriviste* about them—but the tone remained quiet, even genteel, and the pace was leisurely. He put up at one of the larger inns; and though he winced at mention of the price, he found the boniface worthy of his post.

Tom Savage had a weakness for innkeepers, and was frequently tangled in talk with them. So it was at the Crossed Halberds, Tunbridge Wells. The arrival being early, and Tom well turned out, the proprietor accompanied him to his room, an honor ordinarily accorded only to persons of high title or of very low reputation, such as, say, a duke, or one of the King's bed companions. Tom invited him in, and sent for a bottle.

It was not that Tom hoped to hear gossip from this source. Innkeepers, though they might be talkative enough, were leery of talking personalities. This one, Pepper by name, once he had said that no, he had not heard of a Green Bells, was pressed no further. Instead, Tom contrived to get him to talk about his establishment; and they passed a pleasant half-hour discussing wages, linen replacements, differing definitions of the phrase "by act of God or the King's enemies" as it related to the liability of landlords, and also the wine, a Bourgueil.

"I noticed as we entered this room the name 'Salop' on the door. Do you tab your chambers then after the shires of England?"

"Aye. Essex, Sussex, Devon, and so forth."

"There are only thirty-eight counties in England. Or is it thirty-nine? I forget. But what if you enlarged your place here and had more rooms than that? What then?"

"More than thirty-eight rooms? Great God, man, that wouldn't be an *inn*—that'd be a *city*!"

"Still, it could happen. The Wells is growing."

Pepper shrugged.

"Well, there's Wales. Radnor and Montgomery and Pembroke and Cardigan. And there's Scotland. And for that matter, Ireland. They've got counties there too, I think."

"You've picked a wide category. Yet it's like so many of the others—it's limited. I have often wondered about this. One innkeeper calls his rooms Castor and Pollux, Cassiopeia's Chair, Ursa Major. How long will that sky hold out, even though he goes to the Southern Hemisphere? Another uses Cancer and Pisces and Aries, as though there would ever be more than twelve signs of the zodiac, any more than there'll ever be more than twelve months in the year. Come to think of it, I put up one night in a hostelry in Herefordshire that *did* have its chambers named after the months. I slept in April."

"What else would your honor propose?"

"Well, I have wondered why the names of rooms couldn't be simply, A, B, C, D."

"There are only twenty-six letters in the alphabet, sir."

"True . . . And in Greek there are only twenty-four. But— why not ordinary numbers? One, two, three, four, five. There's no limit there."

144

Pepper lowered his head—for the man across from him was a paying guest—but when he spoke his voice was cool in defense.

"Consider the way people *think*, your worship. Figures and letters are for clerks. But when people travel, when they stop at inns, they imagine themselves as among the gentry. No matter what their birth is, or their fortune, they like to be *treated* that way. And consider yourself, sir: Would you rather be in a room called simply M or T or 67 than in one called Cornwall?"

"I can't say that I think it would make any difference."

"Perhaps not to you. But it does to others, I can tell you that." He rose, laughing, and thanked Tom for the wine, and started for the door, to which door Tom courteously conducted him. "The notion of an inn with more than thrity-eight rooms!" He slapped his hip. "Split me, I've only twenty-two myself, yet I run the largest place in Tunbridge Wells!"

"And the best, too, I have no doubt," Tom said. "God be wi' ye, mine host. I'll see you at dinner."

Out on the Parade, the place where Tunbridge Wells went to see itself and be seen by itself, he strolled languidly, his hat canted, the point of his sword peacocked out behind. Other heads might have been twisted as he passed, but his own, like his eyes, remained unswerving; for it was his ears that he chiefly used, concentrating on snatches of talk seined from that fashionable assemblage.

Nothing of significance swam into his net; but he kept walking. In the middle of the morning he took the water, still listening . . . He returned to the inn for dinner, which he ate in one of the most crowded places of the ordinary, the boniface being occupied. He loitered in the tap room for a little while afterward, and then went back to the Parade.

There was a concert making up, the musicians in the gazebo tuning their instruments, while flunkies from the various inns set out chairs. In any other circumstances Tom Savage would have sat down and enjoyed himself, especially since he had heard so much about the man who had arranged the music and composed most of it, the court *Kapellmeister*, an old and half-blind foreigner named Handel, who was said to be very skillful. But in Tom's experience, fribbles, though they do not necessarily fall silent when music is played, do at least lower their voices to show that they have breeding. So he went into an ordinary instead.

He sat at a table near French windows that opened upon a bowling green and the grassy area surrounding it, filled now with chairs and small tables where women were sipping tea. He was not so near to these women as to be deafened by their cackle—in sober truth, a possibility—but he was near enough to gather conversational scraps and strays. Thus he settled back, to any observer just another idle rake who, having nothing else to do, proposes to get drunk, and indeed might be drunk already, though it was scarcely past noon. The glaze of his eye suggested this.

How long the old man had been addressing him he didn't know. Not long, probably. For he looked like a short-tempered old fellow, red of face, crusty, irascible. Tom sprang to his feet.

There was nothing extraordinary about this. On his other visit, Tom had several times been greeted, if fleetingly, by persons he'd never seen before who supposed that they recognized him. The man before him now might have been simply seeking a place to sit—the ordinary was jammed—but it was more probable that he had been honestly mistaken.

"Can't think of the name," he muttered.

"Savage, sir. Thomas Savage."

"Of course. And I'm Colonel Sir Martin Dowd, at your service, sir."

"At yours, Colonel."

A thin hand, knobby with dark blue veins, was waved.

"Damned place is degenerating, don't you think, sir?"

"Absolutely, sir!"

"Not like Bath, eh?"

"Certainly not like Bath," cried Tom, who had never been to Bath.

The colonel had an air of long-standing disgust. At the sound of violins from the common, he belched.

"Fair music. That's that *Messiah* man, ain't it?"

"I believe so, sir. Won't you sit down?"

"Thank you. You alone, Savage? Me too. My females are off to one of those damned card-assemblies. Hate cards."

"So do I," said Tom.

"But sniff. Now that's different! See here: I seem to recall that you played a smart game of sniff. What say we have at it again, for old time's sake? Shilling a point?"

"But we haven't any dominoes—"

"I'll get 'em," said Colonel Sir Martin Dowd.

They played all that afternoon and, by the light of wax candles, well into the night. From Tom's point of view the arrangement was perfect. Colonel Dowd at all times was intent on his game, pondering the tiles as Marlborough might have pondered maps of the terrain just before Ramillies. He was a good player, if slow. His guts were boisterous, but he himself seldom spoke. Sometimes, as though remembering his manners, he would talk dutifully, if bumblingly, about various persons whose names meant nothing to Tom; and Tom would nod knowingly, yet absently, it being his pretense then that he too was absorbed in the intricacies of sniff. In truth he was able to continue listening . . . He lost; but the stake was not large enough to scare him. Neither did the colonel make any objection when from time to time Tom left the table, to go to the necessary room or just to stretch his legs—and listen elsewhere.

Tom himself stayed close with his mouth. There were times when the absurdity of the situation struck him so forcefully that he had all he could do to keep from laughing—he, the pseudo-Harry Tewkes, the man who had held up the King's brother, the most rigorously sought criminal in all the realm, playing dominoes with a half-deaf old codger at an inn!

Yet when what he sought came at last he almost missed it. This was because it came from such an unexpected source— Colonel Dowd.

"—damned silliness, driving ten-twelve miles out into the country just to gawp at a play-actress!"

Tom's head went up.

"What was that?"

"Not that she ain't worth a good long gaze, everything else being equal. Ever see her, Savage?"

"Who?"

"Why, damn it, this woman Evans! Who else was I talking about?"

"Oh. Yes, of course. I saw her as Polly Peachum. Lovely. Pardon me, Colonel. I was thinking of my next play. But—why Molly Evans? She's not here, is she?"

"I've been trying to tell you, sir, that my womenfolks have learned that she *is*. Not in the Wells, no, but at some place called Green Bells, south of here. And so they must traipse off, tomorrow morning, first thing."

"They're missing the promenade?"

"Oho, they'll be back in time for that! They mean to make a *really* early start—dawn."

"I see."

"Damned foolishness. What are we coming to, Savage, when gentlewomen will carriage twenty miles to gawp at a stage person?"

What are we coming to, thought Tom Savage, when gentlewomen think that an actress has no more right to privacy than a tree in the park? He said nothing but totted up the score instead.

"See here, Colonel, I must quit. Have to get up at dawn myself. I've been so fascinated by the game that I forgot— until just now. I owe you a hundred and twenty shillings. That's more than five guineas. I'll send it over first thing tomorrow, of course. Wasn't prepared to play tonight—not to lose like that anyway, ha-ha! Where are you stopping, Colonel?"

He had ten times that sum in his purse, but he needed the address. And on his way back to his own inn, staggering only slightly, he stopped at the stables and ordered his nag to be saddled and ready at dawn.

After which he went to bed, well pleased with a good day's work.

24 FIRST BLOOD, ABSENT-MINDEDLY

THE WAY WAS PLEASANT, FOR ALL THE EARLY HOUR. IT WAS between hop fields, the hills of Sussex humping an horizon on one side, the Medway distantly agleam on the other.

When the sun was fully up—for the sky was clear—there might be a plague of dust. But just now conditions for country carriageing were ideal, the deep-rutted lane being damp with dew, yet not soggy, and opposing no rocks to the small, smart, brightly-varnished cabriolet, a vehicle in truth more suited to city streets than to such a thoroughfare as this.

Mrs. Dowd and her two daughters raised their parasols as soon as ever they had an excuse to, and with small shrieks, took turns holding the reins, while Arthur, smiling in fond condescension, rode in the rear. The Dowd girls looked enough alike to be taken for twins, as indeed they often were, though there was the difference of a year and a half in their ages; but Arthur, a cornet in the King's Guards, knew them apart, being betrothed to one. Arthur thought the whole proceeding rather foolish, but he was in no position to say so, since his future father-in-law, the colonel, was paying his expenses at Tunbridge Wells.

The Green Bells was no disappointment, at first. It was small, it was cozy, and most emphatically it was vine-covered, murmurous with bees, quaint. Mrs. Dowd declared that it was *exactly* the sort of *hideaway* that an actress like the *incomparable*

Molly Evans *would* have, and didn't Arthur think so too? Whereupon Arthur averred that he did.

A closer look brought about some diminution of these raptures.

Under the sign—cracked, chipped, the paint peeling—a door was firmly shut. Nor was there any knocker; and it was only after they had rapped hard for more than a minute that the door was opened.

The woman who stood there was no plump, rose-cheeked, cheery landlady, but gnarled, disagreeable of aspect, with a stringy neck, an Adam's apple that leapt, and sea-green, malevolent eyes. She didn't curtsy, but put her fists on her hips and demanded to know what all this noise was about.

Nonplused, Mrs. Dowd nevertheless rallied, fishing up her broadest smile.

"We're from Tunbridge Wells."

"Well, I'd know that."

"I mean, we don't *live* there—we're *visiting* there."

"Yes."

Arthur shifted from foot to foot. Unsure of himself—he had just turned eighteen—he wondered whether he ought to intervene here and teach this hag to mind her tongue. He decided not to. The woman who was soon to become his mother-in-law could manage it best.

Mrs. Dowd tried. She flashed her most winning smile, put on her most disarming manner, and archly inquired if Miss Evans was still in bed. *She* knew how actresses sometimes were, she said, though she was less than willing to divulge the secret of how she had come by this knowledge.

There was no answer.

"But if you was to tell her that four *very ardent admirers* of her art were here, and that we'd travelled all the way from the Wells to greet her—"

"She won't see you anyway. Why should she? Whyn't you leave the poor thing alone?"

Gone now was cajolery. Not for nothing was Mrs. Dowd the

wife of a colonel. She could be kind; but when kindness was not appreciated, she could be firm too. Minerva-like in her majesty, with forefinger dramatically upthrust, arm raised as though about to summon a thunderbolt, she pointed to the sign.

"See here, my good woman, is this or isn't it a public inn?"

"It ain't, no."

"Then why do you have that sign there?"

"Maybe because I like the looks of it, and maybe because I ain't found time to take it down. It's no business of yours, either way."

Then she stepped back into the house and slammed the door, and they heard a bolt thrown.

Mrs. Dowd, a courageous soul, took it well. She even giggled, though she must have been hurt to the quick, as she proposed that they make the best of a bad bargain by walking around the wee house and seeing if they couldn't catch a glimpse of that so-high-and-mighty stage actress in one of the windows.

It was Beatrice who spotted the stranger again. Beatrice was not the sister who was betrothed to Arthur, and she resented this, as the older of the pair, and often went out of her way to be kind and thoughtful to him, hoping that he might fall to thinking he'd made a mistake. Now she took Arthur's arm, as she pointed across a small hayfield to the corner of a wood, from which a man had just emerged.

"There he is again, see?"

He had followed them all the way from Tunbridge Wells, or at any rate he had been behind them. He had not accosted them, nor had he molested them in any way, or used any menacing gestures; yet his presence back there troubled Arthur, who several times had thought that he ought to order the man away.

Now this fellow was on foot, having turned his horse loose, though still saddled, to munch grass. He was doing nothing—just gazing toward them.

"You really ought to speak to him, Arthur," Beatrice said.

"By God, I will!"

The truth is, Arthur was glad to be about a business he understood—or thought he understood. Uneasy, feeling that he had made a booby of himself by his silence while that countrywoman slanged Mrs. Dowd, he was eager to show, before all three of the ladies, that he had not forgotten how to be a cavalier. He drew. He started on a long stride for the stranger.

"No, no, I forbid it!" he heard Mrs. Dowd call; but he kept going.

His must have been a truculent figure as he marched across that field, swishing steel before him.

"Now see here," he started.

But he stopped, dumbfounded. For the man had turned and run back into the wood.

This was more than Arthur had exected, and indeed it was more than he could bear. His response was compulsive. He didn't really know what he was doing when he ran after the man, but he could not have helped doing it anyway.

He soon learned his mistake.

The wood was tiny, no more than a clump of oak, and on the other side, only a few yards away, there was a field similar to the field the hasty Arthur had only just quit, save that the ground there was smoother, less nubbly.

The stranger had stopped, turning, and had taken off coat and waistcoat. And the stranger drew.

"This is a better place, I think," he said. "On guard, sir!"

Once again Arthur could have acted the gentleman—or at least the man of sense—by pulling himself up and proffering an apology. He didn't even think of this. He was too badly flustered, believing, as he somehow did, that the ladies were watching him—though of course they could not now see him for the trees. So he didn't stop to think. He didn't explain. He simply raised his point and went in.

Arthur was a well-set-up young man, tall, and with a long reach. He'd had a few fencing lessons. But never before had he faced his man with bare steel.

He might have been comforted, if but briefly, to learn that

his opponent too, though much more experienced upon a strip, never before had been called out.

Tom Savage had often wondered if he would in truth one day meet an enemy on the field of honor. He had wondered what he'd feel like, in those circumstances. He had never known any fear in fencing; but then, he'd never known unbuttoned blades. There is all the difference in the world.

He would not have dreamed that it could be like this—that in rage he was proposing to teach an insolent puppy his place. Your first duel should be for something important, something big and significant, not a mere point of manners.

His rage ebbed almost as abruptly as it had risen. He backed away from Arthur's charge. His one fear was that he might kill the lad. He decided to call a halt, and had actually opened his mouth when Arthur charged again.

Again Tom retreated, but not far this time. Arthur had a habit of lunging with a bent right arm, which exposed his elbow. Tom didn't parry or counter. In the proper sense of the word, he didn't riposte. He simply bent low, and reached out and touched that elbow with his point.

Then he did call.

"You beefbrain! You can't go on! You've been hit!"

Arthur came to a halt, blinking, blushing, looking at his right elbow as though he had never seen it before. He had probably not even known until now that it was pricked. He went hot with humiliation.

Tom wiped a fleck of blood from his point.

"Tear your shirt and wrap it around a few times, and it won't show through the coat," he advised. "Better get a surgeon to look at it when you're back at the Wells, though."

Furious, Arthur bowed.

"You'll hear more of this," he mumbled.

"I hope not. I shan't listen, if I do. But mark you *these* words, little boy: If you're going to make a practice of charging up to total strangers and waving a sword at them, you'd better take a few lessons in fencing first. Good morning to you, sir."

From the shadow of the trees Tom watched a baffled caval-cade depart, the women twittering like birds, the puppy stiff and straight, tut-tutting. Tom could not hear what the puppy said, but he could guess.

When the dust had settled—for there was dust on the land by this time, the sun full and fair—he tethered his horse and brushed his coat and straightened his stock with wobbling hands, and went to the Green Bells.

He was bemused by the name, the sign. Why should anyone set up an inn out here? Had this lane been intended as a high-way, and had the builder of the Green Bells believed that he could soon count on heavy traffic? What remote event—for the house was old—had shattered that expectation? Tom neither knew nor cared; and only two things caused him to let his mind dwell upon the matter—a natural, increasing interest in inns and everything that went toward their erection and mainten-ance, and a desire to think of something else besides the woman he was about to meet.

For he was sure she was there. And he was afraid to face her.

He had thought about her too often and too fervently. In the long nights, during the waitings out on Hounslow Heath, he had remembered everything he knew about her; and now he was shaken.

A few moments before, he'd had his first sword fight. He had passed it by, contemptuous. But confronting Molly Evans would be a much more perilous action.

He believed that he was watched as he crossed the field. He drew a deep breath before he rapped on the door, which was instantly opened.

"I too am from the Wells, goodwife, but I am not the—"

"Come right in, sir."

He had little recollection afterward of the two rooms he traversed, dim after the glare outside. Then he was ushered into a paved place behind the house, a place roofed with wisteria. Sunspots wavered before him in a glittering, shifting cloud—oval, round, triangular; some, it could be, all but square—sun-

155

spots that jiggled erratically as a zephyr of a breeze made the leaves go back and forth.

In the middle of this, Molly Evans was rising from a chair.

She wore peach, which in this deceptive light showed sometimes as orange, sometimes as a flaming bright yellow. It was a severe costume, no panniers beneath it, no frills to puff it out; and her hair was caught up into a plain, soft bun behind her head. Grecian, Tom thought. But not, thank God, blonde.

She reached a hand toward him.

"I thought you would come, somehow," she said. "Thank you."

He did not take the hand, only bowed. Once again, he was afraid. If he took the hand he'd kiss it, and if he kissed it he could lose all control of himself. Already he knew that he was lost. Whatever she was, he wanted her.

His muscles screamed at him to grab her. And at the same time, perversely, his muscles begged him to throw himself upon his knees before this lovely woman. He had been stabbed to the heart more accurately and with a more intense force than the puppy of a few minutes ago could ever have stabbed him with that sword. He was in love.

"It is hard to know why you're here," he said.

"And you're entitled to know, Mr. Savage. Sit down."

He didn't obey. And when she had waited a moment, taking back her unaccepted hand:

"There are several reasons. One was that I hoped to get some word here of Harry Tewkes."

Tom swallowed.

"Do you love him so much, then?" he asked in a voice that might have been the whisper of a dying man.

"*Love* him?"

The violet eyes were not violet now, but black. They widened enormously. The sweet small mouth was open as though about to shrill in rage.

"*Love* him? Why, I hate that man as I pray to God I'll never hate anything else on this earth!"

156

"You—hate him?"

"Sit down," said Molly Evans. "Will you have a dish of tea? It could be that I owe you an explanation. And perhaps I'd better start at the beginning?"

"That," said Tom Savage, "would be a good plan."

25 *THE TALE SHE TOLD*

THERE WERE BIRDS IN THE WISTERIA, OUT OF SIGHT, BUT NOISY, fussing, scolding one another. It was not song that they gave forth—it was homelier than that, more rustic too, and it seemed to go with the sunspots. Though not usually moved by the arrangements of nature, or even aware of them, Tom Savage was to remember those sunspots, that wisteria, the indefatigible cheep of birds.

Not that he looked at them! He never turned his head.

Molly Evans sat with her hands in her lap. Her shoulders sagged. She spoke in a voice of grave simplicity. So small, so dainty, she suggested a child, but not a prim schoolgirl who re-cites a lesson. She meant what she said.

"I have never known any life but the life of the stage, Mr. Savage. I've always been stared at."

He nodded, but said nothing.

"Not just the stage either. That's grand. It's only lately that I have seen footlights and a dressing room. It's only lately I have had enough to eat. And I still can't see how this happened. I don't suppose anybody can."

This was like her. As Tom knew from having seen her as Polly Peachum, this woman's naïveté was genuine; she was inno-cence without the simpers; and in truth some of her success must have been due to the very astonishment she displayed at finding herself successful.

"Before that it was streets, public houses, anything. I don't remember a time I wasn't performing. I don't remember when I wasn't holding off men. My mother and father could not help me much, because I was hardly more than a child when they died. They were artists too. Welsh. I'm Welsh, you know?"

"Yes."

"I am not even sure that they were married, my mother and father. I have some reason to believe that I'm a bastard. But my son isn't."

Tom was flabbergasted. She looked so tiny, so young!

"You—you have a child?"

"Why not? I'm a woman. Women often do."

"But—but—"

"There was nothing improper about it, as I told you. We were married. It cost us four shillings, and we got a certificate. It wasn't a Fleet wedding, Mr. Savage. It was a real one."

"I see."

"Robby was young, and very earnest. I won't pretend that I loved him, but I didn't have much of a choice—only a choice between him and a brothel, which is the same as saying between him and the river. And I wanted to live."

"Naturally."

"He was in the troupe too, you see. And I couldn't raise sympathy any longer as a girl. I was a woman then, by everybody's definition. So I needed a protector. I still need one, but nowadays I can afford to hire a lord. I couldn't afford anything then. So I married Rob. And we had a baby.

"I don't wish to detail the story of my life. Heaven knows it's sordid enough, and I fancy not very interesting. But you should know this much."

"Please go on."

"Two months after George was born we were playing Portsmouth, and after the show Robby stopped in the taproom while I was upstairs nursing the baby. He wasn't a man for drinking, ordinarily, but it seems he'd met some old merchant fleeters. He had been a sailor once, for a little while, and he was sentimental about it. He fell to talking their language, and that was a mistake, because when the press gang came, they hauled him off with the others. He tried to explain about me and George, but they never gave him a chance; they beat him with the flats of their hangers until he was unconscious, blood all over his head. And they *carried* him off, literally. I wasn't there, of course, but I heard about it. I did everything I could to get him out, but the Navy doesn't let able-bodied men go. Robby did the best thing *he* could think of—he deserted. Well, they caught him. And they hanged him. Will you have another dish of tea, Mr. Savage?"

"Um . . . If that's brandy I see in that bottle you might pour a little of that in too."

"It was soon after that that I met Mr. Fletcher. I think my success is due to him. He has made a great deal of money out of me, yes, but he's kept his hands to himself. It was Mr. Fletcher who took me up to London and got me the hearing.

"You've seen me, Mr. Savage. You know that a great deal of my charm depends upon my *smallness*, my *helplessness*, isn't that true?"

"It is. But it's strange to hear you say so."

"Why not? This is my profession. I've got to be conscious of it. I can't go walking across the stage in my sleep, like Lady Macbeth. I told you the other morning, at your inn, that I am not a lady—I'm an actress. And I meant that. But the public thinks of me as a lady. It thinks of me as a small, and very lovely, and dainty and fragile *doll*. Well, dolls don't have babies."

"I'm beginning to understand."

"Yes. It would shock people, somehow. It shocked you, a few minutes ago.

She did not face him as she spoke, but sat a bit sideways, gazing at the hands in her lap; and he marvelled that she could be so sensitive.

160

"It was Mr. Fletcher's logic. He said that if people knew about George it would detract from my appeal. He may have been right, he may have been wrong. I owed him too much to argue. Besides, it fitted in with my own hopes. I never did want George to be brought up in the city, or on the road. *I* had to go through all that dirt, but why should *he?* And then, too, I wanted a place where I could go myself and simply be quiet for a while.

"Finding Mrs. Paul was a stroke of luck. She's the woman who let you in just now, and she's a treasure. Finding this house was much, much harder. But I did it at last."

"What's the reason for the inn sign?"

"This used to be an inn. I can't imagine why. Inns have always fascinated me. So I let the sign stay."

He took a careful and very small drink.

"Please go on, ma'am."

"Then Harry Tewkes came along."

"Ah?"

"I have since called for a clause in my contract that I shan't be obliged to meet anybody who happens to push his way into the green room. At that time, five-six months ago, I didn't have that. I don't think it would have kept Tewkes out anyway. He's a man with a genius for getting into places. Does it partly by means of a glib tongue, partly by bribes."

"A quick man with a coin, no doubt. They have to be, in that business."

"Mr. Savage, I didn't know what his profession was when I met him. I wouldn't have agreed to meet him if I had."

"Yes."

"I said the other day that you don't look like Mr. Tewkes, though it's hard to say why. He's only a few years older. He might be a hair taller. But there's all the difference in the world, really. He's—he's—*coarse. A*nd you're not. You're kind."

"Thank you."

"He was hard to hold off. The more I saw him the less I liked him, but as I said, he has a way of worming himself in. And he was infatuated. I knew that. You mustn't think me vain, Mr.

Savage, but I have had men in love with me before this, and I know the signs."

"I can believe it."

"Then one night he proposed to me. I mean, he proposed marriage. I turned him down without a thought. But he kept babbling on. I don't know what had come over him. He certainly wasn't drunk. I doubt that Harry Tewkes has ever been drunk. He isn't that kind. But he was certainly foolish that night. Maudlin. He told me that he had a beautiful house in the country—"

Quickly: "Did he say where?"

"No. And I didn't ask him. I didn't want to seem interested. But when he told me how he made his money, how he spent his nights, then I *was* interested."

"There's something like six thousand pounds on his head."

"I wasn't thinking about that, Mr. Savage."

"Forgive me."

"I don't know why he ever blurted it out. He's anything but an impulsive man. Perhaps he thought he could impress me. The pad is supposed to be such a romantic rascal! Women swoon when a highwayman's hanged! Anyway, he did tell me. But he said he was leaving that life. He said he was rich now, and would retire. We'd get married and go to this place of his, and nobody would ever hear of Harry Tewkes again. He swore it. He hinted that he had some brilliant scheme up his sleeve."

"So he did."

"Aye," dryly. "But I was not interested. I commanded him never to try to see me again. And I went away. Two days later I had a chance to come here to Green Bells. It would mean travelling all night, and I'd only have a few hours anyway, but it would be worth it to see George. But George wasn't here. Mrs. Paul was in distraction, hysterical.

"It had just happened, a little before I came. Mrs. Paul had left him, to go down to the village. On the way she passed a man. She didn't know him, but from the way she described him there

162

isn't the slightest doubt that it was Tewkes. And when she got back George was gone."

"Great God! The man's a kidnabber too?"

The crime of kidnabbing—or kidnapping, as it was sometimes called—a little while ago had been prevalent in the cities, especially the seaports. Such a commotion arose, however, that constables had redoubled their vigilance, and even in the underworld the racket was esteemed so vile that men who would otherwise be mum turned away from it in disgust, and became informers.

The children were needed in America as indentured servants, apprentices, you could even say slaves. They were simply stolen, usually off the streets. The kidnabber worked with a forger, who supplied false parents' permission papers, and turned these, together with the small prisoners themselves, over to some ship's master who knew enough to keep his mouth shut and rake in a good profit. The children, three thousand miles away when they got a chance to tell their stories, weren't heeded. Not one in a hundred ever saw his mother and father again. Tom often thought of America—a place in which he was taking a more lively interest these days—as populated largely by unwanted waifs.

But it passed belief that a successful robber like Harry Tewkes should stoop to a crime so hideous and so dangerous, a crime that had been discredited even among criminals.

"No," said Molly Evans. "No, it wasn't kidnabbing. It wasn't that. I reported it to the sheriff, but I don't think that he took me seriously. An excited mother whose chick had wandered off into the wood, no doubt, and would wander back again. But I knew it wasn't kidnabbing. I knew that from the beginning. And I was sure that I'd see Harry Tewkes in the audience the next night at the theater."

"You—*played?*"

"We must play," simply. "And he was there. I knew he would be. He virtually lived in the Queen's those days. Of course he came backstage afterward. He was plain-spoken. No beating about the bush. He didn't say anything more about marriage. I was to go out to the country with him and live with him. Otherwise I would never see George again."

"What did you do?"

"I believed him. I couldn't help it. I knew him so well. I would have gone with him, right then and there—God help me, Mr. Savage, I was half out of my mind—I would have gone with him. But he insisted that I take another day to think it over. I don't know what he meant. Was it a refinement of cruelty, or just an extra precaution? Maybe a little of each? Anyway, he said he'd be back the next night. But he wasn't. Because he'd just been arrested."

"Rather, *I* had."

"Yes, *you* had. But I didn't know that then. Lord Seares was in France and I didn't have anybody to advise me. I tried to arrange to get into Newgate to visit him—you—but they wouldn't let me at that time. Only robbery victims who might identify him, I was told. Unless I could show that I was his wife or some near relation, which I couldn't. But Pottsy Palmer talked me out of that plan anyway. He said Harry Tewkes would never tell any secrets in jail. We'd have to get him out."

"How did you know Pottsy?"

"I had seen him three or four times, in the theater, with Harry Tewkes. I knew he was some kind of associate, and I guessed he was the fence. But before I could look around for him, *he* came to *me*. They were just as eager to see me as I was to see them. Because it seemed that Tewkes had stolen money from the men, and hidden it. So we agreed to work together to get him out. And I did it. I must have been mad—but I did it."

"Thank God you did," Tom said softly.

She was weeping now. You would never have known it from her voice, that exquisitely controlled instrument. Nor did the tears fall; they hung bright, one in each eye.

Tom Savage rose. His left hand gripped the hilt of his sword, the blade that had so lately been blooded on Arthur, and he squeezed it.

"I'll leave you, ma'am. That's best. You are hoping that Tewkes might be afraid to seek you out in the city, but could come to you here when he learns that *The Beggar's Opera* is closed?"

"Yes, that's it."

"But he won't enter if he sees a strange horse. You have explained a great deal. I'm going back to London, and I have another plan. You know my inn. Call me if you need me, ma'am, no matter what the hour of day or night."

"Thank you," she whispered.

She extended her hand, and this time he took it, and kissed it. He trembled, but he held himself in, though he didn't dare to look at Molly Evans. Mumbling something, he wheeled and went out.

"Guard her," he muttered to Mrs. Paul at the door. He pressed a sovereign into her hand. "Don't let her get hurt."

He kept his head down as he mounted, for he himself was weeping then.

26 *A MATTER OF TIME*

His mind as he rode back to the wells was a turmoil. Until lately an amiable, not to say placid person, he was unaccustomed to hot indignation, which went to his head the way liquor will go to the head of a lad who has never before drunk any. The squalor and stench of Newgate, the overhasty judgment—or rather misjudgment—the japing faces, the screams, Pottsy Palmer's arrogance, the shame and hardships of a criminal life—all these things had combined to disturb him, to shake him out of his student's serenity; but the disclosure of what had been done to Molly Evans all but caused him to explode.

For the first time in his life, he wanted to fight. It was lucky for Arthur the Impetuous that he met Tom on the way *to* the Green Bells, not on the way *back*.

Tom had told Molly that he had a plan of action. This was a white lie, an excuse to leave her with hope. In fact, he didn't know what he'd do next, except that he would go to London, being too badly roiled to laze any longer at the Wells.

It was in this frame of mind, then, that he re-entered the Crossed Halberds, nodded curtly to his friend Penny, the proprietor, and encountered the Honorable Ned Blane.

This was no more than mid-morning, yet Blane already was drunk, a circumstance not in itself unusual, any more than it was unusual to see him in this resort at this season; but to a troubled Tom Savage he was no less unwelcome for that reason. Tom was rash. Without pausing to think, as Blane lurched toward him, impatiently he put out a hand—and pushed.

"Sorry. No, I can't have a drink with you now. I'm busy."

It was no more than that—a push, and hardly a harsh one either. It could not have been called a blow. Yet its effect upon the tall young fop was extraordinary. Blane stiffened. All unsteadiness seemed to flow out of him, so that of a sudden his hands were utterly steady. His eyes cold, on his mouth not the shadow of a smile left, he gave a bow.

This was in the ordinary, crowded now. There was a hush. Faces were lifted, breaths caught up.

"Oh now, see here, I'm sorry—" Tom started.

Blane turned, either not hearing or pretending not to hear. Poised, cool, his voice sounding unnaturally loud only because of the silence, he addressed a youth who had followed him out of the taproom.

"Could I have a word with you, Archy? A personal matter."

They passed back into the taproom.

Everybody was looking at Tom Savage, and fear was loud in most eyes.

He shrugged. He looked toward the taproom for a long moment, then turned away. This was no occasion for apologies, considering his mood. Blane, hurt, was nothing if not formal. There would be plenty of time. Tom got his key, asked that the *valet de chambre* be sent to him, and went upstairs.

Penny the proprietor was at his heels.

"I don't like it, Mr. Savage. I hope you won't fight—here anyway."

"I won't fight anywhere."

"He's a fire-eater. Touchy as a Frenchman. And they do say he's one of the best fencers in the land. If anything was to happen here, at the Crossed Halberds—"

"Cease worrying. To do the thing right Blane'd have to send a message asking me for an explanation, and after that send a written challenge, right? Well, he won't even get the message to me—unless he writes it mighty fast. For I'm leaving, now."

"So soon, Mr. Savage?"

Yet undeniably there was relief in the proprietor's voice. A duel never lent an air to any inn. There was no law about duelling in Great Britain. If the affair ended fatally, it was treated like an ordinary murder.

"I need hardly say it's not because of what just happened downstairs," Tom said.

"Oh, of course not!"

"If anything, that would cause me to stay on."

"Yes, yes."

"But there's something else. Urgent business."

The truth is, he was worried, among other things, about that wallet of loot. He had left it at the Bull in Half Moon Street, not in his own room there but with the proprietor. But even proprietors, though Tom had a great fondness for them, were not without their curiosity. One peek into that wallet—He must get rid of that loot soon, somehow.

Master Penny dismissed the valet and personally helped his guest to pack, chattering the while.

"It's London you return to, Mr. Savage?"

"Oh yes."

"I wonder if you'd be kind enough to leave a message on the way? It has to do with innkeeping, which I know interests you. And it won't take but a few minutes."

"I'd be delighted."

As the event proved, this stop—it was not in any way a digression, the place being smack on the highway, in Lewisham— made a pleasant period of rest that served to put Tom in a somewhat less savage frame of mind.

Master Welt was a plump man with an oleaginous smile, and the westering sun shone upon his pate, all bare, as it shone on the Poole meandering nearby, and shone too on the various inn signs and shop signs with which his yard was filled. For Master Welt, as he told Tom—he was a chatty little man and anxious to please—liked to work outside when the weather was fine. "Like a stonemason." He had never, he added, learned to enjoy the smell of paint, which on rainy days gave him a headache.

The business to be conducted was trifling—Master Penny wished to send the Crossed Halberds sign to Master Welt for refurbishment, but he wished to have the quickest possible job done and sought to learn how much work Master Welt had on hand—and it took only a few minutes; after which the genial artist invited Tom, while his horse rested, to have a glass of wine and inspect the premises.

These were large, as such places went, for Chas. Welt was one of the best in the trade. Not only did he paint on order; when times were slow he would paint on speculation, something that, as far as he knew, no other sign-maker ever did. He was an original.

"Now look at them grapes, your worship. Don't they fair make your mouth water? And this goat! You wouldn't want to meet *him* when you was crossing some field, now would you?"

He laughed, quivering like a jelly, his eyes for a moment completely out of sight.

"What's this?" Tom asked.

"One I'm working on now, from time to time. It's going to be my masterpiece when I get it finished."

"The color's handsome. The red coat . . . the yellow cockade . . . You're saving the face for the last, I take it?"

"Yes, sir. But only because I'm going to do *that* from life."

"Truly? This is to represent a real person, then? How interesting."

"Nobody's ordered it yet. But somebody will. As soon as he's hanged."

"Who?"

"Why, Harry the Horsepad."

"Oh, of course. I should have recognized him."

"I started it when he was nabbed, last spring. As soon as he's hanged, I said to myself, he's going to be a great man—and that means somebody'll name an inn after him. And I want to be right there, with the sign all finished, before they can change their mind."

"An inn . . . I hadn't thought of that."

"Sure to, your worship. Harry Tewkes is a famous man now, what with all them ballads and stories. But once he's been turned off, then he'll be really great. He owes that to his public."

"*He* might have different ideas, himself."

"Tut-tut, your worship. They always gets hanged." He hitched up his green apron, chuckling. "This man got away once, but he won't get away again." He shook his head, the jowls waggling. "That was a sad disappointment, that day. I was up all night, to hold a place on a roof I'd paid three bob for. And then he never got that far. I never even saw him. Was you there that day, sir?"

"Well, yes."

"Ah, that was a terrible morning. Everybody was disappointed. Everybody."

"Excepting the prisoner."

The little man roared with laughter, slapping his hips.

"Ha, ha, that's funny! Everybody but Harry Tewkes, eh? Ha, ha, ha!"

Tom was studying the picture. It was large, depicting the upper half of a horseman. He wore a scarlet coat, a black cocked hat, and there were large brass pistols in his hands. Many details had been painted in—the reins, the stock, the wig-bag—but the face itself was not there: as yet it was but a yellowish blank.

"But I'll finish it, of course, when they get him again and do a proper job on him. I'll be right there, up close. It's only a matter of time, that's all. Will you have another glass of wine, sir?"

"Thank you, no. I'd like to be in the city before dark. An appointment. Uh, good luck with your venture."

"Oh, I'll finish it, and I'll sell it. That's forethought. Acumen."

"Yes."

"God be with ye, sir. I'll see you there, up at the top of Tyburn Hill, when they hang Harry the Horsepad."

170

"Oh, undoubtedly," murmured Tom.

It was indeed getting dark, the shadows stretching themselves along the pavement, when at last he turned into Half Moon Street. He was on foot then, having personally stabled the post horse instead of sending it around by an attendant, and he hurried, thinking of supper.

But he came to a stop when he saw the two men who stood before the inn door, the one with eyes that went back and forth, the other with eyes that were covered by a bandage. There they stood, side by side, blocking the entrance. It was plain that they were waiting for somebody.

They were Saunders Welch, high constable of Holborn and head of the famous Bow Street Flying Squad, and the man who had originated that squad, the chief magistrate of Westminster, John Fielding, sometimes called the Blind Beak.

27 *CONTROL YOURSELF!*

CONSCIENCE, AS SHAKESPEARE HAS POINTED OUT, DOTH MAKE cowards of us all. Tom's impulse was to run; only by an effort that caused his leg muscles to throb did he refrain from doing so. He flushed, furious, for he had told himself that he shouldn't feel guilty, that in truth he *wasn't* guilty. Yet here he was again, jumpy as a hare, his eyes hurting, starting at every small sound.

Yet he made no abrupt movement. He was only a few yards from the Bow Street men when first he saw them; and though the bustle in this, the pre-supper hour, was considerable, any rabbitlike leap would have caught the attention of both, and drawn upon Tom the glance of the sharp-eyed Welch. What Tom did was step behind a barber-surgeon's pole, from where, swathed in shadows, he could study the men who waited.

They were terrible to see, if only because of the contrast they presented.

Welch was the thief-catcher *par excellence.* His hand, falling upon a shoulder, had sent a bolt of panic into the breast of many a felon. His arms were those of a gorilla. His legs were grotesquely bowed, though they showed sturdy enough. Blue-chinned, undeviating, his eyes moving back and forth under those outjutting brows, he gave an impression of tense but exquisitely controlled strength. Motionless, a statue save for the eyes, despite his appearance of awkwardness you were convinced on seeing him that, if needs be, he could and would run like a whippet, pounce like a tiger, wrestle like a bear.

By the side of this horror John Fielding suggested a cherub waiting to take his part in some children's party game—blind-man's buff, say, or pin-the-tail-on-the-ass. The eye bandage enhanced this illusion, if it didn't bring it about. His chin, plump, was somewhat sunken, and he stood with his feet apart, his hands clasped before him. They were pale hands, delicate, with blue veins crisscrossing their backs. His lips were a little open, his head a little tilted, as though he were listening to voices not audible to the seeing world.

Stone, Tom Savage watched. The first move must come from them.

It did; and after the terror these two had struck to Tom's awareness, it was ludicrous, an anticlimax.

A boy approached them, touched his cap, said something that Tom could not hear, accepted thruppence from John Fielding; and then the three of them walked away. That was all—they simply walked away from the Bull; away too from Tom Savage, who, his heart beating thirteen to the dozen, sauntered into the Bull a moment later.

"Who were those hulks?" he asked Patson, the innkeeper. "They came out of here, didn't they?"

"They did that, Mr. Savage. And if I'd known that you were going to return so soon I'd have kept them a bit longer."

"Eh?"

"As it was, they were expecting a messenger from some other premises, though I believe that they had to wait a while for him. I didn't keep them long. What they chiefly wanted was a list of the stolen articles."

"What stolen articles? Stolen from where?"

"Why, from your room, Mr. Savage. But that's the whole point—nothing *was* stolen, as it turned out. I thought that something must have been, when I sent to Bow Street. But we've learned since then that nothing was."

Patson was not one of Tom's favorite innkeepers, but he was efficient and discreet. Now he cleared a cautious throat.

"You had very little here in the first place, Mr. Savage, and you took most of that with you. I assume that any small objects of value were left in the wallet you deposited with me?"

"They didn't get *that,* did they?"

"What does that need matter to you, Mr. Savage? By law, I as an innkeeper would have to repay you every penny of its value."

"But—they didn't *get* it?"

"Oh, no. It's still here. Do you want me to keep it?"

"Please do, for the present. And—thanks. Has my room been set to rights?"

"It's in good condition now, sir. They rolled up the rugs and tore out the wainscoting and pulled the bed apart, but this has all been straightened out."

" 'They'?"

"Well no, probably 'he.' The Bow Street investigators said it looked like the work of one person. And he'd have to be small, because the only way he could have got into that room without passing me here is by climbing the rainpipe to the back window, the one that faces the court. That's a narrow window, Mr. Savage."

"Notice any small men loitering around here lately?"

"Yes, I did. And I reported it to Mr. Fielding and Mr. Welch just now. There's a tiny dark fellow who's been acting in a suspicious manner. I caught him twice in the courtyard yesterday. I believe his name is Joe-something. You may remember him, Mr. Savage. He brought a horse here for you once."

"Oh."

Tom was all rage again, but he kept himself in hand. He had guessed from the beginning that this would prove to be the doing of Pottsy Palmer. Who else knew about that wallet? Denied the privilege of buying the stuff for one-tenth of its worth, he had set out to steal it.

Pottsy was becoming a nuisance. He was doing nothing

toward the exposure of Harry Tewkes, and his bullying tactics were too brazen.

"Thank you, mine host. Yes, I do seem to remember a lad like that. Now, will you send up some hot water? And after that I'll have supper, in my room."

In a minor but significant sense this statement was, for him, a triumph. He had held himself. Tugged this way and that, he was learning to control his impulses. If he went to Alsatia Street now, as he had first thought to do, he might storm and rant— and be beaten. The only way in which Palmer could be brought to heel was by rough treatment, brutality. But not tonight, lest Tom botch the job. Tonight a bottle and a bird, preceded by a bath. He went upstairs—to the sight of Patson, languid as a gentleman should be; but in secret his teeth were set.

28 *AMONG THE MONEY MEN*

LOMBARD STREET WAS A DISAPPOINTMENT. THE TROUBLE WAS, HE had not been clear in his mind when he set forth. He didn't know exactly what he sought; and Lombard Street, a thorough-fare of cold fish-eyes, of mouths clamped shut like sprung steel traps, was no place for a man of indecision.

He knew, at least, that he needed money. Short as was his stay at Tunbridge Wells, it had been crushingly expensive. His room at the Bull he rented by the week, but even so it cost a lot, like all London inns. And he was coming to be something of a sybarite in his personal tastes—drink, food, clothes. In the popular imagination, which enormously exaggerated both the number and the profit of his holdups, Harry the Horsepad, en-crusted with diamonds, drank nothing but champagne and ate nothing but sautéed peacocks' tongues. The truth is, until re-cently Tom Savage had led a Spartan existence. Scholarship and austerity go well together, and it had seemed natural to be a·bit gaunt. Since taking up the life of the road, however—the warm cheerful inns, the rich linen, and richer dishes—he had become, not softened perhaps, but slightly spoiled. A notable thing about the sort of homeless existance he was leading these days, a thing of the greatest immediate importance, was this: it was conducted on a cash basis. And Tom needed cash. He had less than three pounds left.

Pacing the floor the previous night, he had pondered several possible courses.

He couldn't put up the loot as collateral for a loan in any legitimate place, since some of it was sure to be identified, and the possession of any part of it was a suspicious circumstance. Such a tactic would mean going to a professional fence, a man pledged to keep his mouth shut, and Tom knew of only one such—Pottsy Palmer. He had considered this the previous day, riding in from the Wells, though he faced the certainty that Palmer would ask a killing interest—twenty or twenty-five per cent—and the near-certainty that he'd break up the pieces anyway and dispose of them as he saw fit. After he learned of Joe's ransacking job at the Bull, Tom ceased even to dally with any such scheme as this. No matter what the incentive, Pottsy was not to be trusted. Besides, Pottsy needed a lesson, a sharp one.

Tom could go to Molly Evans and ask for a loan. She would have it handy, a woman in her position, and surely she'd advance it without hesitation to a man who was striving to get her son back. But Tom had not thought of this when he talked to Molly at the Green Bells—though even at that time, before he was handed his bill at the Crossed Halberds, he had been troubled in his mind about money and vaguely aware that he would have to do something. And now he was reluctant to go back. He didn't fancy the idea of taking money from a woman anyway, regardless of the provocation.

He might engage a firm of solicitors and put the machinery in motion to recover the cash residue of his heritage, which presumably still was tied up with his cousins' American venture. After all, he *was* Thomas Savage, late of Lincolnshire, so long as he wasn't being seized as Harry Tewkes, knight of the pad. But such a suit would take time. And he was as short of time as he was of money. A tremendous sense of urgency had been added to his quest of Harry Tewkes by the story Molly told. If that poor four-year-old—what was it she had called him?

George?—if he was still alive and still in England, then he was lodged on the very lip of a volcano; for Harry the Horsepad, uneasy in his hiding place, might panic and slaughter the lad.

Tom could go to Lord Seares and say that he'd changed his mind about not accepting a hundred-guinea fee for that historic holdup near Wickford. It was not, here, a matter of embarrassment. It was because he had something else to ask of Lord Seares and his patron Mr. Pitt, something much more valuable. Why take mere gold from a man like that? You can get gold from anyone.

All of these courses he had weighed, one by one.

He could go back to Hounslow Heath—on a black horse. But that would take him out of London just at a time when he might be needed. It would greatly complicate the matter of the jewelry in the wallet Patson guarded. Even from the little he had seen of it, Tom hated the life of a tobyman; and he would return to it only as a last resort. Besides, to ride the heath again might be to stretch his luck too far. He had to remember that it wasn't just his own life he was risking now. There was that boy's as well.

Thus cornered, he fell back upon three new possible plans of action. The first of these, though it delighted him because it had all the charm of poetic justice, he soon put aside as impractical. The thought had come that he might hire himself out as a professional Harry Tewkes-chaser. He could go from inn to inn, discussing the plan with the various proprietors, many of whom he already knew, and setting forth his own peculiar qualifications.

Highway robbery was bad for business. Every boniface for sixty miles around London should be glad to contribute to such a cause, especially when he was assured in writing that his contribution—to be used simply for Tom's expenses—would be returned to him, once Harry the Horsepad had been caught. For Tom meant to collect the rewards posted for Harry Tewkes, rewards totaling six thousand pounds. He had intended this from the beginning. He meant to use the reward money to pay back, in hard cash, what he had stolen from each of his victims—or what each officially declared he had stolen.

This plan, though it tempted, was imperfect. It would take time to launch. It would keep him away from the capital, and from Molly. It would leave him liable to another chance confrontation by somebody who knew his face, like the Wife of Bath or the driver of the Ipswich diligence. The organization of it would involve too many questions about his identity and background. And what was there to prove that it would work? If Tom's private activities had failed to flush the fugitive, what cause was there to believe that a Tom hired by innkeepers could do so? Harry Tewkes, wherever he was, had only to keep his head in like a turtle to be safe. A single horseman, no matter how agile, no matter how daring, could not catch him if he didn't show himself. A whole flying squad, a whole regiment of horse couldn't.

This left Tom with but two alternatives, and it was in pursuit of the first of these that immediately after breakfast he had started for Lombard Street.

The connection of money with Lombard Street was a natural one. Tom was thinking of underwriting activities. Perhaps he might yet be able to salvage something out of the previous scheme? At least he could learn about coach liability insurance.

Lloyd's coffee-house was large and it was clean. More, it was quiet. Though it was crowded, Tom seldom saw more than a few men together, and there was no babble of talk, no swirl of words and laughter such as hung over the company of most coffee-houses like a cloud of tobacco smoke—which often enough was there as well. In Lloyd's there were tables, but they were boxed off by high-backed benches or pews. This made for cubicles of various sizes. Newcomers appeared to know just which enclosure to go to, paying no attention to any of the others. The talk was low, earnest, with no graciousness in it. Indeed, Lloyd's was a serious sort of place. Nobody smiled. Nobody rallied the waitresses, plain, plump women. Even the host, a dignified, middle-aged man named Saunders—Edward

Lloyd, who founded the original establishment in Tower Street, had died years ago—though assiduous in his greetings, never emitted a beam, much less a guffaw. This was July; but if there had been a fire in the fireplace, doubtless it would have burned stodgily, without any crackle.

The place was after all a public house, and Tom was served, but he was looked at with astonishment and disapproval, and he had the feeling that he had somehow invaded a private club, that his presence was resented.

He was conducted to a small enclosure in the rear. After a waitress, nobody came there; nobody even passed. The isolation booth, he dubbed it, and stirred his coffee. He was obliged to admit that it was extremely good coffee.

At last the proprietor appeared.

"Are you expecting to meet anybody, sir?"

"I had hoped," Tom replied pointedly, "to meet somebody who might tell me something about the insurance business."

He had already dropped the fuzzy plan of raising expense money as a tobyman-catcher. Indeed, he'd dropped it before he had reached Lloyd's, after looking at the faces of the men in the street. The best he could hope for now was information.

Guardedly: "Well, what, for instance?"

"I have a little money to invest," Tom lied, "and I've been thinking about highway robbery insurance. I *assume* that all coaches are insured, just as I assume that it's done here?"

"My dear sir, certainly not!"

"Oh?"

"They are insured, yes. But not here. That would be a risky business and a small one at best. My associates and I—I speak only for myself, but I have no doubt that any of the others would tell you the same thing—we deal only in S's, G's, Mo's, B's, and Ra's."

"I—I'm afraid that only bewilders me."

"Those are all marine risks. Ships, Goods, Money, Bottomry, and Respondentias."

180

"I see. And—none of those has anything to do with highway robbery?"

"Certainly not, sir."

"You sound amazed, sir. Yet I had always understood that insurance men were gamblers?"

If he had called them adulterers he could not have offended Samuel Saunders more.

Saunders bowed. From a man's bow, much can be told of how he feels. Saunders was furious.

"You have been gravely misinformed, sir. Perhaps you came to the wrong place? Perhaps it would be better if you applied to some"—he spoke as though referring to a reptile—"some *sporting* man?"

"Y'know, by God," Tom cried, "I think you've got something there!"

He rose, and bowed.

"Your servant."

"Your servant, sir."

Tom paid for his coffee, and went outside, and hailed a chair, and gave an address.

The chair men were Irish. They almost always were.

"Never heard of it," stolidly.

Tom sighed. He was used to this. After all the enterprise was, technically at least, against the law; and chair men thought that they should be paid something extra for going there.

"Two shillings."

"Well, we *might* be able to find it. Get in, sir."

And so he went to Jack Broughton's academy of pugilism in the Tottenham Court Road.

He was down to his last device. It was also the most dangerous one.

29 *A STROLL DOWN THE STREET*

HE FOUND THE FORMER CHAMPION PRIMPING—FRILLED SHIRT, stiff linen cravat, an embroidered waistcoat, a new wig. Solicitously if sarcastically attending him—Jack Broughton lived on the premises—was a one-time butcher called Carey, who was employed by the great man as a trainer and sparring partner, occasionally doubling as a manservant.

"Something special?" Tom asked.

"Good morning, sir. No, this is a routine task, but it's such a fine morning that I thought I'd go on foot—and strut a bit. You didn't come for a lesson, Mr. Savage?"

"No. Some other business."

"Your coat, me lord," Carey falsettoed, holding out a handsome mulberry-velvet creation.

Broughton looped a quizzing glass around his neck, clapped on a tricorn, picked up a stick.

"As a matter of fact, it's a friend of yours I'm going to Bow Street to bail out. Croucher Givens."

"Drunk again?"

"Drunk again. *And* disorderly. It will cost a few pounds, which I'll take out of his wages, of course. It isn't that, Mr. Savage. It's the bad name this kind of thing gives the profession. Would you care to come along, keep me company?"

"I'd admire very much to," Tom replied.

182

In all conscience, it was an honor, a privilege, and Tom treated it as such. Everywhere they went heads were turned. Not only was Jack Broughton a celebrity, he was also the handsomest man in town. He wore his clothes with a quiet, if perhaps over-earnest, air of elegance. Tall, strong, he carried himself well, and he was not muscle-lumpy: he had a truly striking leg.

Though not unaware of the glances he won, he paid Tom polite attention all the while.

"You mentioned business, sir?"

"Yes. A man in your position, Mr. Broughton, often is asked to arrange fights, hold the stakes. That is, you might be entrusted with a prize."

"As it happens, I have been. A certain party has offered to put up two hundred pounds if I can find a pair of worthy bruisers. There has been no notable prize fight in some months, Mr. Savage, and no doubt a great deal of money would be bet on this—if I can arrange it."

"Ah? Do you know a man named Pottsy Palmer?"

The great man gave ever so slight a frown.

"I've heard of him. And once I saw him fight. A sailor named Norcross. That was in a field near Bristol, last year. Norcross never had a chance. Palmer is slow, and he knows nothing of the art of boxing, Mr. Savage, but he's prodigiously strong."

"Um . . . I hadn't known that Pottsy was a pugilist."

"I believe that that's the only time he was ever actually in a ring. He'd fight more, I am told, if he could only get somebody to meet him. Jack Slack's too fond of being champion. Corny Harris is afraid of him, and so's Moreton. What he did to that sailor, Mr. Savage, truly was gruesome."

Though he strove to keep an impartial attitude, as became a man in his position, it was clear from Broughton's voice that he disapproved of Pottsy Palmer. In the first place, the man had no fistic science, and properly wasn't a pug at all. In the second place, as an underworld figure he was not to be desired in the ranks of honest bruisers; and no doubt Broughton thought about his criminal connections, as he did on a lesser scale about Croucher Givens' intemperance, that they tended to give the profession a bad name. From an everyday pugilist this might have amused. From Jack Broughton, with his obvious sincerity, it was touching.

"The two hundred pounds is available?"

"Any time I wish to ask for it."

"It would be awarded on a winner-take-all basis, I assume?"

"Of course."

"Mr. Broughton, what would you say if I told you I think I have an opponent for Pottsy Palmer?"

"I would say that I am flabbergasted. I'd supposed I knew my fighters, but I can't think of any worthy of the name who could be induced to climb into the same ring with that man."

"Mr. Broughton, what would you say if I told you that I would?"

They had been strolling at a fashionable pace, and nobody would have guessed, looking at them, that they were discussing a serious subject, for their voices by habit drawled, while their actions were languid. But now the former champion forgot his manners, and stopped short, turning to gawp at his companion. He didn't even remember to raise the quizzing glass.

"*You?* But—but you're a *gentleman!*"

"A debatable point. But even if I was, is there anything about a gentleman that would forbid him to fight?"

"But you—"

"Maybe I need that prize?"

"See here, Mr. Savage, if a few pounds would help—"

He was reaching for his purse, but Tom, with a smile, put a hand on his arm.

"Thanks, Mr. Broughton, but I'm afraid it's a matter of much more than a few pounds."

"But—what if you lose?"

"With you in my corner I should have a good chance. And if I do lose—why, there'll be time enough to worry about that then. Now here's Bow Street. I wonder how the Croucher feels."

184

The Croucher felt mighty poor: that was clear at a glance. His hands trembled; his face gleamed with sweat; his reddened eyes were hollows of self-reproach, and he looked as though he might at any moment start to vomit. In addition, he needed a shave, and his clothes were filthy.

"Been sleeping on some stable floor?" the ex-champion asked cheerfully.

"Gawd bless you for coming, Jack! You're the best friend I got in the world! And Master Savage too! Awr, I ain't worth it that such good men should be put out because of me! I just ain't worth it!"

He went on, and on. Morning-after expressions of repentance rarely are entertaining, and the newcomers were glad when a clerk told them that the magistrate—who evidently had *sensed* their presence, since their arrival had not been announced— would see them at the bench.

Tom was worried about Croucher Givens. Aside from a perfectly human—and humane—dislike of seeing any man in such a condition, Tom could not help remembering from time to time that he and the Croucher had been accomplices in a crime that would not soon be forgiven. Croucher's was not a noble character, nor was it strong. He had been shaken by the sight of that man hanging in chains near Wickford. Like so many of his fellows, he feared gibbeting more than hanging itself. We must all die, but to be denied a decent Christian burial was for Croucher the most horrid fate of all.

Neither was the Croucher ever likely to forget that he had laid unholy hands upon a duke. Nor that he had glimpsed in Master Savage's saddlebag the purple silk mask and yellow cockade that could be said to make up the very device, the identifying ordinaries, the charges with which the escutcheon of Harry Tewkes was emblazoned. The Croucher couldn't *know* that Tom was Harry the Horsepad; but he might surmise it, for the man, sober, was no beefwit.

The Croucher had always shown a fondness for the bottle, but his behavior since he returned to London had been nothing short of scandalous, and it argued a conscience that was ill at ease. What might not Andrew Givens do if, while in the throes of a hang-over, he was threatened with the gibbet? Tom did not like to see him in a police station, even on a trifling charge such as this.

John Fielding and the former champion were not strangers to one another. Fielding didn't defer to the famous man, who for his part remained respectful, never condescending. They might have been two members of the same club, who didn't often meet.

The magistrate readily consented to let Croucher Givens off with a reprimand, but he released him only in the custody of his employer, warning him that another such offense would be handled more severely, and suggesting that if he must get drunk, he stay off the streets, where he was wont to challenge one and all to a set-to.

Croucher started to babble his thanks, but the magistrate cut him short by turning to Tom. He always faced the person he addressed, clearly as a matter of courtesy. It was startling, now, when he called Tom by name.

"I take it that you didn't get to Newgate the other day in time to talk to Ase Mellish, Mr. Savage?"

"Not quite, your honor."

"That was a beastly business—but not unexected, as you know. What was stranger was that breaking at the Bull yesterday, when your own room was ransacked—and no other. Can you conceive what they were after, Mr. Savage?"

"I simply can't," said Tom, acutely conscious that he was trembling before the gaze of eyes he couldn't even see.

"We have some reason to believe that it was the work of a cat burglar named Joseph Dunne. Do you know him?"

Tom shugged, then immediately spoke.

"I may have met him. I can't rightly say I *know* him."

"He's a member of the Pottsy Palmer gang. A bad lot. We would be a great deal happier here if Palmer was put away for a while."

"If your honor please," interposed the former champion, "it may be that he will be 'put away' soon, though not as you meant it."

"Eh?" The bandaged face was turned toward him, and Broughton instantly regretted his words. "You planning another fight? You've got a patron again? Well, you'd better not hold it in my bailiwick, Mr. Broughton. After all, it *is* against the law."

"There isn't any turf left anywhere in Westminster anyway."

"But it'll be near here? You might tell me when you know yourself, if you'll be so kind? Unofficially, of course. If I can find the time I might go."

"But your honor, you can't—well, I mean—"

"Of course I can't see anything," imperturbably. "But it might be very helpful for me anyway to attend such an event. You'd be amazed how much you can learn with your ears, Mr. Broughton, especially when men are excited."

Outside, a still abashed Croucher, pleased to have something to take his mind off his headache, eagerly asked about this proposed fight. For some moments, as they walked, Broughton was unwilling to tell him. When he did so, the Croucher stopped dead, gawping, as his master had done a little while before. Then he crowed with delight.

"I think you got a good chance, Master Savage. I'll train you myself—me and Jack here. We'll start right in soaking your hands in brine this afternoon."

"We'll start tonight," Tom corrected him. "This afternoon I plan to visit a lovely lady."

The Croucher had a misgiving.

"But look: What if Pottsy won't fight?"

"He'll fight," said Tom Savage, "if I have to break every bone in his body to make him."

30 THE HOUSE THAT STOOD ALONE

IF IT WAS LOVE THAT HAD LED HIM TO THE GREEN BELLS, AND desperation that caused him to throw down a gage before the land's most formidable fighter, it was nothing but plain curiosity that took him to the house in Hackney.

Here was a dreary neighborhood—a road, all ruts, flanked for the most part by small drab houses and by fens. To make matters worse, the sky lowered, and rain drove diagonally into mire that was like glue, so that the hooves of the horse Tom rode sank and were withdrawn to sickly, sticky, sucking sounds.

Yet there were a few fine houses, or houses that had been fine, and the one he visited could be numbered among these.

Its gentility sagged. It stood alone, square, low, needing paint. The fence that fronted it was red with rust. The garden was weeds. It had about it an air of desolation and decay.

He recognized it from the answers to cursory questions made on the way out from town, but he believed that he would have known it on sight anyway. All the same, he checked at the nearest building, a shabby tavern about a hundred yards away. Yes, she lived there, a drawer attested. Unless, he added, she had lately died. Nobody ever had seen much of her, and for months now nobody had seen her at all, not so much as a glimpse at a window.

The place did have a sepulchrous air, Tom reflected as he

strode up the path. To enter it must be like entering a tomb. Quite possibly nobody *was* alive in there? The house could have swallowed a corpse or two, leaving no sign.

He marveled that anybody ever moved to a district like this. It was neither country nor town; some aged person whose income was small might go there to die as cheaply as possible. But the woman Tom was about to visit was young, scarcely more than a girl; and her income, while it might not be massive, certainly was sure.

He knocked, waited a while, then knocked once more. The door at last was opened, though gingerly, a few inches. A hag peeped out. Seamed, sere, hatchet-faced, chin and nose trying to meet, she might have come from some Bavarian fairy story. She could not have been less than fifty, and she had an unpleasant expression.

Tom Savage hesitated. To bow before this crone would have been unseemly, but if he mounted a high horse, he might have the door slammed in his face. He hadn't a smitch of authority for what he was about to do.

He compromised by leaning close, and though there was nobody else in sight, his voice was the whisper of a thief.

"I should like to see Mrs. Isaac Axford."

The name sounded made-up, concocted for some particular occasion.

"Who are you?"

"I come," said Tom with a confidential leer, "from Mr. Pitt."

Even on the Hackney Road, he reasoned, the dropping of names could do no harm.

"She oughtn't to be bothered."

"I shall only need a few minutes. It's a matter of consequence to—to, uh, the man I mentioned."

He felt ashamed of these lies, as he stepped into a large unlit entrance hall, and even more ashamed of himself for obtruding upon the privacy of a lady in order to satisfy his own curiosity. Well, no, it wasn't only that. He wished, as well, to verify what he had read in those two papers taken from His Royal Highness William Augustus, Duke of Cumberland. The price he meant to ask Pitt to pay would be a high one—when the time came. He wanted to be sure that the papers were worth it.

He was ushered into a large square room that had about it the air of a Nonconformist chapel. What furniture there was was plain, though solid. The curtains were drawn. The day was dim, growing dimmer as night approached, making it difficult for Tom to peek out at his horse, tethered to the gate. It was a hired nag, and in a neighborhood like this, you couldn't be too careful.

The hag, who had been holding one hand behind her, now brought this forward. There was a large carving knife in it.

"Damn it, grannie, d'ye take me for a roast of mutton?"

"I'll treat you like one if you do anything to hurt this girl."

"Strong words, grannie. But quell your misgivings. My designs are pacific."

"They'd better be, whatever that is. I'll not be far off, mister. One scream—even if it's only a little one—and you'll have me to contend with."

In other circumstances the scene would have been ridiculous, but in that large gloomy room, the hag's sincerity and her passionate determination to defend her charge were so plain that they lent her a touch of nobility. Tom Savage even granted her a short bow as she backed out.

"I see that unlike your mistress, you, grannie, are no Quaker."

Alone, he paced the floor. He had many things on his mind. A letter had been left for him at the Bull, but it was not from Molly Evans, though he had hoped to hear from her. He worried about her, out in the country alone, or virtually alone. If Harry Tewkes knew about the hideaway—as clearly he did, since he had kidnabbed the boy—what was to prevent him from visiting it again, this time to carry off the boy's mother? He might not even have to carry her off. She had told Tom

190

that she'd do anything to get her child back. He swallowed, wincing at the thought.

The letter at the Bull in fact had been from the Honorable Ned Blane, who evidently was back in London, since it had come by messenger, not by post. It was little else but a challenge, demanding as it did an explanation of Tom's extraordinary behavior in the presence of many persons of *ton* on the occasion of, etc., etc. It did not greatly trouble Tom. Blane was merely keeping up his reputation as a ruffler, a reputation that was meat and drink to him. Blane wouldn't fight unless he was forced to. He simply wished the world of fashion—and the world of politics—to hear that he had been out again. His fame as a swordsman, together with the triviality of the reasons he gave for challenging, each time made an apology easy; and Blane would accept that apology, preferably, for the dramatic effect, upon the very field.

Pottsy Palmer was another matter. Tom wasn't worried about what the big man might say when Jack Broughton himself made an offer. For a chance to win two hundred pounds, Pottsy Palmer would have climbed through the ropes to slug it out with Lucifer, Prince of Darkness, himself. What Tom fretted about was how he himself would behave when the time came. He would be pitted against a larger and much stronger man, a man, moreover, who if he wasn't a skilled boxer knew every dirty trick of street fighting. Tom would be handicapped by the knowledge that so much depended upon the outcome, and additionally, by his awareness of the crowd. Pottsy, not one to have qualms, had been in the ring at least once. Tom Savage, who never had, who never even had witnessed a prize fight, might be gripped by what Molly Evans and her confrères would call stage fright.

"Did thee wish to see me?"

Tom turned slowly, as a man might sip a rare wine, almost afraid that it would prove bitter. Then, again slowly, inwardly, showing nothing on his face, he glowed. For Hannah Lightfoot was as lovely as he had hoped.

191

31 *A TALE OF TWO MARRIAGES*

SHE WAS WELL NAMED. HER MOST NOTABLE CHARACTERISTIC WAS her lightness. She was of medium height, and though slim, not skinny nor bony; yet somehow she seemed ethereal. Her feet were not visible, but she gave the impression of one who stood on tiptoe. Her presence in this world, you would have said, was fortuitous, and wouldn't last long. She was poised as a bird that has just alighted and is ready to fly off again at the least alarm.

This is not to say that she *fluttered*. Gravity was the very essence of her. Not pomposity, not solemnity—she was no vinegar-eyed prude—but an acceptance of the seriousness of life. You would have trusted her with anything. She was pure-souled.

She was also comely. Her face was an exquisite oval. Her skin recalled peaches and cream. She had a tiny mouth. She had long, very dark, slightly upslanted eyes, a touch of the Oriental in them. Her hair, unfashionably straight, dark brown or perhaps even black, was glossy and soft; she wore it in a bun behind. Her French-gray dress, though it avoided the extreme severity that marked so many members of her sect, was plain; but it fitted well, and could not have concealed the lines of a body that was young, fresh, sweet.

192

"Ma'am, I have been ordered by Mr. Pitt to ask you if you have lately seen Mr. Axford."

She showed puzzled, yet at the same time resigned. She would never struggle against anything.

"Thee knows I met Friend Axford but once, for ten minutes, when we were wed. I have not seen him since. William Pitt knows this."

"Um . . . Perhaps he simply wishes to be sure, ma'am. Now— that was after the other wedding, the first one, of course?"

"Thee means when I was joined to George Hanover? But I take that to be my only true marriage."

"But you must know, ma'am, that the law doesn't agree with you?"

She made no reply to this, standing with eyes downcast, hands folded before her, doubtless aware of his gaze but not blushing.

He himself might have blushed, instead, for he felt a wave of impatience pass over him at that "George Hanover." These Quakers were so damned smug! Tom was no devotee of the ruling house of Great Britain, the members of which he, in company with so many of his fellow men, rather despised. But he could respect position, rank, while he disregarded the man. It has been pointed out that *somebody* has to go through a door first. A cult could be made of "plainness," and titles eschewed. "Friend Axford" and "William Pitt" rather than "Mr. Axford" and "Mr. Pitt" might be considered quaint, albeit a trifle silly. But to call the lad who would be the next King of England "George Hanover" was going too far. How- ever, Tom refrained from comment, still regarding this young woman.

Back in the shadows of the hall a smaller shadow moved— the hag. Fleetingly Tom Savage thought of Molly and her fierce protectress. But there was no sound analogy. The mistress of the Green Bells was as different from this meek, unblinking lass as the vine-covered Kent cottage was from the drab and lugubrious house in which he found himself.

"About that first marriage. I regret this intrusion, but I'd go over a few details once more, if you will bear with me."

She said nothing. Did she think anything? It was unlikely.

The story of Hannah Lightfoot had been whispered about for months; but there are always stories concerning the amorous doings of royal persons, and it is doubtful that anybody took this one seriously, the lad in question being himself so slow, so sluggish. Hannah came from Yorkshire, an orphan, and she had worked in the linen-draper's shop run by her uncle, one Wheeler, at the southeast corner of Carlton Street and St. Alban's Place. About a year ago she had disappeared.

The Wheeler shop was halfway between Leicester House, the town seat of Augusta, Dowager Princess of Wales, and St. James's Palace, where the crusty old king slept when in London. Princess Augusta's older son, the King's grandson, sixteen-year-old George, heir to the throne, must have passed the shop many times. A shy, excessively dull boy, brought up by a possessive mother in ignorance of all worldly things—what Hannah Lightfoot would have called "creaturely activity"—he nevertheless was human, as princes go. That there had been some sort of flirtation was generally assumed. That there had been a marriage was something Tom Savage, to his great astonishment, had learned from the two papers Cumberland carried. One of those papers had been a page of the marriage registry, duly signed and sealed, with the names and titles spelled out. The other had been a letter written by the Great Commoner himself half a year ago. There could be no question about the hand: at Lord Seares's insistence Tom had studied several samples of it, at the Adam and Eve. It was from this letter that Tom learned about the house in the Hackney Road. The letter, written to Pitt's cousin Hester Grenville, set forth in lively and highly irreverent language the particulars of the rite.

For Mr. Pitt had been present. He had signed the registry as a witness.

This was the most extraordinary part of the whole extraordinary business, the part Tom Savage found it hardest to believe.

How the letter and the registry page had come to be in the possession of the Duke of Cumberland did not matter now, but what would happen if the King ever saw them could not be in doubt. That a man of Mr. Pitt's probity, one whose whole life lay in his political career, could have let himself become involved in such an affair smacked almost of suicide. What could his motive have been? An outspoken foe of the house of Stuart, he could not have been hoping to bolster the Jacobite cause by making the family of the *de facto* king appear absurd—or at any rate, even more absurd than it was. He knew well enough that that cause was lost, and that the Young Pretender, though he might still be Bonnie Prince Charlie to a few die-hards in the highlands of Scotland, in truth was a discredited adventurer skulking about the Continent, fat before his time, soft, enfeebled, an habitual drunkard, and—childless. A prank? A whim or freak of humor? No. Not in any of its many forms did humor have a part in the make-up of the Great Commoner. He was the last man in the world who would have played a joke. To curry favor with him who would soon be king? Yet surely Mr. Pitt, that astute manipulator, knew that any prince would hate and distrust a man with whom he shared a secret that was either shameful or ludicrous, or both. Blackmail? Aside from Mr. Pitt's all but painful honesty, there was the circumstance that the marriage had no validity. *He* knew that. When the Prince of Wales died, four years ago, Parliament, leery at seeing a minor in line for the throne, after much debate—a debate in which Mr. Pitt took part—had passed the Regency Bill, which provided, among other things, that if Prince George married without the consent of the Regent and the council, the marriage should be null and void.

What the Great Commoner might have forgotten was that this same bill also provided that everybody concerned in such a marriage should be deemed guilty of high treason.

It was unthinkable that any such charge would be moved against Mr. Pitt; but it was likewise unthinkable that George II would entrust to an abettor of that secret ceremony the highest ministry in the land. And after all, as Seares had pointed out, the King still did have some authority.

Tom could think of only one possible explanation, now that he stood face to face with the bride who, her marriage of the previous summer declared invalid, had been wed against her will to some fetched-in figurehead named Axford—a marriage she would not permit to be consummated, since she still esteemed herself the wife of Prince George—and then hustled into obscurity.

The Great Commer had been in love.

There was no other way in which to account for it.

Stern, irascible, in his middle forties when these events occurred, a man who had never had time to think of women, he had suddenly been smitten by the charms of his Grenville cousin, Hester, an infatuation that had caused much amusement in high circles. They had subsequently been married. The marriage of Prince George and Hannah Lightfoot, however, had taken place before this event, at the height of Mr. Pitt's courtship. It was conceivable, if just barely, that in promoting the illegitimate affair—the clergyman had been the Rev. James Wilmot, a Pitt family retainer, as Tom Savage knew from the registry page, and the other witness had been Elizabeth Chudleigh, lady-in-wating to the Dowager Princess of Wales, and one of Mr. Pitt's closest friends—the Great Commoner had somehow thought of himself as putting his personal stamp of approval upon romance. Love does strange things to men, especially men of middle age who are experiencing it for the first time. Surely nothing less than love could have caused him to be fool enough to write a description of the marriage in his own hand. It was bad enough that in a maudlin moment he had witnessed the joining and signed the registry. He should never have confirmed this by means of a long letter, no matter how intimate, no matter what his trust in the lady of his heart. "Do right, and fear no man," goes the adage, to which many a grim one, wise after the event, has added: "Don't write, and

196

fear no woman." Mr. Pitt, seemingly impeccable, had slipped twice. Once would have been too often.

"And Miss Chudleigh was there?"

"Elizabeth Chudleigh was there. She works for George Hanover's mother."

The answer was a parrot's. There was no touch of wonderment in it. This beautiful Quaker had not even begun to marvel that such inane questions should be put to her by a stranger. She was more than merely stupid, Tom surmised; she was a half-wit.

Not so the old woman in the hall. No doubt still clutching her knife, she must have overheard all of this, and *she*'d seen through Tom's impromptu catechism, possibly cursing herself the while for having let him in.

He sighed, and turned away. Somehow he thought that he could not look at that lovely, empty face for another moment. After all, he had learned what he came to learn.

Uneasy, he went to a window. He fingered aside the curtain. He looked out.

The rain still slanted down, and his horse was still tethered out there, where the afternoon was darkening. There was another horse tied to the hitching post before the tavern down the road to London; but no man was in sight.

He turned back.

"Do you have many visitors, Mrs. Axford?"

"No. Thee is the only one who's ever come here."

"God help you!"

"The Lord will do that without prompting from a mortal, friend."

"But—you don't understand why you're here?"

"No. But I have no complaint. Though it is a bit drafty sometimes."

She had raised her eyes, fairly stunning him with the glory of that gaze; but now she lowered them again, her cheeks for the first time touched by color, as she realized that she actually *had*, for an instant, complained.

He pitied her from the bottom of his heart. Yet it was as well for everybody concerned that she *didn't* have visitors. She had nothing to hide, for she knew nothing. She was simple almost to the point of imbecility, and any rascal who suspected who she was could have had the story out of her within ten minutes.

Tom made a deep, old-fashioned court bow.

"Ma'am, I won't bother you again. And—thanks."

She dropped him a curtsy as unexpected as it was ungraceful —for members of the friendly persuasion do not believe in formal greetings—yet it had about it a girlishness that brought a lump to Tom's throat as he made in haste for the door.

The rain slanted at the same angle, unwavering, relentless. It looked as though it had been coming down this way forever, and would continue. The mud was glue, as before. The road was deserted.

That other horse, richly saddled, still was tied before the tavern, where it stood disconsolate. But Tom paid it no heed when he rode past, chin on chest, for he had many things to think about.

32 *RIDE TO A HAYBARN*

HE LOOKED FOR A LONG WHILE AT HIS HANDS, THINKING THEM the ugliest things he ever had seen. For a week, off and on, he had been pickling them in brine, a dreary process, an ordeal for one who hated to sit still while so much was going on around him. Tom, who formerly had been so amiable, was restless and morose these days. He was sullen, snappish. This is the way they wished him to be, Jack and Croucher and the others. Traditionally, the trainers strove to get the trainee into an angry and impatient mood. Good nature should be allowed no part in pugilism. The fighter should climb through the ropes in a let's-get-this-over-with spirit. In Tom Savage's case, however, it was not the training that could be called to account for his taut nerves, as Broughton and the rest supposed. It was the fact that he hadn't heard from Molly.

The cart bumped and thudded over cobbles, throwing Broughton and Tom against each other. "The last time I rode in a thing like this," was Tom's uneasy thought, "they were taking me to the gallows." The present vehicle indeed was much the same in shape and size as the one from which Pottsy Palmer had plucked him on the way to Tyburn. There was one important difference: that cart, with cut-away sides and no cover, had been designed to exhibit him as much as possible, whereas this one was meant to hide him. It was dark in there, like a tent. He could hear street sounds, and wondering where they were now, reached up to push back the canvas.

"No, no," cried Jack Broughton, and slapped his hand down.

That was typical of the way they had been treating him these past eight days and nights—like a naughty child who must be watched. Broughton was riding with him now, in part because as a past champion he was so well known that his very appearance in public at a time like this, when the sporting world was asking where the fight would be and when, would infallibly collect a crowd; but he also rode in the cart to keep an eye on Tom. Less famous, Croucher Givens trailed them on a nag. Between them, they never left him alone for a minute, but even went to the jakes with him as though he were a condemned prisoner who might try to kill himself. Croucher slept on a pallet in Tom's bedroom at the Bull.

The cart bumped on. For three days it had been like this— a series of false starts, either in this cart or under cover of darkness. Again and again they would set forth, only to receive some message that sent them sneaking back to the academy in the Tottenham Court Road, where once more they'd submerge Tom's hands in salt water. There was a tremendous amount of coming and going, of whispered conferences, plans on paper, cryptic messages, significant glances. It was clear that there was a great deal more to a prize fight than just the fighting.

Broughton never mentioned his anonymous patron, but he seemed certain that the two hundred pounds would be forthcoming at the right time. He expressed the belief, too, that the patron would get this, or most of it, back, by reason of the sale of information. There were no tickets to a prize fight, Tom gathered. It was not like a theater or a recreation garden. The erection of any sort of fence or enclosure would attract attention. All London and all the surrounding countryside as well knew that there was to be a fight soon, somewhere. It was not only the law officers who were alert; everybody was. It would be impossible to reserve positions at the ringside, in such a rough unruly crowd, and of course there would be no benches or stools. Anybody who knew when and where the show was to be staged could go there for nothing. Only those who paid for it—who "subscribed," as Jack Broughton preferred to say— were given this information. But since there were several hundred of these, and since the information itself was changed from time to time as the sheriff's men in this county or in that learned of the arrangements and moved to block them, it took a deal of scurrying to keep matters straight.

Meanwhile, Tom Savage would spar, using the mufflers, or, more often, sit silent and glum, soaking his hands.

The ancient Greeks, he had read, used to strap a cestus on each pugilist's fist. This was nothing like the girdle of the same name that Aphrodite wore for quite a different purpose, but was a broad strap of bullhide set with lead or iron strips. Tom previously had supposed that it was worn for the purpose of lending weight to the fist, making the punch more powerful. He now learned that the cestus had a protective function as well. It kept the hand bones from getting broken. More, it kept the fist itself from swelling.

Few bare-knuckle fights, in fact, were fought with bare knuckles. Some manner of glove was usually used. It might be rough-ribbed across the back, a sort of modern refinement of the cestus; but its primary purpose was to keep the fist down to effective proportions. It was not unusual for a fight to go fifty or sixty rounds or more, and the fist, again and again slammed against the head or against the blocking elbows or forearms, took a terrific pounding. Unless something was done to confine it, it would soon swell to the size—and the softness—of a bed pillow. Hence the gloves. Yet if the gloves were thick and heavy, they slowed the punches and tended to soften them as well; whereas if they were thin—and they were usually thin, skin-tight leather—they might split in a dozen places, either because of the pounding from the outside or because of the swelling of the hand within. It was for this reason that the secondary precaution of pickling the hands was taken. A treatment of brine, repeated at frequent intervals, was supposed to make the skin tough and at the same time keep swelling down to a minimum.

He would learn soon, he reflected as he looked down at his hands, whether the treatment really had rendered them tough. It certainly hadn't rendered them pretty.

The cart had quit the cobbles and was trundling along what must have been, from the sounds, a country road.

What sounds was Molly Evans hearing? Did she still wait, with hard-beating heart, for that step that might mean news of her child? Could she endure this torture alone, unconsoled, while the man who vowed that he loved her was sneaking out of London in a covered cart to act a clown's part for the benefit of gamblers, drunkards, and pimps?

Bitterly he cursed himself, calling himself selfish, even cowardly. He shouldn't be here! He should be in that cottage in Kent. *He,* not the poor frail mother, should be waiting for the step that announced the arrival of Harry Tewkes. He should have known as soon as he heard Molly's story that *here* was the man's weakness, his Achilles' heel. *Here* was where Tom should have taken his stand, pistols ready, sword loose in its scabbard. He should never have left Molly Evans's side.

The sounds that came to Tom now were not all rustic. True, he did occasionally hear the low of cattle, chickens chittering, the creak of a rusty weathervane, the sudden scritches of a jay. But the more immediate noises were urban in character—the voices of men who travelled this road, of whom, it became clear, there was a growing number.

There was a great deal of cursing, of chaffering, some of it bawdy. Bets were made from carriage to carriage, saddle to saddle. Gin was offered for sale by somebody with a whining voice. And intermittently somebody sang.

> His steed's the speed of wind, sir,
> In color black as night;
> His sword's not far behind, sir,
> When Harry's in a fight.

They must have made a queer cavalcade as they trudged that country road, and Tom, concealed, covered like an Oriental woman, still could picture in his mind's eye the farmers looking up from the fields, the goodwives coming to the doors of their cottages, open-mouthed, goggle-eyed, while even the poultry and livestock stared. It was not often that men such as these, from the backwash of London, from cellars and even sewers, went for a ride in the country. They might have been as much bemused by the peasants as the peasants were by them.

It was mid-morning of a dry day. The horses' hooves poofed wearily on the road, and dust rose on all sides. Dust slid and slithered into crevices of the canvas that was stretched over the cart. It sifted across the floor between Tom's feet, taking the form of fans or of tiny, fragile arabesques, figures that shifted and changed and disappeared, to be replaced by others as the humping of the cart and vagrant movements of air stirred them.

Imperceptibly the pace of this caravan had quickened. There were more shouts now, more bets being made. There was no longer the slightest show of furtiveness. The "fancy"—that is, the followers of pugilism, the knowing ones, insiders, *aficionados* —were making a field day of it. Tom could deduce that they were at last sure of themselves. They had cast off all attempt at disguise. They were not afraid to be known for what they were, their destination guessed. This would imply bribery, this confidence. Some sheriff or under-sheriff, his heart light but not so his purse, had consented to look the other way.

> His pistols, made of brass, sir,
> Are bright as any fire—

Here was yet another of those ballads that tooted the crimes, loves, and hairbreadth escapes of that folk-hero, Harry the Horsepad. Tom wondered whether Croucher Givens, riding behind them, heard it. He glanced at Jack Broughton, but Broughton was peering out through a slit in the canvas, obviously nervous, under a tighter strain, it would seem, than was Tom himself.

He's conquer'd many a lass, sir.
He's oftentimes a sire.

The cart jolted to a stop, and Broughton, as excited as a boy, scrambled out.

There was a small, rickety haybarn at the edge of a pasture. On either side of the entranceway stood a ruffian. They suggested sentries, each with a scowl, each with a cudgel.

Horses were being tethered there, but few men ventured into the barn or even loitered in its vicinity. Instead they made for a crowd of men clustered in the very middle of the pasture, a level space, where, it could be assumed, a ring had been pitched. Some paused long enough to cheer Jack Broughton, and a few took a good look at the man with him, no doubt speculating as to whether Tom was indeed the former champion's "mystery pug." But most of them scurried for the center of the pasture, no doubt to get as near to the ropes as they could.

Blinking in the sunlight, Tom was led into the barn, and the door was closed behind him. Once again plunged into darkness, after the dazzle outside, he stood confused, making out only vaguely the figure of the man he confronted.

"Your highness, this is my friend Mr. Thomas Savage. Tom, it's my honor to present you to the man whose gracious generosity made this sporting event possible, his royal and illustrious highness—the Duke of Cumberland."

"Billy the Butcher again," muttered Tom as he bowed.

33 *"SAID A SPIDER TO A FLY"*

THE PLACED SMELLED OF NEW-MOWN HAY, WHICH SET HIM TO
sneezing. This sharpened his impatience, making him more ir-
ritable than before, but it did supply a sort of shield from behind which he could nurse his astonishment and survey the
situation in which he found himself.

Surely it should not have come as a surprise that Duke William Augustus was backing Jack Broughton again. For some
time the sporting world had been abuzz with rumors of such a
reconciliation. Much was at stake. It was not merely a matter
of personalities. Since that historic occasion five years before,
when Jack Slack had punched the blinded Broughton to a pulp,
a defeat that had cost the duke a fortune, Cumberland's accusa-
tion of a sell-out, and the scandal this created, coupled with the
withdrawal of all his support of pugilism by Cumberland—who
until that time had been by far its wealthiest and most influen-
tial patron—had threatened the very existence of the pastime.
No longer were big purses put up, and for what else but cash
prizes could you get bruisers to fight? Rich men of sporting pro-
clivities feared to incur the disfavor, not to say outright hostility,
of the Duke of Cumberland, an exceptionally vindictive man
with the memory of an elephant. Sheriff's agents everywhere,
and the Bow Street runners in town, were made more alert. The
academy in the Tottenham Court Road was closed by order of

the municipal council, thus for a long while depriving the sport of its headquarters.

This ban lately, if unofficially, had been lifted. And there were other signs that the duke, bored, was about to come back into the fighters' fold. Doubtless this was the reason for Broughton's secrecy about the patron: he wished—or perhaps it was the duke who wished—to save the announcement for a dramatic occasion, just before the fight itself.

Not being a professional, Tom Savage was indifferent to this aspect of the case. He was more concerned with the personal side.

The duke, in that dim place, loomed enormous, a monster, square-headed, cold-eyed, arrogant. He made no acknowledgment of the presentation of Tom, on whom he gazed with all the contempt of a man who is offered shoddy goods at a high price. His eyes were the blue of ice deep in some crevasse. His straight, thin mouth, that ordinarily looked as though it had been slashed into the lower part of his face with a saber, now was curled a little in scorn.

"This is not much of a man, Broughton," he said in his curiously high, squeaking voice, a voice that issued from that great frame as unexpectedly as might the cheep of a canary.

"Your highness will find that he's very strong, though."

"Humph! He's no more than a boy!"

At this moment, fortunately, Tom sneezed. Otherwise, furious, he might have made some sharp retort. That sneeze brought him to his senses. He must hold in his temper. He mustn't speak. Hateful, this royal personage assuredly was, but he was far from stupid. "I shall remember you." Tom could see him now, barefooted, bare-legged, his shirttails flapping, huge bony fists pressing his waist on either side, while he cocked that great head, regarding intently, in a cold rage, the man who had just robbed him of two papers an ordinary highwayman would never have noticed. "I shall remember you. . . I'll be there when they turn you off."

That had been on the plain near Wickford. This was in a hay-

206

barn near—where? It didn't matter. Cumberland, not a man to forget anything, might well remember Tom's voice. Tom sneezed again, and stayed silent.

"Very well," said the duke. "Have him undress."

Here was humiliation only in part anticipated. Jack Broughton and his protégé had been squabbling for several days about the matter of ring costume. The ex-champion, a stickler for etiquette, with the traditions of his calling dear to his heart, insisted upon tight doeskin breeches, cotton stockings, spiked shoes, a gaudy sash—and no shirt. A barber would not be called for. Tom's hair, like that of any man who wore a wig, was cropped very short.

Tom Savage conceded the breeches and stockings. He agreed to the spiked shoes: "Palmer'll wear 'em, and you make sure he don't use 'em on you in the falls!" He had held out successfully against the sash. But his loudest protest was against the lack of a shirt, or even undershirt, which he said would be immodest.

"There won't be any women there!"

"It'd be indecent anyway, even just with men."

However, Broughton had been inflexible, and Tom had at last capitulated.

But Tom had never thought to have to strip before the insolent stare of William Augustus, Duke of Cumberland. He started to refuse—but checked himself.

"Come, come," said his royal highness. "We haven't got all day. I want to see what I've bought," he added.

With trembling hands—though it was anger now, not nervousness—Tom took off his shirt and his undershirt.

In the manner of a farmer at a fair who examines a prize hog, or a racetrack tout who studies, for the first time, a horse he means to bet on, the Duke of Cumberland nodded portentously.

"Aye, he's bigger than he looks. And he should be fast. But that man Palmer is a high mountain to climb, I can tell you."

"Tom'll do it," Broughton said earnestly, making himself smile—or smirk.

At that moment Tom Savage disliked his teacher almost as much as he disliked the duke who so coldly appraised his points. Jack Broughton, to Tom's way of thinking, was ten times the man that Cumberland was; yet now he fairly grovelled before his patron, who treated him with an offhandedness that could not even be called condescension. But Tom kept his mouth shut.

"Have him turn around," said William Augustus.

Tom, in a rage, at the same time had to confess that there was a certain amount of poetic justice here. He could only pray that William Augustus did not see why.

His back was slapped, his biceps felt as he flexed them. The hand from behind was clammy. It made Tom start.

"Tut, edgy, eh? Stand still, damn it."

"It's good for 'em to be that way, your highness. He's in the pink. Trained perfect."

"Um . . . Well, we'll see, soon. Now let's be about the business. They tell me Palmer's already here. Come along."

Then there was no Croucher Givens, look where they may. He had certainly followed them in, but must have slipped away. Broughton, flustered, made an abject apology to the duke.

"He was to be our bottle-holder. I can't imagine what's happened to him."

But Tom could imagine it.

"Andy Givens. They called him the Croucher, and he was devoted to Tom here—taught him everything he knew. You remember the Croucher, don't you, your highness?"

"No. But what of it? Get somebody else."

"If your highness will just wait half a minute—"

One of the bruisers posted outside the door was brought in, a large lout named Fisher, who seemed stunned by this unchased honor, and dropped his cudgel to take up the sponge, the towels, and the water bottle, as though they made up the royal regalia at London Tower.

Thus equipped, they sallied forth.

They had been in the barn no more than a quarter-hour, but in that time the crowd had trebled. Men were pouring across the fields from all directions, converging upon the pasture where the ring had been pitched. The nearby trees already were filled. There might have been close to a thousand men and boys there —though, as Jack Broughton had promised, no women.

There was a shout as soon as Tom was seen, for they knew from his bare torso that he was to be one of the fighters. Most of the calls were encouraging, though flippant, and a few insulting. Marching stolidly behind the duke, flanked on one side by Jack Broughton, on the other by Fisher, Tom paid them no attention.

No one seemed to think that there was anything unethical in the fact that Jack Broughton, the promoter of this fight, should act as second to one of the fighters, or that the Duke of Cumberland, who was now seen to be the patron, should accompany that same pug to the ring. Broughton occupied a unique place in the world of pugilism anyway, being much of a myth in his own lifetime, a man who could do no wrong; and as for Cumberland, though clearly the crowd didn't like him, they were so glad to see him and their beloved Jack Broughton together again that they raised many a lusty cheer.

It gives me an advantage to start, was Tom's thought.

That advantage, as far as William Augustus' part in it was concerned, he would willingly have foregone. He stared hard at the duke's broad, square shoulders, at the all but neckless head, the rigid back, and he was suddenly seized with an almost irresistible temptation to kick that man in the bum. He *did* resist, but the effort made him giggle. Assuredly he was nervous.

The crowd parted, and Fisher on one side, Broughton on the other, held open the ropes. Tom drew a deep breath. He ducked, and stepped through the ropes.

"Come right in," said Pottsy Palmer.

34 *TIMIDITY WAS NOT THERE*

WAS THERE NEVER TO BE AN END TO THE DELAY?

That madhouse in Moorsfield known as Bedlam (it had originally been a priory for the sisters and brothers of the Order of the Star of *Bethlehem*—nobody knows how the name came to be corrupted) was an institution much visited by a certain type of morbid, thrill-seeking Londoner. It was one of the sights of the city. For a mere two shillings you could be admitted to that noisome place where, at leisure, perhaps through a quizzing glass or monocle, you could watch the lunatics. Protected by grills and gateways, you could sit and see them flogged until their backs were like raw beef; you could hear them gibber and jabber, screaming obscenities; you could gaze at them as they squirmed in strait jackets, or were hanged by the thumbs, or lay naked on a stone floor, screeching, while buckets of icy water were thrown over them—all of which was considered good fun, especially if you were in a party and everybody was a bit drunk.

Tom Savage had not visited Bedlam, but he fancied that in the matter of noise at least, it must have been much like this once-placid pasture. True, the members of the fancy, though they rolled their eyes, were not in chains; but many of them looked as if they *should* be, and more than a few no doubt *would* be, ere long.

For they were ferocious of mien. Though nothing more than

fists were brandished, it could be taken that there was many a knife hidden in that crowd.

"Keep back from the ropes," the great Broughton whispered. There was a touch of embarrassment in his voice, like that of one who introduces rude relations from the country. "They're not all of 'em as sportsmanlike as they should be, and maybe some who bet on Palmer'll bash you from behind—if they can reach you."

The ring had four sides, each twenty-four feet long. This made a considerable square, floored not by grass but by a very close-cut hay stubble. Despite the confusion on all sides of this space, the ring itself was limited to the two principals and their four helpers.

Like Tom, Pottsy Palmer had nothing to sit on, nothing to do save stand there while yammering "fans" shrieked encouragement or abuse at him; or else, cold-eyed, as the duke had been, calculating, moving their lips to add mental sums, they studied him from this angle and from that, walking around him like the possible purchasers of a prize bull. Tom, of course, was experiencing this same unease; but Pottsy had been subjected to it longer. Pottsy scowled in the direction of his adversary, but it was a somewhat defensive scowl, and suddenly Tom Savage realized that Pottsy too was on edge.

At first this was unthinkable. Could such a hulk have nerves? Yet Tom came to believe that it was so, and the belief did him good.

Still, Pottsy's was a magnificent figure. Unnaturally heavy, he wouldn't be fast; but there was not an ounce of fat on him, and his skin was clear and firm without being taut, the muscles rippling like satin when he stirred.

The betting rose in frenzy. What he could make of it did not encourage Tom, who gathered that Pottsy Palmer was a favorite for first throw, first knockdown, and final victory, Tom himself rating odds only for first blood—"first claret," they called it.

Seemingly, part of the delay was caused by the Duke of Cumberland, who had not yet made up his mind as to how to lay his bets. Cumberland stared steadily at Tom Savage. This disconcerted Tom. Common sense said that the duke was merely appraising him, was thinking of him only as a money-making—or money-losing—pugilist. All the same, the steady, hard gaze, those cavernous eyes, set Tom to fidgeting. How well had the mask fitted, that afternoon near Wickford?

There seemed to be no judge or referee. The only person who even pretended to assert any authority was Jack Broughton, whose prestige was so great that when he bellowed for silence, he did bring about a certain temporary diminution of the noise. Thus favored, he announced that it was because of the gracious generosity of His Royal Highness the Duke of Cumberland that they were present in this place on this auspicious occasion.

Here was no bombshell, and little more than a murmur of acknowledgment greeted it. The duke had been spotted as the sponsor, and the prize itself, while not mean, wasn't princely.

Taking advantage of the comparative quiet, Broughton went on to name the fighters and to recite the simplest of the rules: no gouging, no kicking, a man to be considered down and not touchable when one hand or one knee was on the ground, no hitting below the belt. Finally, and most important, a man who was carried to the scratch by his seconds, after the usual half-minute rest, *but who could not stand at the scratch unassisted,* should be declared beaten.

Broughton signalled to two men, one in each neutral corner, each holding a large watch.

"Five more minutes for betting," he shouted.

The hubbub was resumed.

Broughton hurried to Tom Savage and started to pull on Tom's gloves, which were thin, dark brown, made of leather. There were no fingers in them, though they did cover the lower knuckles.

"It won't be long now," Broughton muttered.

Nor was it. Tom never did understand how they got the signal. He heard no sort of bell or whistle. Perhaps the bettors kept their eyes on the two men with watches, who at the proper time raised arms or made some other manner of motion. Whatever the reason, silence fell upon that pasture like a great smothering blanket. There was not even an echo. It was as if the whole world had been shut off by the closing of a door. Every tree for two hundred yards around was black with men and boys. They leaned forward, tense, holding their breath, just as the men at the ringside, straining against the ropes, were leaning forward.

"Go ahead," whispered Jack Broughton, and put a hand against the small of Tom's back and pushed. "Hit him!"

Pottsy's seconds might have given him that same sort of push. He took a hesitant forward step and blinked, bewildered. He was like a pit bear suddenly released to face the dogs after weeks of confinement in a dark cage.

Tom already had decided not to edge up to the scratch—a line scraped across the middle of the ring from timekeeper to timekeeper. Instead, he would walk at a rapid stride clear over to the opposite corner, bearding the lion, as it were, in its den. Now he changed this plan in only one particular: instead of walking rapidly to Pottsy Palmer, he *ran*.

The surprise was complete. Palmer had only started to raise his elbows when Tom swung a long, overhand right. It was Tom's best punch, as he knew, and he'd hoped to catch Pottsy between the eyes with it. But Pottsy, though he didn't have his guard up in time, did jerk his head back, and the blow landed on the bridge of his nose.

Tom hit him twice again, in the face, with quick jabbing lefts, and then sprang back.

There was good reason to spring back. Pottsy Palmer, outraged, his elbows up, his knees outjutting, charged.

Pottsy's nose bled, a torrential stream. The crowd liked this. A crowd always likes gore. There is something satisfying about it. "Shed tears, and men doubt;" goes a French saying. "Shed blood, and they believe."

Aggressiveness counts too. An instant later, the men who had been cheering Tom jeered him. For Tom didn't wait to be hit. He jumped away.

Pottsy's advance was not swift. He leaned back from the waist in the conventional posture of the pugilist: Had he been taking lessons? His feet were wide apart and in a line with Tom, like the feet of a fencer. His fists were high, elbows out. Weeping with mortification, while blood dribbled off his chin, he moved in; and Tom moved back.

It was Tom's plan to retreat until Palmer was winded. For four or five minutes he skipped backward, laughing, while an infuriated Pottsy, spitting blood, stamped after him.

Then Tom got too close to the ropes.

Momentarily he thought that he had stepped into a fire. That was the way it stung—like a burn, not of his feet but of the lower part of his legs. Pain streaked up those legs, and he pitched forward.

He couldn't have kept his balance, in that instant, had his life depended upon it. Yet his guard remained high, covering the top of his head, so that Pottsy Palmer, as he passed, could do little more than put out a thigh, and help Tom on his way by clouting him across the back of his neck.

Tom fell face down. Palmer, trying to make it seem an accident, fell on top of him.

Broughton was a quick-thinking second, one who knew all the tricks. By the rules of this contest, such as they were, seconds and bottle-holders were allowed to stay inside the ropes during the fight, though prohibited from touching their principals until the end of a round, and from touching the opposite principals at any time whatever. Broughton briskly flouted this rule. He peeled Palmer off Tom and lifted Tom to an outstretched knee, where like some marionette, gasping, Tom gawped.

"I told you to stay away from those ropes. No, don't talk! Fisher, let's have that water."

Fisher was not the bottle-holder Croucher Givens would have been. He didn't know the game as well. He was slow, clumsy, over-excited; he fumbled. The Croucher was nowhere in sight.

214

"There we are! *Up!* Want me to carry you?"

"No."

Tom ran to the scratch. He had forgotten his shins.

He lost the second fall as well, though Pottsy hadn't laid a fist against him. It was less a throw than a slip. Tom, dodging, rolled as he dropped, so that he put a good distance between himself and Pottsy, who did not get a chance to spike him.

Tom didn't wait for Broughton's knee this time. He was up immediately—and retreating again.

He did win the first knockdown, as he had won first claret. He had danced away from Pottsy for fully ten minutes, when Pottsy—whether as a gesture of impatience or from sheer absent-mindedness—stopped charging and lowered his fists a little. Tom sprang in with a left rounder and then a right. Each met an ear. Then Tom whipped in another left, a straight one this time, to the point of the chin.

It had happened so quickly that it startled Tom almost as much as it did Pottsy, whose eyes got like glass. Had Tom been prepared for that opening, had he been more experienced, he might have delivered one or even two more punches before Pottsy Palmer went down. For Pottsy didn't sprawl full-length. He crumpled, to sway a moment on his knees, as though in grotesque imitation of a man at prayer, and then toppled forward.

His seconds lifted him, and half-carried, half-dragged him away from the scratch. He would take the full thirty seconds. That was certain.

Tom sauntered about his part of the ring, thoughtful. He spurned Broughton's knee, Fisher's wet towel. He was not breathing hard; his shins no longer hurt; and indeed, except for his hands, he was feeling better than he had felt when the fight started. The hands did hurt, however, and when he looked at them, he saw that the gloves were beginning to split in several places.

Musing, thumbs under the sash that held up his breeches—for he had consented to wear a sash, though not the polychromatic one Jack Broughton favored—he found himself standing before William Augustus, Duke of Cumberland. He grinned.

"*Ave, Caesar! Morituri te salutamus!*"

"You don't look it," laconically.

"I trust that your highness has wagered on me?"

His highness kept his own counsel here, only nodding toward Pottsy's group.

"He's getting up. Go on with the fight—if you could call it that."

Tom turned, and ran to the scratch, raising his fists as he did so.

He was wearied of backing away, and had decided to stand and punch it out. But he underestimated Pottsy Palmer. Pottsy was faster than Tom had thought to find him; he puffed, but he continued; and most important of all, he was oaken of texture, a hard man to pulp.

Yet Pottsy's eyes were glazed. He had been stunned. That knockdown took away his heart. Never before had he met anybody he couldn't flatten. And now he was losing, and knew it. Self-respect had been snicked out of him as neatly as a housewife snicks the spine out of a mackerel; and though he still was incalculably strong, he was discovered, as he stumbled about, cursing, for what in truth he always had been—a man who lacked the first requirement of a fist fighter, "bottom," or courage.

Yet he was hard to reach, being so large. Tom, having backed away for several long rounds, now pushed forward, bending low, as Croucher Givens had taught him to do, and hooking his blows to the body just under the ribs. This was unconventional fighting, and there were boos from the crowd. But Pottsy found a way to meet it. He would take a backward step, holding out a knee, at the same time clubbing the top of Tom's unprotected head. Twice he put Tom to the ground in this manner.

Hell, thought Tom. And thereafter he fought it straight. He simply stood up to the scratch and kept hitting, right and left. It was a brutal, beastly thing to do, and it was terrible to his

216

hands, for not more than half the blows met Pottsy's face, the others being blocked by forearms and elbows, which stung. Soon Tom's gloves were shredded off entirely, and every blow meant a crash of pain; but he kept pounding.

Sport? No more than the axman in a slaughterhouse finds it sport to kill sheep as they are driven past him, swinging and swinging until his arms ache.

Palmer stood up to it. He couldn't do much more than this, being too awkward to retreat; and had the fight been supervised by somebody with a sense of decency, it would have been stopped. But the spectators had expected it to go on half a day. Besides, most of the fans had bet on Pottsy Palmer, at least for knockout. They screeched at him to get up. They called him a dog.

Five times Tom knocked him down, and five times Pottsy's seconds somehow got him back to the scratch. The fifth time Tom shook his head, turning away. Pottsy could not even lift his hands. And when his seconds released him, he collapsed.

The fans, howling like disappointed wolves, broke into the ring. They kicked the prone, mute Pottsy. They called him a coward.

Nor was any cheer raised for the victor. The men who had lost bets yelled abuse after him. He had "framed" the fight, they cried. He was a damned thief, damn him.

Tom shrugged. At the ropes he turned to face them—not from bravado but because he was afraid to turn his back upon such a pack. No longer were weapons concealed. The fans had sling shots, knucks, knives.

Snarling, panting, they eyed him.

This, Tom thought, would be the ultimate degradation: to be trampled to death by the fans. He spread his feet, leaning a little forward. His fists were clenched, but those fists, soft now, wouldn't be much good against a mob.

"Stand back, *canaille*!"

At Tom's elbow, from behind, appeared a silver pistol. At

Tom's sweat-sheened shoulder appeared a square, uncompromising warrior's face.

"*Kerl! Lump! 'Raus sofort!*"

The mob had no acquaintance with German, but they could read the message in the shouter's face. And they froze. Billy the Butcher, the first general of Europe, had many despicable qualities, but timidity was not one of them.

He spread open the ropes.

"Come along, Savage. I have some money for you."

On the way back to the barn the great Jack Broughton stammered his excuses. "I'm—I'm sorry they are acting like that, your highness."

He was like a fond mother whose children, at all other times angelic, have misbehaved before guests. The Duke of Cumberland snorted.

"Broughton, you're an ass!"

* * * *

"Great God, what happened to *you*?" cried Lord Seares, who was waiting for Tom at the inn in Half Moon Street.

Tom looked into a mirror. His face wasn't much discolored.

"A sort of duel," he said.

"A duel? Damn it, that's what I'm here for. You asked me to make your excuses to Ned Blane. Well, he won't take 'em."

Tom started to strip, eyeing his bath.

"I don't *have* to fight him, do I? There's no *law* to that effect?"

"Of course not. The law's the other way. But I thought I'd warn you. For some reason, Ned wants to get you out. I thought you ought to know that."

"To the devil with Ned Blane," Tom cried. "I'm glad you're here, my lord. I want to dictate my price for having held up that, uh, that illustrious personage. Who—" At the edge of the basin he turned and waggled a finger. "Well, he's no weakling, my lord!"

"Did I ever say he was?"

Tom, sighing, immersed himself as far as possible.

218

"It may take a bit of time for me to explain. So why don't you come along?"

"Where?"

"To the Green Bells, in Kent. And I hope you carry a pistol?"

"You're being mysterious, Savage."

"The towel . . . Good! . . . You might hire a couple of horses."

35 *ALL THAT GLISTERS—*

GOLD SHONE AND JEWELS GLISTERED IN THE SUNLIGHT THAT speared through the wisteria. Topaz and emerald, ruby and sapphire, and the proud diamond, smashed by that light, shattered, flew in the form of tiny reflections to the side of the house —red, green, violet, yellow—wavering there, jigging crazily.

"Impressive," Lord Seares conceded. He flipped back the lace at his wrist, and with a pale, blue-veined hand, picked from the table a watch studded with pearls. It was of Dresden workmanship, minute, dainty, a delight to the eye. "What I don't see," he added, as he put this back after a fond examination, "is why you brought me all the way out here to show me these. Why couldn't we have done that in London?"

"Because," said Tom, "I was in a hurry."

He glanced at Molly Evans, then at the floor of the terrace outside the house. And she studied her hands with an intentness that those hands, lovely as they were, did not deserve. The truth is, these two persons, a student, an actress, were behaving like a couple of rustics in love for the first time. When they had met, a few minutes before, it was with a rush, with glad cries, and so impulsive had they been that it was only with an effort that they restrained themselves from falling into each other's arms, behavior that would not have been seemly in the presence of a peer. Since that time, stunned by the strength of their own emotions, they had sat apart, eyes downcast, cheeks bright.

Lord Seares, the corners of his mouth uplifted, looked from one to the other.

"I see," he said softly. "No doubt as the lady's, uh, protector, I should fly into a rage and challenge you, sir. But I am forced to remember—and I wish you would too—that you already have one affair of honor pending."

"He must not go there," Molly said quickly, and then bit her lip.

Seares surveyed again the rings, watches, bracelets, snuffboxes, necklaces. He had a connoisseur's eye, a jeweller's touch. But he shook his head.

"Impressive," he said again, "but hardly the fabled loot of that colossus among criminals, Harry the Horsepad."

"It's all *I* stole," Tom snapped. "I've kept track of every piece, no matter how tawdry, starting with these—" He held up a snuffbox and watch, each engraved with the Carnborough lion. "They can all be got back to their proper owners, provided you have the organization. And I believe you have, my lord?"

"Hm . . . It wouldn't be easy, on a no-questions-asked basis. But—the money?"

"The money I'll get. There are claims in for all of that. It would call for some work to tabulate those claims, but it could be done."

"They'd be puffed. D'ye seek to be cheated by persons you've robbed?"

"I'm afraid I have no other choice, my lord."

"And then this matter of the detailed confession, which you have written so well—" He tapped a paper on the table beside the gauds. "You seek a full pardon before you're tried. In truth, without *being* tried."

"It can be done, can't it?"

"Conceivably. It's irregular, but much will be allowed of the king's first minister, which my patron virtually is—"

"Thanks to certain news that did not reach King George."

"No need to rub it in. You've said you would name your terms, and you have, and I will do everything I can to comply with 'em."

"You think it can be accomplished, then?"

"I will do everything I can," Lord Seares repeated. "There're two things about this affair I still don't see."

"Yes?"

"First, the pardon. It might be the most ticklish part of the whole business. Why do you seek it? The money, the trinkets—they can be a matter of conscience. But why a pardon for crimes you haven't been accused of, when you are walking around undetected all the while anyway?"

"I might *be* detected."

"How? You don't plan to go into politics. You have no property that might be expropriated. No relatives who might be harassed. You could easily return to France."

"I don't wish to return to France, my lord. I'm for the American colonies."

"*Chacun à son goût.* That's still another reason why you need not trouble yourself with a questionable pardon. Theoretically the long arm of the law reaches to His Majesty's colonies in America for everyone, but actually, only for men of high importance. You'd be perfectly safe in Massachusetts or Virginia. Both places are filled with fugitives from justice."

"My lord, I am not thinking of my own safety."

"You've never done that."

"I am thinking of somebody else," went on Tom Savage, and he looked at Molly. "When I am finished with this business—when not only my conscience is clear but also my name—then I mean to ask Mrs. Evans to marry me. Before that time"—and he spread his hands—"I don't see how I decently can."

She gave the smallest of sobs, but did not move, still staring down at the hands in her lap. Lord Seares, genuinely touched, raised his eyebrows.

Then Lord Seares harrumphed portentously.

"This may be malapropos," he began, "but I still think that

222

you should go back to town with me and clear up the spat with Ned Blane."

"Oh, damn Ned Blane!"

"Many have, but he's still there. He is a most extraordinarily pesky person."

"My place is here," woodenly.

"Blane," the nobleman pursued, "has the wiliness of the serpent and the persistence of a Bow Street runner. But he has something else besides—the bumpiest bump of curiosity in the land. He pokes into everything. It's a passion with him. He can be more inquisitive than any cat. I don't think there's anything malicious in the lad, but his tastes are expensive, and he has too much time to himself. He'd do anything whatever for money. In secret he despises his uncle, who's a despicable character, I can tell you, but Ned needs the cash so badly that he wouldn't stop short of anything to tickle Lord Sutton."

"I take it that you have such high respect for the Honorable Ned that you long to see him laid low?"

"I shouldn't weep. He'll drink himself to death eventually anyway, but we can't afford to wait for that. You must not suppose that because he's an indefatigable gossip, Ned Blane is empty-headed. Not at all! He has an uncanny knack of putting two and two together and getting four."

"Clever of him."

"I suspect that he's already wondering about you. Who you are, where you came from. I know it was Ned Blane I saw sneak around a corner of the corridor the day you were at my office. It's like him. You'll find him behind all sorts of things. And you being a Pitt man will stir his curiosity the more. If on top of all that you refuse to go out in the field—and that would damage his name, for a man in his position only has to be laughed at once—*then* he would truly turn on you. And he can be venomous, make no mistake about it! There must be some chink in your armor. Somebody besides Mrs. Evans here and myself must know who you are." He waved at the jewelry. "Has anybody seen these?"

"Pottsy Palmer. At least he knows about them. But I've confessed every crime that's represented here, and I am offering to make restitution. Pottsy doesn't know anything about—well—"

"Does anybody know about that?"

Tom paused. The thought of Andrew Givens was in his mind. The Croucher was unreliable, no denying it. He loved his gin, as he feared his betters. And Ned Blane, who patronized the boxing academy, would know of the Croucher's weakness. A casual question would elicit the news that it was Givens who brought Tom Savage to the academy, and that this introduction occurred the very day after the Duke of Cumberland was robbed. "He has an uncanny knack of putting two and two together . . ." Had he done so already?

Lord Seares returned to his point.

"You've given me a hard enough task, returning all this *bijouterie* without scandal. I certainly don't relish the prospect of having Ned Blane buzz around me like a gadfly while I do it."

"Tom mustn't go," Molly said.

"There isn't a trace of peril, ma'am, believe me. Even if Blane hated Mr. Savage here—and I'm sure he doesn't—even then, he'd have no choice but to accept a straightforward apology on the field. Why not? He'd get his flash-in-the-pan, which is what he seeks. Then he would go looking for trouble somewhere else, and be out of our way. Nor is there anything about an apology that would reflect upon your own honor, sir."

"I wasn't thinking about my own honor," Tom said.

He changed the subject slightly.

"You said that there were two things about this affair that you could not understand, my lord. You've only told us one."

"The other is simple. Here's the gemmery and such. But where will the money come from?"

"You forget, my lord, that there is six thousand pounds reward for the capture of Harry Tewkes, dead or alive."

"You still think you're going to get him?"

"I have never been so sure of anything in my life."

"You won't do it by staying out here in the country."

"I wouldn't be too sure of that," said a voice from the house.

Tom sprang to his feet. Lord Seares quick-mindedly tossed a riding-cloak over the table. Molly, who had placed the voice as Mrs. Paul's, did not rise, but she looked up in wild expectancy.

Tom strode to the side door of the house, a few yards from where they had been sitting under the lattice.

"I saw that man again, just now," said Mrs. Paul, coming out of the house.

Dust was fresh on her: she was just off the road, perhaps by way of the front door. Her "milkmaid" straw hat was still fastened under her chin. Those slats, her hands, fluttered like limed sparrows.

"Did he look like me?" Tom cried.

"Well, something. But you're younger. And you're a gentleman."

"Where was this?"

"Down a little t'other side of the village. I was calling on Bessie Limpus, seeing as how my mistress here had such good protection, and I'd just stepped outside when he rode past."

"Making this way?"

"No, going toward the Lunnon road. I was afeared he'd *come* from here. That's why I ran back, nigh the whole distance."

She was in truth badly out of breath and had been as badly scared: this was easy to see.

Tom turned upon Lord Seares.

"That settles it. I stay."

"Just because Harry Tewkes was seen four or five miles from here, headed the other way?"

"He must be hiding in Kent, near here."

"Nonsense, Savage."

"Don't nonsense me, my lord. Nobody can tell where that man Tewkes might be. He could come here any time—at any *minute!*"

There was a knock on the front door.

This time they all came to their feet, Molly Evans at least as startled and as fearful as any of them. As for Mrs. Paul, though plainly she was determined to shield her chick, she had gone pale with fright. It was she who should have answered that knock, but for the instant she was paralyzed and could scarcely swallow, her Adam's apple bobbing hysterically.

The knock came again.

It was Tom who acted. He had a high-surging hope that now at last he would face his mortal enemy. All spring, all summer, he had been living for this moment. He tossed the others a let-me-take-care-of-this look, and passed into the house.

He might have reached the front door by walking around the corner of the house, but he preferred to confront the man directly, not to seem to sneak up to him. He went through the side door, crossed two rooms, reached the front door, fetched a full breath.

The knocker was sounded again, imperiously.

Tom threw open the door.

"Who the devil are *you?*" a sandy little man snapped.

Tom smiled, and indeed almost giggled, so sudden was the letdown. For this most assuredly was not Harry Tewkes. This was an oldish, irascible, peppery, impatient small man in mulberry, a gamecock of a man who, however, carried no weapon more formidable than a riding-rod.

"The question," Tom said, "might be asked the other way."

"Eh?"

"It was *you* who knocked, sir."

"I did. And I asked what the devil *you're* doing here. I came to see Molly Evans—and I'm met by a macaroni!"

Tom bowed, rather pleased to be thought a macaroni.

"You know Mistress Evans?"

"I damned well should! I've managed her for five years!"

"Oh. Come in, Mr. Fletcher."

They talked it over well into the night. It was clear that Molly and her manager had no secrets from one another, but the stage man had only now learned about the kidnabbing of little George. He was furious. He had known Tewkes, though he described him somewhat differently than others had done; and indeed, Tom Savage reflected that everybody who had met him had a somewhat different way of looking at Harry Tewkes, who if he wasn't all things to all men, at least was a good many things to a good many men. Robert Fletcher hated Tewkes. But hatred, he was quick to admit, was not enough.

"I came to see what was keeping you out here in the country, my dear, and to talk over plans. But I'm sure you don't feel like talking now. Damn it, if I ever lay hands on that rascal—"

"Mr. Fletcher," Lord Seares interposed, "no doubt you would have stayed a day or so? Mr. Savage, here, and I have some business in town. It should not take long. But Mr. Savage was reluctant to make the trip if it meant leaving Miss Evans unprotected. But if *you* was here—"

"Delighted, my boy. Though I don't happen to have a sword."

Tom saw what Lord Seares meant, and brought forth his brass-barrelled pistols.

"I wouldn't load 'em," he advised. "But they ought to scare even a man like Harry Tewkes."

"I don't know about Tewkes, but they damned well scare *me!*"

"But you'll stay?"

"Of course I'll stay. It'll probably do Moll good to weep on my shoulder. Wouldn't be the first time. You take as long as you like in London, you two."

Immediately after breakfast Tom had a moment alone with his hostess. Mrs. Paul was in the kitchen. Fletcher was chatting with Lord Seares, who was booted and spurred, mounted too.

The day threatened rain, but there was only sunshine in Tom Savage's heart.

"I—I meant what I said yesterday, about what I'd ask you when my name has been cleared. But I won't embarrass you."

They stood close together, and her head was down.

"You don't embarrass me," she whispered.

"I thought you'd heard it so many times—"

"Not that. And—not from you."

She looked up, the light of her violet eyes flooding him so that for a spell he was speechless.

"I'm sorry about my face," he muttered at last.

"Your face is—your face—"

Then she gave a small low cry of gladness, and threw her arms around him.

Thunder spoke, far away. The sky was the color of a rat's back. But these two didn't know it.

"Split me, you took a long time," Lord Seares complained when Tom joined him, mounting.

"Did I?" said Tom, and burst into a song as they started away.

"For a man who is about to meet the best fencer in the kingdom, you're most marvelously gay, my robber friend."

"Am I?" said Tom.

The thunder mumbled and bumbled, and lightning flashed tentatively across the sky. Tom's horse shied, but Tom paid no attention.

36 *BLOOD IN BIRDCAGE WALK*

THE SURGEON PUT DOWN HIS BLACK BAG. THIS WAS DAWN; THE sky was iridescent. A last wan star was being washed away, and the last sliver of the moon.

The ground behind the cockpit in Birdcage Walk had been picked rather than Hyde Park, because in the park, that skulking place of lechers and pimps, prostitutes and snatchpurses, an affair of honor, no matter what the hour, inevitably drew a crowd. Not that Birdcage Walk was uninhabited. It had been dark when the first comers, a friend of Ned Blane and a friend of Lord Seares, arrived to examine the ground and to shake their heads over the presence of dew. Each of these had come in a chair, preceded by a linkboy; and the linkboys, like the four chair men, smelling trouble, had lingered. Then had come Ned Blane, in a coach, and his remaining second, and Lord Seares, and Tom Savage, and the surgeon, and sundry others whose function never was to be made clear to Tom, so that what with them, and the coachmen, chair men, horse-holders, and the like, the crowd swelled.

It was not in any way like the crowd that had witnessed the downcrash of Pottsy Palmer a few days ago. Not only was it smaller, it was more orderly, being indeed silent, almost reverent.

"The thing will be a farce, of course," Lord Seares had said, but there was no hint of farce here.

Most of them stood stock-still, awed. Those who did move about moved solemnly, like priests who perform some rite, and when they spoke it was low.

The swords had been measured, the ground paced and pegged, the spectators warned to stay back. The surgeon opened his bag, spread a startlingly white serviette on the startlingly green wet grass, and laid out his instruments, which twinkled in the uncertain sunlight.

"It won't be long now," said Lord Seares; and Tom reflected whimsically that the last time those words had been addressed to him was by the great Jack Broughton in much the same circumstances.

The delays had irritated him to a point of near-frenzy, not because of apprehension, as before, but because he was eager to get back to the hideaway in Kent, to scour the countryside thereabouts. It was three days since he had left the Green Bells, expecting then to go to the field the very next morning.

Word had not come from either Molly or the explosive Mr. Fletcher. "No news is good news" goes the saw; but Tom Savage did not feel that way.

Seares was responsible for most of the delay. It had taken him all one afternoon, the first, to find a supplementary representative for Tom, though London was full of military men who would fight at the drop of a hat and supervise a fight even sooner. Seares finally secured the services of a Major Armstrong, who scarcely said a word to Tom himself, and never asked the cause of the quarrel, but knew his job.

Then there was the matter of the field. Seares agreed to Birdcage Walk, but it had rained a good part of the time for the past two days, and he argued that a duel with swords on wet ground would not be fair to either principal. It might be different, he added, if they fought with pistols; but nobody had proposed this.

Finally he protested against a prompt meeting for the reason

230

that Mr. Savage's hands had of late been pounded, so that neither muscles nor nerves were normal. Once again, he had pointed out, while anybody can pull a trigger, the grip a duellist has on his sword is of paramount importance. His principal, Seares had said, required a few days to regain the complete use of his right hand. He offered to have Tom submit to an examination by any surgeon the Blane camp might bring forth—an invitation that was not accepted.

"My lord is utterly right," Major Armstrong had said.

It was true that, until the previous day, Tom's hands had showed puffiness, and had not felt right: he wasn't sure, when he picked up an article, that it would not slip through his fingers.

But, he had raged, what of that—as long as they weren't really going to fight *anyway?*

"Mr. Savage, it is my duty to see that every possible precaution is taken, regardless of what mental reservation you may have made. I must prepare for the worst. *You* go into this thing hotheadedly, and that is correct. Any other attitude would be shameful. But *I* must be cool-headed, or I am no friend of yours."

"My lord is utterly right," said Major Armstrong.

Of all that company, the only man who did not act like a bishop or the manager of a funeral was the Honorable Ned Blane. He chatted with his companions, never so much as glancing at the other end of the cleared space where Tom Savage stood, for he knew that it would be in the worst of taste to acknowledge Tom's existence just now. Blane was not merely at ease; he seemed to be enjoying himself. Redolent of musk and bergamot, clad in white with a silver lace overlay, his heels red, his wig exquisitely powdered, while at his chin a fan of needle-point flared, surely he was not drunk; yet he was vivacious. Save that his scabbard was empty—Tom's seconds were engaged in measuring his sword—he might have stepped away from some splendid ball. Perhaps he had?

Yet there were black thoughts behind that gloss, as Tom was to learn.

The comedy approached its climax. Lord Seares, after a talk with his principal, formally confronted one of Ned Blane's representatives and proposed that a last-minute effort at reconciliation be made. Blane's second agreed. Seares then suggested that the two principals meet face to face, without weapons, and converse. Blane's second said that he would be obliged now to speak to his principal. He did so, and then reported back to Lord Seares that the Honorable Ned Blane had pronounced this suggestion to be acceptable. Whereupon the duellists, empty-handed, advanced upon each other from opposite ends of the field.

The seconds would have accompanied them had not Blane signalled a request for privacy. Blane wasn't imperious, only polite; but he was obeyed.

His mouth was commendably grave, his carriage had dignity, as he faced Tom Savage; but his fine blue eyes twinkled. He was like a boy excitedly holding in a secret.

"Before you speak the apology," he said in a swift low voice, "d'ye know where I think you and I should go, once we've got this nonsense past us?"

Astounded, Tom said: "No."

"I think we ought to go to that house in the Hackney Road."

The horse that had been tethered before the tavern! Tom had remarked at the time how good the saddle was, the accouterments.

He was sure that his face showed shock; sure, too, that Blane was watching him with perspicacious eyes.

Blane gave a deprecating wave of his hand, which scintillated in the early sunlight. He had not removed the rings, in itself proof that he never meant to fight.

"I have so much time, these days . . . And I chanced to see you, and took after you out of sheer idle curiosity, I'll confess."

(This man, Lord Seares had said, had the biggest bump of curiosity in all the land.)

"Such an odd place for a person of *ton* to go," Blane continued, a touch of his accustomed drawl back in his voice. "Hackney!"

Tom swallowed carefully, deliberately.

"Did you go to that house?" he asked at last.

"Oh, to be sure! And I've been there twice since."

"And you—met somebody?"

"Only old Hatchet-Face. She wouldn't let me in. I took a wild chance and said I had come from Mr. Pitt—and *then* she slammed in my face."

Tom emitted a small bitter grin.

"The other two times she wouldn't even open the door. Must have seen me coming. But, if you and I went there together—"

"Yes?"

"—I think we might learn that we've discovered a gold mine. Oh, *you* discovered it, I'll grant! But a mine's no good unless you dig in it, and I happen to be a most prodigious digger. Because unless I'm being bubbled, from what I learned from the neighbors the person Hatchet-Face is shielding is—well, a certain fair Quakeress."

Tom said nothing. He knew that Blane was guessing, but the guesses were shrewd, and this dandy had the persistence of an ant. Even if he wasn't helped he would succeed somehow, sooner or later, in getting into that house in the Hackney Road. And once he met Mrs. Isaac Axford, with his wit and his glib charm he'd have the whole story in a matter of minutes. He'd know what to do with it, too. He would ruin the career of the only man who could guide England through the war that seemed to be just ahead. He would shake public confidence in the probity of the ruling house. He would drag Hannah Lightfoot's name through the mud. And he'd fill his purse in the process.

There was only one thing to do with the Honorable Ned Blane—kill him.

"What are you looking at me like that for?"

Tom, not answering, turned away.

"See here, you've forgotten that apology, Savage. Uh, make it in a good loud voice now, won't you?"

"I have no apology," said Tom, and returned to his own end of the field.

He took off his coat and took off his shoes.

"Bring me my sword," he said.

Because the preliminaries had been conducted with such care, the ground so well laid, there was not excuse for further fuss. There was little left to do but fight.

Too well-bred to show astonishment, the Honorable Ned Blane prepared himself. He pulled off his rings, worked off his shoes. He stripped to shirt and small clothes. He flexed his legs.

The chair men and linkboys, fascinated, moved a little nearer.

Lord Seares all but sobbed. Frightened, he was also furious.

"You *can't* do this!"

"I can't do anything else."

"When did you decide to fight?"

"Just now."

"In God's name, *why?*"

"Because I learned that Ned Blane knows about that house out on the Hackney Road."

"Oh."

Armstrong was more practical. He had already examined every inch of the field, and now as he circled his principal, tightening, tucking in, he gave forth pauselessly with low, unemotional advice.

"I've seen him at Angelo's. And he's good, make no mistake! He's taller than you. Longer arms, longer legs. I'd say he has three inches in the reach."

"That's not much."

"Young man, three inches, if it happens to be in the form of steel that's thrust through your heart, is a very great deal indeed. And remember this too, that he's faster than he looks. Much faster. When you attack, do it with a leap. Don't try to inch up."

Tom took his sword. He simply held it before him, being careful not to let the point graze the ground. He refrained from making any passes. That would have been deemed bad form.

234

All four seconds now met for a final, mercifully brief conference in the middle of the field, and then broke up, going four ways.

"Gentlemen, *advance and engage!*"

Tom strode forward at a brisk pace, for two reasons: he did not wish to seem in any way timorous, and the more field he had behind him, the better it would be in case of an attack he wasn't sure of. His experience had taught him that for a fencer who is in doubt, howsoever fleetingly, the best defense is retreat.

Ned Blane, on the other hand, positively *strolled* toward the middle of the field. He might have been wandering among daisies. He carried his blade carelessly across his shoulder, as though it had been some stick picked up from the side of the road. There was even that which was girlish about his gait.

When he fell into guard position, which he did with an easy grace, he retained this air of languor, this lazy, feline way of moving. And as soon as Tom tried a few tentative passes, Ned Blaine went back. He was wonderfully graceful about this, if slow.

Tom couldn't comprehend. Blane might well be a swordsman who preferred the defensive. There were many such. By backing away, refusing to answer any move save when an actual parry or counter was called for, they could learn a lot about their opponents, at the same time conserving their own energy and wind. But Blane was *suspiciously* slow, whom Armstrong had described as fast. In a fencing academy under the critical eyes of fellow students, that might make sense. Blane after all was a show-off, an exhibitionist. But—why such risky behavior without masks, and with the buttons off?

Tom ceased to attack, and stood watchful.

Blane smiled. Granted that Tom was rather straightforward, and certainly not subtle like his adversary, nevertheless it was eerie the way Blane knew of a decision as soon as it was made.

Blane lunged.

They had been a large distance apart, their points barely

kissing. Blane had not edged forward, to give himself all the advantage his reach entitled him to. Instead he leapt like a tiger.

Tom had no chance to retreat. Neither was he able to riposte. It was all he could do, with a rather clumsy counter, to pin Blane's guard low, almost on the ground, the point having passed within an inch of Tom's breast. The quillons clashed, not unmusically. The men's faces, like their hands, were only a few inches apart, and neither one dared to move.

"So you'd let me dig that mine alone, eh? You're a fool!"

Tom made no reply.

Major Armstrong was the first to reach them, and he slapped both blades clangingly with his own sword, a heavy cavalry saber.

"You will disengage and each go back three steps! If either man lunges before I give the signal, he'll be shot dead!"

They obeyed willingly enough, both being glad to get out of that awkward—and perilous—position.

As soon as Armstrong had called the word, Tom Savage moved in again. He attacked full-length.

Blane parried, but his riposte was high. Perhaps he had not expected Tom to go in all the way or had not supposed that Tom would have such a long low lunge. At any rate, his point, meant for Tom's heart, slithered across the top of Tom's right shoulder, pricking the shirt, and came up to rest by the right side of Tom's neck. Tom could even feel it there, for an instant. It felt cold.

He backed away, countering.

He heard somebody call something about a hit. He shook an impatient head.

"I haven't been touched!"

Even as he said it, he realized that it wasn't the truth. Blane's point had passed not only through the loose of the shirt but also through some of the skin beneath, the skin on top of the shoulder. Tom had felt no pain then, and felt none now, but he did feel the blood that began to roll down toward his armpit. It tickled.

He said nothing about this. He didn't want the fight stopped for the sake of a silly scratch. And if Ned Blane knew that he had touched flesh, he too said nothing, being intent, like Tom, on death.

For some time neither man moved. Tom refused to do what he knew Blane wished him to do—jig around, circling, making false lunges and feints, beating the other's blade. Instead he stood immobile in a strong position, watching his adversary's eyes, his own point steady as a rock.

That was when, for the first time, Ned Blane began to show annoyance. He lost a mite of that curled, coiled grace, and with something akin to a snarl began to press the fight. He was wonderfully fast, feinting here, feinting there.

Tom retreated. He did this very slowly, even dragging his feet, as though in imitation of the way Blane had fought a little earlier.

This effect wasn't lost on Blane, who swore under his breath. His ears, it could be, were cocked for a titter, though in fact nobody made a sound. Blane was a man who could not bear to be laughed at.

He leapt, sliding into a lunge.

It was fast, but Tom was ready for it. Tom bent his knees and brought his guard up high, catching Blane's blade from beneath as he straightened his own arm.

Blane's point passed over the top of Tom's head. Tom's point, as the other came forward, sank into Ned Blane's throat.

Tom sprang back, yanking his sword out; it might have been snapped, otherwise.

Blane fell forward, but instantly, and with amazing strength, flipped over like some great grotesque fish. Both his hands went to his throat, though it is doubtful that he knew what he was doing.

Blood gushed from that throat, great gouts of it, warm, wet, thick, red in the morning sunlight, and it stained the needle-point. It seemed incredible that there should be so much blood in any one man. His hands fell away; and though the blood still charged and boiled at his throat, it was clear to everybody who saw him that the Honorable Ned Blane was dead.

37 *RUN AWAY! RUN AWAY!*

THE MESSAGE OF CHEER SQUEALED PITIFULLY. AS SHE DROPPED down the river, lumbering like a lame bear, she seemed intent upon making as much complaint as she could, every timber rubbing against its neighbors, every joint a source of squeak.

This was odd in view of her work, ordinarily associated with silence and sneakiness. She was a smuggler.

Any customs man would have spotted her as such. A hoy, she carried a huge gaffsail, an enormous course, two jibs, and a topsail, being perilously over-canvased for her size. She would be fast in fair weather, but hell to handle in a blow. From the way she rolled, on a morning of little chop and only faint wind, it was plain that she had not much in the way of a keel, having been designed to work in and out of creeks and small shallow bays. This would account, too, for the leeboards slotted to her sides, a Dutch trick.

However, *Message of Cheer,* sad though she looked, had been up to Deptford on legitimate business, a matter of re-rigging, and since she carried nothing but crew and ballast, she might have welcomed a hail from a revenue cutter, being all righteous indignation—for it is known that a thief who has no chance to steal esteems himself honest—except for one thing, one man rather, who stood on the deck forward, glumly staring at the Greenwich shore, where the windows of the palace gleamed.

The skipper was worried about this man. Undoubtedly he was in trouble of some sort, and though his passage had been handsomely paid, he might yet prove more costly to have aboard than the usual brandy, olive oil, and such. Peter van Straalen didn't like it.

"If you went below, *mijnheer*—"

"It stinks there."

"True, true, but you soon get used to that."

"Lookee, Captain: if you're eager to get rid of me, why don't you put me ashore?"

"*Blijf af*! The gentleman is very funny. Ha, ha, ha!"

And he strode aft.

"Ha, ha, ha," muttered Tom Savage, glaring at the shore.

He had been granted scant chance to balk. He'd been hustled off the scene so fast that the party was halfway to the river before he could catch his breath.

"See here, I'm no criminal!"

"You are now," Seares had said crisply. "If you weren't before, you certainly are now."

"Beautiful swordplay," Major Armstrong kept mumbling, though all the while he pressed the pace. "Split me, that was beautiful!"

The noble lord was nothing if not thorough. Tom had been infuriated by his second's quibbling, but he thanked God now that Seares, though he had not expected a fight, had taken every precaution. Seares had known where *Message of Cheer* was docked, and he had known her skipper—and his price. Seares had had that price in his purse. He even had another purse, in French money, to press into Tom Savage's hands at the last moment.

"Write me as soon as you have an address."

"But damn it, man, there have been duels before this! Ned Blane himself has fought some, and stayed in England."

"Ned Blane's the nephew of Lord Sutton—or was."

"And you are the secretary of William Pitt!"

"Mr. Pitt would never intercede in a scandal like this. He holds himself above such things."

"He has a secretary who doesn't seem to hold himself above receivers and highwaymen—and smugglers."

"Beautiful swordsmanship," Major Armstrong said.

"Mr. Savage, it's no time to go into that."

"People might just be sick of Ned Blane. They might think that he got what was coming to him."

"I tell you, you don't know politics. Now—get aboard!"

"The way you went low when he came in, but holding your point up—that was lovely. That was worth the whole try."

The day was bright, but not Tom Savage's heart. There were those who might have been exultant at so sensational a win, at the ease of escape, the purse, the prospect of France, even at the sight of the river. Tom wasn't. The lower Thames at its best was a dirty, smelly stream, and he had no fondness for it, even on a morning like this. He felt neither pride nor compunction at having skewered Ned Blane. But he hated to leave things half-done. Also, he was in love.

It happened that he had a second purse in his pocket, one he'd forgotten about when Lord Seares pressed the purse of French money upon him. Seares himself had in his custody the stolen jewelry, but Pottsy Palmer did not know that, and Pottsy, a stubborn man, might make another attempt to burglarize Tom's room in Half Moon Street. It was for this reason that Tom had carried to the field all the ready cash he possessed, a matter of more than sixty pounds.

He could buy a horse for less than that, a good one too. And he still had his sword.

He surveyed the water. It was filthy. Tom could swim; but if he leapt into the river, he probably would be overtaken and boathooked out, thereafter to be more carefully guarded. Even if he made the Greenwich shore, he would have to buy, besides a horse, new clothes and possibly a new wig, all of which would take time.

He remembered what he had thought after performing his

first robbery: that there is nothing a fugitive needs so much as cash. But the French money wouldn't do him any good in Kent.

When he had proposed that he be put ashore, he had been sardonic, and a somewhat confused skipper had elected to take it as a joke. But why not?

He made for the captain's cabin, where Peter van Straalen spread pudgy hands.

"*Mijnheer,* I mislike to refuse anything to a passenger, but don't you see that if I put you ashore I'd have to return the money? And I *have* the money."

"Why not put me ashore *without* paying the money back?"

Van Straalen popped his eyes. "But that would be *dishonest!*"

His sincerity was so clear that Tom, baffled, tried another tack.

"Captain, if you made one deal, and then before you'd delivered the goods you had a chance to make a better one, wouldn't it be all right to take the second offer?"

The skipper was looking sidewise at him.

"Specifically, *mijnheer,* what do you mean?"

"Specifically, I believe that Lord Seares gave you ten gold louis to take me to France, right?"

"That is correct."

"But you haven't spent this money? You still have it?"

"How could I have spent it?"

"Then the deal hasn't been completed. It hasn't been consummated, as they say of marriages. So suppose that I was to offer you *twelve* louis to put me ashore? Wouldn't you be justified in accepting that, when you knew that on your next voyage here you'll be in a position to pay Lord Seares back?"

Peter van Straalen was a smart man in the worldly sense, a driver of a hard bargain, but he was not notably intelligent. He took some time to ponder this latest proposition, for he feared a trick, which, in fact, he couldn't find. At last he slammed down his fist.

"*God verdomme,* I think all Englishmen are mad!"

"You may have something there. But—"

"Come along. I'll get you ashore."

*　　*　　*　　*

The Green Bells was faintly pinked by sunset—its chimney, its eaves—and birds fluttered in the wisteria, while the garden was murmurous with bees. Nevertheless the Green Bells looked not asleep, not quaint, but rather deserted. There was an air of desolation about it.

Tom was tired, for he had been riding hard; but at the same time he was tense. Without tethering his horse he strode to the door. He knocked.

"Come in," said a muffled voice.

It did not sound like Molly or Mrs. Paul, and as Tom remembered Fletcher's voice, that too had been high and thin rather than, like this one, low.

He frowned. He opened the door and stepped in.

"Oh," he said, coming to a halt.

"Yes," said the man with the pistol.

Tom gazed for a long moment, then shook his head.

"You don't look a damned bit like me," he decided.

"By God, I don't think so either," said Harry Tewkes. "But I'm glad you came. No, don't sit down, Mr. Savage. You and I are going for a ride—a long one."

38 *A HARD MAN TO KILL*

Tom did sit down.

This was not mere bravado, though it was that too. Tom had seen too many coach passengers shrink like worms when a firearm was pointed. Men who might have shown spunk if threatened by any other weapon cringed shamelessly when they looked into the cavernous mouths of the pistols Tom carried in his capacity of Harry the Horsepad. They lost all sense of manliness, all judgment as well. This was one reason why they gave such garbled reports of the holdups. Tom, some time since, had determined that if he were ever so menaced, he wouldn't crawl.

Yet he did not underrate this gun, any more than he belittled the man who held it. It was no quasi-toy like the one Molly had pointed at him, nor yet a small cannon of the sort he was wont to carry—but didn't have now, for he'd left the pair of them here with Robert Fletcher. It was a Forsyth patent, a fulminator, with a long, thin, octagonal, steel barrel, a piece meant for use, not display. Even in the half-light, Tom Savage could see the priming pan, and it was filled with powder. Yet Tom believed that Harry Tewkes was cool enough to refrain from firing at the first provocation.

Besides, Tom was very tired. So he sat down.

He was less interested in the pistol than in the man who held it. And just at first he was disappointed. If this was a mirror, then his vanity was chafed.

Harry Tewkes was indeed of the same general proportions as Tom, but he was *coarser*. Somehow, no matter what the measuring rods might say, he was *larger*. It was in the face that Tom thought he saw the greatest dissimilarity (though it must be granted that no man is a good judge of his own appearance). Harry Tewkes looked ten years older than his prisoner, to that prisoner. But if there was vulgarity in the face, there was also intelligence—not simply Cockney cunning, but true intelligence. The eyes and mouth were hard, the nose thin, if scarcely sensitive. Features aside, you knew at a glance that a great deal of thinking went on inside that head. Here was a schemer, a planner, a man who constantly altered his own ideas and dusted his designs, ready for any shift that might occur. Here was a man of action, but not just brutal action. Tom wondered indeed, looking at him, why Harry Tewkes had gone in for highway robbery, which Tom now knew to be hard, fraught with peril, and not notably lucrative. Why hadn't the man taken to some equally dirty but more nearly legitimate profession, like politics or the law? His talents would not have been wasted in either of those fields, and he would have made a fortune. But perhaps he had been given no choice? Tom shrugged. This was not what concerned him at the moment, anyway.

"Where are the women? And Fletcher?" he asked coldly.

"Beating the countryside looking for me, I gather. Fletcher, too, eh? They must have pressed him into service also. But they'll never find me. I've got a little spot tucked away that no one—Well, seems they've been gone quite a while. The stove was cold when I broke in a little while ago."

"Versatile man! So you are a burglar too?"

"No, but I have an assistant who is. How did you make out with Ned Blane this morning?"

"You know everything. Why, I killed him."

"*What!*"

Tewkes had been gazing upon Tom with as much curiosity as Tom showed toward him, if anything, being somewhat more frank about it. Now Tom all but chuckled to sense his consternation.

"You *killed* him? How?"

"With a sword, sir. A riposte from the low line. He came in very fast, all the way out—"

"Yes?"

"—and I crouched and tapped off his blade from underneath. It went over my head. Mine went through his throat."

"My God, man, then why aren't you on your way to France? Couldn't Seares, with all his influence—"

"I didn't go to France because I didn't want to. I have somebody else to kill, here."

"You're bloodthirsty, Mr. Savage."

"Right now, yes."

"Is that why you walked straight into my spiderweb?"

Tom Savage did not answer at first. He had nothing to fight with but his wits, yet he had won what the fancy would have called first claret by calmly sitting down when he'd been ordered, at pistol-point, to remain standing, and he could only think to better this advantage, such as it was, by liberal applications of contempt. *Despise this man!* Harry Tewkes was used to abject obedience. Tom sneered at him.

"How did *you* know *I* was coming?" Tom asked at last.

"I didn't. I got here only a little while ago, and your arrival was pure luck. Just as it was luck that night at Tom King's when I spotted you, so obviously a passer-through, and alone. And right behind you was one of the best pickpockets in London, looking for a drink. *That* was luck too. I had several other plans for disappearing, but there was my favorite one."

"And then your gang had to go and ruin it by rescuing me."

"They did. I can't blame 'em, in a way. Though it wasn't loyalty that moved them—it was loot. And then you, damn your eyes, instead of holing up somewhere and never being heard from again, *you* had to take to the pad—on a black horse!"

Tom released a small smile. It pleased him to see Harry

Tewkes so unsettled. Tewkes had suffered while he skulked, hearing about the brave deeds of Harry the Horsepad. Tewkes was an angry man. His voice twanged with passion.

"I can't love you much, Savage!"

"A pity."

The door had been left open, and sunset streamed over the floor, but the gloom elsewhere thickened, making Tewkes's pale face a blur, and when he gestured with his left arm, his shadow on the wall loomed enormous, monstrous, bobbing erratically, swooping, then falling back. Yet he held the pistol steadily enough.

"And now I'm sought even more than when I retired!"

Tom grinned.

"Why, so you are. But just think of the excitement when Harry the Horsepad is killed."

Unexpectedly, Harry Tewkes snickered.

"I *am* thinking of that," he confided. "The ballads will increase, but those reward notices will begin to come down. All over the country. I shall enjoy that as I ride about, looking at the places where they used to be."

The change of tone, the triumph, were not lost on Tom Savage, whose neck went tight, his mouth drying.

"You have—plans?"

"Oh, you may count on that!"

"And they include murdering me?"

"Assuredly they do, sir. Assuredly. You ought to've run while you still could. It's too late now."

Tom wet his lips. He did not fear to do this, for he knew that his own face was in shadow now.

"Here?"

"Certainly not! I shall leave this place as I found it, as soon as it gets really dark. Then we will go to my box in the country. It's not so many miles from here."

"I shall of course ride in silence whenever we pass through a village?"

"You'll have no alternative, Mr. Savage. Your ankles will be roped under the belly of your horse. Your wrists will be tied behind you. And you will wear a bandage over your mouth. What's more, I shall keep a grip on your reins to make sure that there'll be no bolting."

A hush falls on the world at dusk, and that might have been why they were speaking in whispers. Tom, truly tired, nevertheless worked a taunt into his voice.

"This is a large task you've taken upon yourself, Mr. Tewkes. Or is it that you think I'll co-operate by somehow tying *myself* up?"

"You misheard me, sir. I said I had an assistant." Over one shoulder he called: "Come in now."

The moment he saw that great frame, and before he could have made out details, Tom recognized the man who emerged from the kitchen.

"Well, I'll be bubbled," he muttered. "You've made your peace, eh? Not with the blessing of the rest of the gang, I'll warrant?"

"Why, no. Pottsy never mentioned it to them. He's not as big a fool as he looks, Mr. Savage."

"How could he be?"

Even Pottsy, though no longer his old arrogant self, could not endure this. He started with long strides for Tom, his arms swinging.

"*Palmer!*"

Pottsy stopped as though struck by lightning.

"Get the rope from my saddlebag, and do with it as I told you. Never mind how you feel about Mr. Savage here! I need him whole—unmutilated."

Tom asked, negligently, "And how long are you planning to maintain me in that condition?"

"Until tomorrow night. Go on, Pottsy."

All this time the pistol was steady, flicks of sunset licking its underside like small flames. Using only his left hand, Tewkes placed a chair near the open doorway, and sat down, resting the gun on one knee. From there he could see the road and Tom too. He was in better control of himself now, and even managed a drawl, playing the gentleman again, as he jerked his head to indicate the departing Pottsy Palmer.

"A week ago he would never have done that, even for me. You slammed something out of him, Mr. Savage. And by God, it was a magnificent performance! Magnificent!"

Tom cried: "You were there?"

"I risked it, yes. I'm a cautious man, Mr. Savage. I have not been as ready as you to show my countenance almost anywhere. Each of us has his own peculiar little fears, and this is one of mine. That's why it hurt me when you continued my career— after I'd retired."

"Good."

"But when you and Pottsy had that set-to, I reckoned that all attention would be on the ring. Nobody would look for a criminal."

Tom remembered John Fielding and wondered if the Blind Beak had made it. Fielding, in any event, would not have known the Tewkes voice. Harry the Horsepad's crimes—with the exception of the first one that Tom performed for him, the holdup of Carnborough's heir—all had been performed outside the municipal limits.

"Frankly, I was hoping you'd be killed," Tewkes went on. "Or at least," he amended, "maimed."

"I damned near was. Though not by Pottsy."

"I know. I was egging them on as much as I dared without calling attention to myself. But your friend Cumberland came along."

"Don't call him my friend!"

"No matter. Perhaps you might even have got out alone. You seem an extremely hard man to kill, Mr. Savage."

"I could be."

"Tomorrow night, of course, we will learn—for sure."

He looked at Tom and smiled. He had beautiful teeth.

39 "YESTEREVE A NIGHTINGALE—"

TOM HAD THOUGHT OF POTTSY PALMER AS A BIG MAN—BIG IN every way. Not only were his proportions vast, but his fame as a criminal was great, and properly so. His ambition soared: he would be nothing less than a second Jonathan Wild, king of the underworld. His grip on one of the most workmanlike gangs in the East End was a grip of iron. Pottsy was more than a thug. He was a schemer; and his schemes, though low, as befitted his background, were marked by craft and penetration—and executed with skill. Indeed, the first time Tom Savage had seen this giant was as the planner and principal actor in a rescue so masterful of conception and so brilliantly carried out that it would be talked about, and sung about, for many a year to come.

It was the more amazing then, when Pottsy, reduced to taking rather than giving orders, proved petty. As he tied Tom's wrists, for example, though watching his master, the man who sat in the doorway, under his breath he was whispering meaningless insults, childish blasphemies that did not so much annoy as amuse their target; twice he surreptitiously kicked Tom's shins; and again and again, until reprimanded by Tewkes, he gave the rope a vicious jerk, causing pain to streak up Tom's arms.

"That's enough of that. I want this man *unmutilated*. You'll get your go at him tomorrow night."

They started as soon as the sun had set, leaving a tidy house. The night was dark, before the rise of the moon, and Tom did not know this part of the county, for they did not turn toward Tunbridge but made off in what he thought to be a generally northern direction. He never glimpsed the Medway, nor indeed any mentionable stream, though he came to believe, as the countryside flattened, that they must be approaching the Thames, perhaps somewhere near Gravesend or Rochester. But it was hard to know, for they travelled only by small back lanes, and never stopped; and in addition, Tom, trussed and gagged, was damnably uncomfortable. It is difficult to be observant when you itch.

Tewkes rode ahead, a fine figure of a horseman. Tom followed, his tricorn shoved low over his forehead, the gag, the bound wrists, perhaps even the bound feet, concealed from the gaze of any possible passer by a high-collared and very long *roquelaure*, or riding cape, which on this warm night added to his unhappiness. Palmer rode sometimes just behind Tom, sometimes, when it might appear prudent to shield him from possible onlookers—when they were passing a lighted hut, say—by his side. In any case, Palmer never lost a chance to jab him with an elbow, nudge him violently with a knee, or kick him.

To busy his mind, to hold himself away from worrying about Molly, Tom, as he rode, speculated on this small meanness of Pottsy Palmer.

He believed that he could account for it. In the first place, Palmer hated and still feared the only man who had beaten him with fists—and that before a crowd of the fancy. Pottsy's *amour propre* had been punctured, his status in the nether world brought low; and he was no man to be quick with forgiveness. Indeed, as Tom saw sometimes when there was a little light, Pottsy still bore on his face bluish reminders of that battle of almost a week back, and his eyes and mouth were puffed.

More important, possibly, was the fear in which Pottsy held Harry Tewkes. The horsepad did not break into bluster of the sort Pottsy might have understood, and counteracted. He was cold, exact, rude. He was a man who was accustomed to obedience, one who would not accept excuses for blundering, and he was at all times in command of the situation.

There might have been a third reason for Pottsy's pettiness. Even he, that monster, must have had some manner of conscience, and it was likely that, according to his own crooked code, he was doing a shameful thing, consorting with the enemy, selling out his own gang. Realization of this would make him the more angry at Tom Savage, a scapegoat again.

Yet it was not Pottsy but Tewkes whom Tom should study, if he hoped to come out of this adventure alive.

He had no chance for this. Tewkes set a brisk pace. He seldom turned, and still less often did he speak, yet it was patent from his back that he was aware of the beat of hooves behind him, and any straggling surely would have brought him around.

Once, indeed, he did turn, reining to a stop.

The bandage that covered Tom Savage's mouth had worked itself too high, so that it was blocking his nostrils. At that rapid pace, and with the weight of the cloak and the heat it caused, Tom ordinarily would have relieved his breathing with his mouth; but now, of course, he was not able to do this. He retched horribly, or tried to retch. He tried too to swallow. His eyes stung, his face became filmed with sweat, and there was a harsh hammering at his temples. Truly, he thought that he might suffocate, sitting right there in saddle.

He leaned forward, striving to work the thing down upon the horse's mane or the pommel of the saddle, but because of the way his feet were tied, he could not bend that far. The pain was excruciating.

Pottsy Palmer came up from behind and punched Tom over the right ear.

"Don't like it when you can't talk, eh? Well, you always did talk too much. Now stop going forward like that."

It was then that Harry Tewkes turned. Whether he had heard Pottsy's voice—this was unlikely, for Pottsy had no more than whispered—or whether he somehow *sensed* the situation, Tom Savage never was to know. But he did not hesitate. He drew his pistol, examined its priming, cocked it. He nodded coldly at Tom, who, convulsed as he was in his struggles to breathe, must have looked like a man having a fit.

"Take off the kerchief."

He didn't berate Pottsy, and made no move to commiserate with Tom, but after a few minutes he gave a signal that the gag should be tied back into place, and when this had been done he examined it personally, satisfying himself that it would not ride up again; after which he uncocked his pistol and pocketed it, and rode on ahead.

Relieved a little, Tom felt himself sagging. It was as though somebody had snipped his muscles, as scissors snip thread. There was no pain, but abruptly he became as weak as a baby and could hardly hold his eyes open. Though this was to be expected, it astonished him. He had been up before dawn. He'd fought a sword duel. He had started to drop down Thames toward the sea. He had ridden hard for half the morning and almost all the afternoon. And for several hours now he'd been bound hand and foot. No wonder he was weary!

Yet he struggled to retain his senses. It could be he feared that if he went to sleep now, he would never wake up.

By this time the moon had risen, and he strove to study the countryside to get a clue to his whereabouts. His eyes, at least, were free. But he could make nothing of what he saw, which was fuzzy, the edges blurred. Twice he all but slithered upside down as he nodded, and had to be caught by a watchful Pottsy, who seized each occasion to give Tom a knee-kick as he straightened him.

Tom didn't even remember stopping, or having his ankles untied, or being lifted down. As he staggered and lurched into the house, being helped by Pottsy on one side, Harry Tewkes on the other, it occurred to him that he had never even seen the structure he was entering.

He couldn't care. He was grateful when they took the bandage off his mouth; but he hardly noticed it, so numb were his hands and arms, when his wrists were untied. Without so much as a grunt, he fell upon a bed he could scarcely see.

He never heard them leave, never heard the door locked.

Yet there were some sounds that he did hear, briefly, before he lost all consciousness.

One was the song of a nightingale. It was not far away. There was but one bird, and it warbled superbly. Tom, then, was near a wood.

The other sound was rather a cacophony of sounds, immediately more familiar. It came from far away, for the night was clear, the land flat, and there wasn't any breeze. It was the creak of leather, the crunch of iron-shod wheels on a "made" road, the squeal of axles and of linchpins, also the dull and dogged hoofbeats of horses. It was a coach. So—he was somewhere near a highway.

He fell asleep.

40 *THERE WAS THIS BOY*

WHEN HE AWOKE, IT WAS TO HEAR THE NIGHTINGALE AGAIN. OR
perhaps here was a different bird? They sing in the daylight
hours too, Tom knew, and are associated with darkness only
because that is the most convenient time to listen to them.

He lay for some minutes, heeding the song, before he opened
his eyes. This was late in the summer for nightingales, and
somehow, lying there, Tom drowsily assumed that he was being
favored with a good omen. He needed all the good omens he
could get.

He grinned. Muscles aching, he got up. He was very thirsty,
hungry too; but his head was clear.

It was no dungeon he found himself in, but a large, square
bedroom, agreeably if scantily furnished, with windows on two
sides. He tried the door and found it locked, then made for a
window.

It was plain before he got there that this was an upper-story
chamber, though Tom had no recollection of climbing stairs.
The trees told him that he was about twenty feet above the
ground.

Not trees, however, but something more distant, at first
caught his eye. Twinkling in the morning sun, some miles away,
was a stream so wide and so dirty that it could only have been

255

the lower Thames, an estuary in fact. Tom could make out a few boats.

Nearer, less than half a mile away, was a well-marked, wide highway. He could assume that this was the Dover-Canterbury road to London. Tom himself had traveled it on his return from France, and he reflected now that the hill to the left was surely familiar. Shooter's Hill—there it was! He had studied that eminence with a special interest when he came up from Dover to town, for it was famous: together with its companion, Gad's Hill, it was a favorite striking place for highwaymen, and many a murder had been committed there.

The surrounding countryside, however, was in no way glum, like Hounslow Heath, nor yet bare like Finchley Common, but rather was lush, lavishly hedged, a quiet, happy place, shimmering in the sunshine.

Below this window was another surprise. The house would seem to be a substantial one, though probably not large, and beneath the window at which Tom stood, there was a garden, gorgeous with color, rimmed by a twelve-foot stone wall spiked along its top with glass. Tom chose to by-pass the stern, prison aspect of this in his joy at the sight of the flowers. Late June in south England can be polychromatic almost beyond belief, a merry heaven. They were all there—roses, Canterbury bells, pinks, delphiniums, foxgloves, stock, and a dozen others that he didn't know the names of—and they nodded or swayed with becoming carelessness, each growth assured of its own beauty and acting with no thought of the morrow. Tom could not remember ever having looked down upon such a riot of color. The gardens of France were formal, and in Lincolnshire he had never known any such madness of blooming. It took the breath out of him. He was about to die, and the woman he loved was in an agony of suspense for her child; yet somehow, just for that precious moment, nothing but the flowers mattered.

In that Eden the only "off note," as a musician might have said, was Pottsy Palmer. Wearing a coat of dun-brown satin, much like the one in which Tom Savage first had seen him,

256

Pottsy leaned against a sundial. What were blossoms to him, who longed for the streets and stinks of Whitefriars? To that nose—broken in a contest for Cumberland's prize—the mingled heady odors of an English country garden could never smell as sweet as Billingsgate-under-the-Bridge. Palmer, in short, was homesick. It told in his stance, and in the slouch of his shoulders.

As though he had heard Tom's gasp, he looked up. A scowl overspread his face, its natural habitant; yet this passed, and when he spoke his voice was unexpectedly mild.

"Would you like to have some breakfast?"

Tom could not have been more astounded. But he managed a nod, and Pottsy humped away.

Soon afterward the bedroom door was opened.

Tom bridled. "Well, where's that breakfast?"

"I thought you might want to eat it in the garden."

This was harder for Tom to take than the sneaked kicks of last night, since he felt a trick; but he left the room, Pottsy standing politely aside.

Pottsy did not precede but followed him downstairs and out. The big man was not unprepared. He toted a two-foot oaken cudgel, and there was a bulge at his hip that might have been a knife or pistol. He never got close to Tom Savage, but neither did he get far away. And he was alert.

The garden was snug, a miracle of neatness, plat after plat perfectly set out, impeccably bordered. There seemed to be no entrance to it save by way of the house. And the sun crashing against that broken glass on the top of the wall that ran around three sides of the garden—the house itself formed the fourth side—was a reminder that this was, after all, a prison. Not only was no tree near that wall, but neither was there any potting shed, forcing frame, or other object that might have afforded footing. The wall itself was lined with hollyhock and snapdragon, flimsy stuff.

There was a table set out under a willow tree, and a real English breakfast spread.

257

"If you'd like a bath first I could heat the water? And Mr. Tewkes will lend you his razor."

Tom shook a vigorous head.

"Food first, wash after. I'm starved. Besides, I can't comprehend. Am I to be—well, fattened for the slaughter?"

Pottsy nodded, a gleam of triumph in his eyes.

"Yes, that's it," he said. "That's it exactly."

Then he went back to the sundial and sat down.

It was disconcerting, even creepy; but hunger is hunger, and Tom addressed himself to chocolate, scones, marmalade, jam, butter, kippered herring, richly yellow eggs, sausages, bacon, even a mutton chop. As one who had spent years in France, he could appreciate an English breakfast. He thought, as he ate, of various morning meals he had enjoyed at various English inns, and thought, too, that if ever he came to own an inn (a chance that of late had been increasingly in his mind) he would make it famous for all its food, but especially for its breakfasts. He believed that many a traveller would push on further, even if it meant riding after dark, in order to reach a hostelry that served the better steak, the more flavorsome pot of coffee.

He must have been vulgar, in that dainty place. Grunting, when he had finished eating, he wiped his mouth.

It was then that he became conscious that he was being watched. He looked up; it was not Pottsy but a small, serious boy who regarded him from the other side of the table.

"Hello," said Tom.

The lad was handsome. His face was thin, fine. He had his mother's expressive purple eyes. He didn't stir.

"You come from Nan-Paul?"

Tom reckoned this to be a pet name for the nurse, and he nodded.

"From her and from your mother," he replied.

"Take me back to them."

"I mean to, George. I will. But—not right now."

"Right now," said the boy.

258

"*You*, brat!" This was Palmer. "Back to the house!"

The boy turned without another word, his eyes flashing a last appeal to Tom Savage. Tom looked after him. As the boy started through the door he seemed to shrink into himself. Tom had failed him! He became even smaller than he was, his shoulders cringing, his fingers curled. A moment later there was a curse, a slap, another slap. Then it sounded as though somebody had been knocked down, somebody small and light.

Tom sprang to his feet.

"I wouldn't," Pottsy Palmer advised, coming toward him, the cudgel half-raised. "Harry Tewkes is rough with that kid sometimes, but not as rough as I'll be with you if you let me."

Tom turned to stare at him for a long moment, in contempt. There was no other sound from the house.

At last Tom said: "Get me that bath, then."

"Yes, sir," said Pottsy Palmer.

41 *TO HIM WHO WAITS*

THE BEES OF THE GARDEN WERE INDEFATIGABLE, AND IN SOME
nearby thicket or wood, that nightingale continued to pour
forth song. Inside the house itself, however, all was silent. Tom
never saw or heard a servant. Pottsy escorted him to his bedroom, and it was there that he had his bath. Afterward, and
after shaving and dressing, he listened for a long time at the
hall door. He thought he could hear somebody sobbing in a
distant part of the house. He tried the door. It was unlocked.
He opened it and stepped out.

Pottsy was there.

"The garden again?"

Tom sighed. "Yes," he said, "the garden again."

The nightingale sang on.

Tom walked around the garden. He had the curious conviction—he'd had it at breakfast, but then he was too much
taken up with food to mind——that he was being watched.
Not watched by Pottsy, but by the other. Several times he
whirled around to face the house, his glance butterflying past
windows, but he never saw anyone.

Human curiosity—assuming that this man Tewkes *was*
human—should prompt an examination of the physical appearance of Tom Savage. Could it be more than that? What was

260

Tewkes's plan? He was a man to *have* a plan, surely. He'd said as much, and Pottsy had confirmed it.

Tom waxed sore. What was the reason for this cat-and mousing? If they meant to kill him, why didn't they go ahead and do it? Harry Tewkes did not look like a man given to theatrical effects—unless he hoped to profit by them. And the longer Tom was permitted to live, the greater became the chance that he might spot an escape hole.

This whole business was insulting. Death should have a certain dignity. Tom was entitled to an explanation, and abruptly he decided to demand it, Palmer or no Palmer. He spun on his heel and started for the house.

Harry Tewkes came out. As though by signal the nightingale ceased to sing.

Tewkes was well-dressed, though for Tom Savage to have said so would smack of complacency, since the man wore much the same togs as Tom himself—bottle-green coat, embroidered waistcoat, tricorn, buff smallclothes, high black jackboots. The outfit was conventional enough, and this could have been coincidence. Or—it could have been something else.

Tewkes took snuff. He did not offer his mull to Tom.

"I have just heard from the Wells. Mrs. Evans is not there. I wonder where the devil she is. Do you know, Savage?"

"No. And if I did I wouldn't tell you."

"I can believe that."

Tewkes had a jaw that might have been closed by a steel clamp, eyes that never had been glazed by remorse. Somehow, fleetingly—though there was little enough of physical resemblance—he made Tom think of William Augustus, Duke of Cumberland. He had that same damn-you stare. But if he, too, was used to seeing men kowtow before him, they kowtowed not because of his birth but because he held a whip—a whip he was always prepared to use.

Now he studied Tom, whom clearly he did not like. He put his snuffbox away, and waved negligently toward a couple of garden chairs.

"No doubt you are wondering why we didn't kill you right away?"

"That thought had crossed my mind, yes."

"La, you have a right to know. Sit down, Mr. Savage, and I'll tell you."

As Tewkes outlined it, the plan was simplicity itself. No doubt he had other plans as well, designed to fit other sets of circumstances, for he was a calculating man, as he had shown.

Pottsy Palmer had been riding the Dover-London road lately, showing himself at the principal coaching places, letting it be known that he was in search of Harry the Horsepad. No license was needed by one who would practice this profession; but Pottsy at least had, as it were, put his intentions on record. He said he was gambling. Harry the Horsepad never had worked the Dover road, perhaps the most heavily travelled in all England, and maybe now Harry would. Pottsy was, frankly, seeking the reward. Ruined after his fight with the fashionable Mr. Savage, his prestige at a low ebb, his credit almost gone, he was doing this as a desperate measure.

The diligence would pass early this evening, pushing ahead for the capital. It should surmount Shooter's Hill just after sunset, a time when nobody really expects to be held up, a time tonight, too, of no moon. In a nearby wood—they'd been back and forth over every inch of the ground—Tom Savage would lie, bound and gagged, a yellow cockade in his hat, a purple silk kerchief tied across his face.

"This becomes clear," Tom murmured.

Tewkes would hold up the coach. He would do this at the foot of the hill, just after the passengers, who were required to climb that hill on foot, had tumbled out, stretching their legs. Tewkes would be astride a black stallion, and he'd wear the purple mask, the yellow cockade. Also, he would carry two brass-barrelled pistols.

Pottsy would come along, as though providentially. Tewkes would discharge a pistol at him. There would be no ball in that pistol, but the passengers wouldn't know this. Then Tewkes, as though in panic, would turn and race for the wood, which lay on the opposite side of the road from his house here. Pottsy would pursue him. Just inside the wood, there would be an explosion. Passengers and the driver would hear it. Pottsy would reappear, crowing that he'd killed Harry the Horsepad. Tewkes himself would leave his pistols and the black mount with the body, from which he had removed the bonds and gag. Then Tewkes would make his way out of the wood by another route, and return to the house, which would be empty, the servants having been sent on an errand to London. Who would suspect him, that quiet man who tended his garden?

"And I would be dead?"

"Harry the Horsepad *must* die! I'll have no peace until he does!"

"And what will you do about Molly Evans?"

"I don't know, yet. I've got to get the Horsepad legally put away first. But I'll soon have a plan."

"I don't doubt it," dryly.

"This time there won't be any trouble about identification, no matter how many of my former associates they fetch from town. You'll be recognized by your clothes and certain stolen articles in your pockets. Not by your face. In fact, your face won't be *there*. I'm going to use a very large pistol—at close range."

"I see. And of course Pottsy will claim the rewards?"

"Of course. And split with me."

Tom regarded the garden, quiet, serene, and sniffed the slightly spiced odor that came from the pinks. He smiled a small smile. He took snuff from his own box, afterward poofing the residue away.

"And what if I don't go?"

"Why, we'll take you!"

"If I struggle? You've said you want an *unmutilated* corpse—except for the fact that the face will be blown to bits?"

"We'd prefer that. But I believe that a man holds on to life as long as he can. And so will you."

Tewkes rose. Though he was but a little larger than Tom, ne looked incalculably strong. He looked sure of himself, a man who would think of everything. The pinks behind him, by contrast, nodding and rocking in the sunlight, heightened this effect.

"You will doubtless make plans of your own, Mr. Savage. You're human. But I must warn you against a dash. You'd be cut down. And we *could* do the thing with a cold body."

He backed a few steps, unwilling to turn his back to his prisoner.

"Another thing. You are assuming I'll give you back your sword. We could hardly find the just-dead Harry the Horsepad without a sword, could we? And you're thinking that as soon as you get it, you'll lug it out and lay about you, which at least would be better than getting slaughtered in cold blood. Isn't that so, Mr. Savage?"

Tom did not answer.

"I am not a cruel man," Harry Tewkes went on. "I shall kill you not for the joy of killing but purely and simply because you have got in my way. But I have no wish to torture you. And this is why I'll tell you right now that we won't strap that sword around you again until you have been thoroughly bound. Spare yourself *those* dreams anyway."

"You are very kind."

"And now, if you will precede me—This garden is a charming spot. It's one of the reasons I bought the property, last year. But Pottsy and I still have certain preparations, and only one of us will be guarding you at a time. You'll be safer in your room."

Tom had slept late and had breakfasted in a leisurely manner, so that it was already noon. He had the afternoon to wait, and the early part of the evening. It did not prove as wearisome as might have been expected. It was as nothing, for example, compared with his last hours at Newgate; for this place at least was clean.

It was also uncommonly strong. Left alone, he now made a

thorough inspection of the room, even tapping the walls. He found no weak point, nor yet did he discover anything from which a serviceable club could be made, nor any manner of writing materials. True, the windows all worked, but they were narrow and it would take some time for him to squeeze through one of them. They creaked. There was no time when one or the other of Tom's jailers was not posted in the garden below, heavily armed. Even if Tom succeeded in jumping unseen, succeeded too in not turning an ankle, he would be trapped and cut to pieces.

He stretched out on the bed. He thought of Molly Evans, and that was a good thought, for he remembered how she had blushed, looking down, when he announced that if he ever got out of this scrape alive, he meant to propose marriage to her. If—

He sighed; yet he wasn't unhappy. He believed he knew what the answer would be—*if* he survived.

Smiling at the ceiling, he did not notice that dusk had gathered in the room. He was nursing his strength. He might even have dozed for a while there, nodding. At any rate the room was completely dark when first he heard the sounds.

They came from the east, and were very faint, yet distinct— the creak of leather, the squeal of axles, the tired clomp of hooves.

The Dover diligence!

The door was opened, and in a cloud of candlelight Pottsy Palmer and Harry Tewkes entered the room. Tewkes was grave, even solemn, the perfect executioner. Not so Pottsy. He carried a length of light rope, and when Tom sat up, Pottsy swept him a low, mock bow.

"The carriage awaits, me lord."

42 *"YOUR PURSE, NOT YOUR OPINIONS!"*

TOM SAVAGE WAS NOT A SUPERSTITIOUS MAN; AND PHILOSOPHI-
cally—though he had scant time for philosophy these days!—
he found the concept of predestination untenable. Neither did
he believe in evil as a positive force, esteeming it to be, rather,
an absence of goodness, an error, deviation, misguidedness.

Yet when he was hustled out of the house near Shooter's Hill
that night, he took a sideways glance at Harry Tewkes, and he
shuddered. He could not help wondering whether Hamlet had
been right in telling Horatio that there were more things in
Heaven and earth than were dreamt of in his philosophy. Riding before Tom was a being whom he had not even heard of a
few months ago, and who had not heard of him, a man who
had tried to have him judicially killed, and who was trying once
again to do away with him—why? Could it be that there was,
after all, such a thing as malice incarnate? Could it be that Harry
Tewkes was possessed by the devil?

Here was an eerie thought. Yet—Tewkes was not superhu-
man. He was worried, even he; and the knowledge of this
brought to Tom some slight comfort.

They were running short of time. The diligence was near.
There would be no chance for a last-minute check. Whether the
coach was moving ahead of schedule, or whether either Pottsy

or Tewkes had failed to keep sharp watch, Tom neither knew nor cared. The fact was that they would have to move fast.

It was not to be thought that Tewkes mistrusted himself. But he was used to operating alone, and he might have misgivings about his co-conspirator.

If so, those doubts were justified. Pottsy was in a funk. Out of his *milieu* in the first place, his nerve pulped by the beating of the previous week, dismayed by Tom Savage's contempt, uneasy on horseback at best, probably he (to make matters even worse) did not trust his leader.

Tom had played on this. While he was being fastened, and before the gag had been stuffed into his mouth, taking advantage of Pottsy's proximity (whereas Tewkes had stayed well away, a cocked pistol in his hand), Tom had been busily whispering.

". . . if you think that gun doesn't hold a ball . . . What an easy way to get rid of a partner! . . . He'll simply shoot you in front of them all, and then gallop over and do the same to me. . . . How he'll manage to get the rewards I don't know, but he'll have a plan, don't worry! . . . Why should he split six thousand with you? . . . He's got a houseful of booty here, and has he offered to split any of *that*? . . ."

"Shut up!"

"Well, go ahead and get your guts blown out," Tom had whispered. "I never liked you anyway."

"Hurry," Harry Tewkes had called.

The wood was a tiny one at the base of the hill, startingly close to the highway, from which it was separated by a meadow. Nobody was in sight. The sky was dark, and there was a smell of rain, even a few wan, tentative streamers of fog from the direction of the river; but the moon battled to break through clustered clouds, and there were a few defiant stars.

When the party crossed the highway, being careful to avoid clatter, they could hear the coach, though they couldn't see it, for it had at least one more curve before it reached Shooter's Hill.

The two men were barbarously abrupt with Tom, hauling him out of saddle, re-tying his ankles while he lay on the ground, swiftly strapping his swordbelt. This was under the outermost trees, and he could scarcely see the men who handled him, though he could feel their breath.

The coach came nearer. They could hear the wheels.

Tewkes looked at the horses. His own black stallion was the most mettlesome, though Tom's brown mare, a rented animal, was by no means docile. The steed Palmer had, on the other hand, was a ludicrously muscular creature, slow, phlegmatic.

"Use the mare," snapped Tewkes.

"But it's too—"

"You heard what I said."

Tewkes was edgy as he mounted. Pottsy Palmer took time enough to aim a final kick at Tom's head. The Horsepad, watching for the emergence of the coach, didn't see this. Tom did, if none too clearly, and he rolled his face away, so that the toe of the boot only struck him over the left ear. Tom was grinning under the mask, and it was as well that in that light Pottsy couldn't see his eyes. For Tom had got his bound hands to the hilt of his sword, and already, with his thumbs, he was inching the thing up.

As Pottsy rode away, he clutched the pommel, unsure of himself. He went east, toward the coach, but keeping to the shadow of the wood: evidently the plan was that he should appear to have been riding behind the coach in the hope that a highwayman might halt it this night—a hope that would be fulfilled at the foot of Shooter's Hill. After that—the false rescue, the shot, the triumph.

Harry Tewkes was an equestrian statue, barely seen. He did not stir as he stared out across the meadow.

From where he lay, Tom could not see the Dover diligence when it reached the foot of the hill. Anyway, he was engaged in working his sword out. He might have displayed too much haste here. Tewkes's head turned. Tom sucked in his breath.

For a moment nothing whatever stirred.

Harry Tewkes, suspicious, dismounted. He felt the rope at Tom's ankles. He felt the gag. He touched the rope that lashed the wrists together. He could not see those wrists, nor could he see the sword beside them, half out.

Tom did not budge.

Tewkes grunted, and remounted. He put on his mask. He drew and cocked his pistols.

As quietly as he could, Tom went on working the sword out. The farther it came, the easier it was.

He would have given ten such swords for a knife. The blade was a small-sword, or court-sword, and had no edge, being strictly a sticker, not like a cavalryman's saber, or the cutlass a mariner might carry. It did, however, have an extremely sharp point.

The coach stopped, the creaking too. The men in the wood could hear the driver's voice.

"All out! Everybody out and climb!"

They heard the door opened.

Harry the Horsepad started across the meadow. Tom Savage, for the first time not concerned about noise, flipped over to his other shoulder, and with eager, sweating hands got the sword all the way out—and then dropped it.

Sobbing with exasperation, he rocked back and forth, feeling for it. How could he possibly lose a sword in a small place like this? Even though he could see nothing, or next to nothing, and even though his hands were numb, he could certainly locate a *sword*.

He did; and moving more carefully this time, he started to prick his bonds with the point.

Tewkes had broken into a trot. Tom, writhing on the ground, heard somebody gasp, heard a woman give a chopped-off scream. Then Tewkes's voice came—clear, loud, authoritative.

"You—driver! Never mind that blunderbuss! Climb down—or by God I'll blow you to bits!"

Tom's hands and wrists were sopped. It couldn't all be sweat. He must be cutting himself. But he struggled on.

"See here, you're not going to—"

"What I want is your purse, not your opinions!"

The second voice was Tewkes's. But—the first? There was something tantalizingly familiar about it. Without ceasing to tug at his bonds and to hack with the sword, Tom edged forward on his chest, using his shoulders as though they were the oars of a boat, until, at the very edge of the tree-shadow, he could see and hear everything.

"Tewkes! I've been riding all over the country to find you— Molly's just down the road at the inn—"

No mistaking the voice now. It was Robert Fletcher, Molly's manager. Apparently, in his quest for information around the shire, he had taken to the public vehicles. But there was no acknowledgment in Harry Tewkes's voice.

"Stand still, grandpa!"

Instead of obeying the order, Fletcher dove back into the coach, to emerge with one of Tom's large brass pistols. He was trying to cock it, using both thumbs, when Tewkes rode forward and fired. A fat blob of yellow smoke rose, was caught by a breeze, wavered, and broke into streamers. Pottsy's fears had been groundless: the pistol indeed *had* been—as planned— empty of lead.

But it accomplished its purpose—to frighten Harry's victims. Fletcher, the driver, and two passengers fell to the ground beneath the coach—a perilous thing to do, for by this time the horses were rearing and pawing.

Hoofbeats on the road from the direction of Dover, just around the next bend, stopped. They started again an instant later, but this time they were receding, not advancing. Pottsy Palmer had heard the shot and decided to get away from there.

Tewkes had a second pistol, one that did hold a ball. He might have shot Fletcher dead, for at that range he couldn't possibly have missed. But he had another use for the bullet.

He started back across the meadow to where he had left Tom. Tom was the one to kill.

Tom, at the very edge of the wood, had just snapped the rope around his wrists. He had a grip on the sword, but at the wrong end. His ankles were tied, and there was a mask across his face, a gag in his mouth. He couldn't possibly fight. He did the next best thing—he rolled.

There was no underbrush. He bumped a few trees, but he might have covered twenty feet before he sensed that Harry Tewkes was dismounting at the edge of the wood. Then he lay still.

This was the moment that would tell.

He could hear but not see Tewkes. By that same token, thank God, Tewkes couldn't see *him*.

Tom heard the man stamp around, heard him go down on his knees and pat the ground, heard him curse. Tewkes couldn't have seen much there, but his hands might have found the very spot where Tom had been lying, knowing it by the warmth. Possibly the hands found Tom's hat, perhaps even a wisp of the violated rope, which would tell its own story. The hands did not find Tom.

Tewkes rose. For all he knew, his mortal enemy was only a few feet away. But he might spend hours—who had only seconds at his command—in searching this wood.

He mounted and rode off. He rode—Tom could tell it by the hoofbeats—back toward his own house.

The boy!

When Tom himself, having freed his ankles, raced across that meadow and past the coach, he must have been a fearsome sight. Hatless, his wig askew, he bestrode a loutish, badly frightened beast, and the hand that held his naked sword, like the hand that held the reins, was red with blood.

"Hurry! Get help! Get Molly!" he cried to Fletcher. "He's got the boy—George—in a house no more than a half-mile through the trees," pointing as he flashed past.

The stableyard gate still was open, and the stallion stood saddled. On the ground lay a brass-barrelled pistol, no doubt flung away as the rider dismounted. Tom paid no attention to that pistol—it would be the fired one. Instead, he ran into the house.

Harry the Horsepad was coming down the stairs. He had just reached the bottom. Over his left shoulder he carried a canvas bag that must have been heavy. In his right hand he held the other pistol.

Tom had misjudged him. Not the kid he had nabbed but the cream of the stuff he had stolen was what Harry Tewkes would take away.

When he saw Tom he stopped short. He didn't smile, for he was not a smiling man, but a bright light of pleasure came into his eyes.

He raised the pistol. He pulled the trigger.

There was a *"clack!"* and a flash of light in the flashpan. There was nothing more.

Before Tewkes could have cocked that heavy striker again and coaxed powder back into the pan for a second try, Tom Savage would be upon him. Tewkes knew this. He threw the pistol at Tom, hitting him on the chest, and he turned and ran away.

It might have been the only time in his life that Harry Tewkes lost control of himself, being touched for an instant by panic. There was no other way to account for it. He sprang through the nearest door—and found himself in the garden. There was no escape from the garden.

Tom was after him with a bound.

The moon at last broke out of that rack of clouds, flooding the countryside, the flowerbeds.

Tewkes spun about, beside the pinks. He dropped the pack from off his back, and it clanked as it struck the ground.

He drew.

"Ah," whispered Tom Savage.

43 *GO TO A GAUDY GRAVE*

HE WENT IN WITH HIS GUARD HIGH, HIS POINT STRAIGHT OUT, using quick small steps. Tewkes, though his face was threatened, didn't flinch. Instead, he dropped to a low stance and reached for Tom's right armpit. It might have been only a feint, but Tom couldn't take the chance, being vulnerable there. Tom stepped back, falling into a more conventional guard position, and Harry Tewkes charged.

It was a wild attack, unplanned, for their blades in truth had not yet kissed, so that neither really knew anything about the other's defense, his favorite parries and counters, his instinctive movements, what he did when pressed, what he might do if frightened. But time was against Harry Tewkes; and between him and the house, his only means of escape, stood his mortal enemy, who smiled. So Tewkes went in.

Tom had no difficulty with that attack, fierce though it was, and in the course of the flurry he made at least one riposte on the left shoulder, high. This surely did not hurt Tewkes, who perhaps didn't even know that he had been hit. But Tom was thoughtful. He had pictured Tewkes as a brute, not a gentleman; yet fencing was a gentlemen's sport. Tewkes was long-limbed, and he was fast. He was no Ned Blane, but neither was he a novice. And he had on his side something that might be a handicap, but again might well prove the telling force: he had desperation.

He was preparing to attack again—Tom could sense this—but he had been impressed by his previous reception, and he would have a plan this time. Tom took two backward steps and lowered his point a little, while holding it still in line. Puzzled, Tewkes edged closer. His plan of attack, whatever it was, was not complete. To keep him off balance, Tom half-lunged, once high, once low for the hip. Then Tom beat the blade, slithering in.

Tewkes retreated. His left foot, behind him, met the canvas bag both of them had forgotten. He teetered, windmilling his left arm, then for an instant even his sword arm, to avert a fall.

Tom could have skewered him, and perhaps should have done so. Tewkes expected it; Tom could tell this from his eyes.

But Tom only stepped back; and when he had recovered, Harry the Horsepad, far from showing any gratitude, nodded significantly, his eyes cold with scorn. So that was the sort of lily-livered fool he was fighting! A man who wouldn't go in for the kill!

Tewkes advanced. Now he was suffering from a bad case of over-confidence, and it grew worse as Tom Savage backed away.

Tewkes's advance was tighter than the previous one had been, but it was clear to Tom that the man was getting poised for a full-length lunge. Tom retreated still further.

Tewkes swept in, low. It was done very fast and very gracefully, and against an opponent who was not at least equally fast and who had not been expecting this very lunge, it would infallibly have ended the fight. It did so, anyway, at one remove. Tom met it from an even lower position, his buttocks all but touching the sanded path. Scarcely moving his arm, except to straighten it, he lifted the lunge past his right shoulder, while his own blade, underneath Tewkes's, slipped soundlessly into Tewkes's right side.

It might have been a little low for the heart, but it went deep. When Tewkes fell—and he fell forward—the force of the move-

274

ment yanked Tom's weapon right out of Tom's hand, slapping it on the path.

Tom leaned down and pulled the steel out. He had to give a hard jerk to free it, and it was red for five inches from the tip. He was wiping it with a handkerchief as he ran back into the house. He paid no further heed to Harry Tewkes.

It was dim in the hall. Somebody—Fletcher perhaps—was pelting into the stableyard, but Tom didn't pause to see who it was. He ran up the stairs and turned left, making for the part of the house from which, that afternoon, he'd heard the sobbing.

He tried two doors, and they were locked. But a third door had a stout balk on the outside, and he threw this and opened it.

The room was smaller than his own, but it faced the same garden, and moonlight, streaming through the windows, lighted it. The boy was seated on a stool at one of those windows, and it occurred to Tom that he might have witnessed the fight. He rose, not defiant but not grovelling either.

"You've come to kill me," he accused.

"Why, no."

"I don't want to die."

"Who does?"

Tom sheathed. He held out a hand as voices came from below—Fletcher's, and yes, hers—

"Come on, George. Your mother wants to see you. I think she's coming into the house right now."

The scene in the downstairs hall was embarrassing for Robert Fletcher, grizzled theatrical man though he was. Molly, that magnificent actress, that paragon of courage, broke down—and they weren't stage tears! When she was not kissing her son, she was throwing her arms around young Tom Savage, who beamed inanely.

"I'll never let you go again, either of you!"

"That's a promise." Tom grinned down at the boy. "We'll remember it, won't we, George?"

Molly Evans was feeling giddy. Not the fainting type, she

knew that she might faint here. She started to move around the dim hall, arms outstretched.

"Let's go somewhere else, where there's more air . . ."

She opened the first door she came upon. As luck would have it, this was the door that led to the garden, closed by Tom when he came in. The boy George, thoughtful beyond his four years, tried to hold her back. So he *had* seen the fight, that little one! He knew what was out there. Tom, too, hurried to her side.

They were both late. And both were astounded by what they saw.

Harry Tewkes, though surely he was dying—for his whole right side was soggy with blood—had got to his feet. Dead-pale, his eyes closed, his lips mumbling, somehow, with one last effort, he had succeeded in hoisting the canvas bag to his shoulder.

It was too much for him. As Molly Evans opened the door, he collapsed.

Undoubtedly he died in that instant. He fell on his back in the bed of pinks, which nodded and swayed all around him, and his arms were spread-eagled, his knees high. The bag had broken open, and its contents splattered all over the corpse—watches and bracelets and diamond rings blinking bravely in the moonlight; snuffboxes, earrings, necklaces of emerald, topaz, sapphire, ruby; silver chains, pomanders of gold filigree, and bangles and brooches.

Tom closed the door without a sound.

"Let's leave him with his booty."

44 *NET PROFITS*

LORD SEARES RODE DOWN TO PLYMOUTH TO GODSPEED THEM. ELE-gant in cherry and dark blue, he even gave them a case of Joppa soap balls, for he said that he'd heard it was unspeakably dirty in the American colonies.

"I shall miss you, my dear," he told Molly.

"Lord, won't *I*!" Robert Fletcher groaned.

"But there'll be less of the kind of work we used to do to-gether, now that Mr. Pitt is on top."

"There's no question of it, then?" Tom asked.

"None. He is the designated first minister. Oddly enough, the thing that really clinched it was your pardon."

"Oh?"

"When my patron's enemies saw that he could even get a royal pardon for the man who killed Ned Blane and who had confessed to a whole series of highway robberies—though granted, Blane deserved it, and granted that the thief made full restitution—*then* they admitted defeat. And England is saved."

"Speaking of that restitution—"

"Oh, yes! Well, every piece of jewelry you handed over to me has been restored to its owner. No squabbles there. But—I couldn't collect quite the full reward."

"Why not?" Molly demanded indignantly.

"It was adjudged that certain others were entitled to some of it. The coach driver, for example, was allotted a hundred

277

pounds for giving the first alarm in the westerly direction, toward London."

"He only did that because he was running away!"

"True, my dear, but your husband instructed me not to quibble."

"Go on," said Tom.

"Mr. Fletcher, here, was allotted three hundred pounds because he had the high courage to threaten Harry the Horsepad with a gun. But he refused to accept it, so that goes to your own assignment."

"Oh now, see here—"

"No, no," Fletcher said hastily. "Call it a wedding present."

"And finally, there was Pottsy Palmer, who did give the alarm in the easterly direction—though only because he fell off his horse and broke his leg and howled so loudly that he brought a crowd. But anyway, they paid him fifty pounds."

"Let him keep it," said Tom, "with my love."

"Now with that out, and the driver's out, and the various commissions and fees taken out as well, I was left with the sum of five thousand, seven hundred and sixty-eight pounds. But the cash claims against that—"

"Why, they couldn't have come to a *third* of it! Not a *quarter*!"

Seares shrugged.

"You were warned. And you insisted that I make everything good."

"But—five thousand, seven hundred—How much is left?"

Seares took Tom's right hand and upturned it, and ceremoniously he placed upon its palm five coins—three one-shilling pieces, a sixpence, a tuppence.

"Three and eight," he replied.

Tom roared with laughter. He tossed the coins over the rail, to hear them splash into Plymouth Sound.

"My net profits," he cried, "for half a year as the most successful highwayman in England! God's feet, darling—"

"Sh-sh!" glancing at George, who was entoiled by the sights

along the Hoe.

"—let's at least hope that the innkeeping business in America pays better than *that*!"

"It's a curious thing," Lord Seares pursued, "but the only real objection to the royal pardon—the only one in exalted circles, that is—came from His Grace of Cumberland."

"Oh?" said Tom Savage, his heart sinking.

They were so near to departure! At any moment the visitors would be sent ashore, the anchor hauled up. But—Cumberland? What had happened that that cold-eyed soldier took it upon himself to interpose? What did he know? Had somebody got to Croucher Givens when the Croucher was in gin?

"When I say he objected, I don't mean that he objected to the pardon itself, no. What he objected to was the provision that it would apply only if you left England. Cumberland didn't fancy that provision."

"In Heaven's name, why?"

"Why, he said that anybody who can fight like Tom Savage shouldn't be sent away. He said England needs men like that. But he was overruled."

The visitors' barge was alongside, and warnings had been called. There was a general embracing.

"What are you going to call this tavern?" Mr. Fletcher asked, his voice husky as he tried to change the topic of talk.

"Well, Molly saved the sign from her cottage, and she wants to call it the Green Bells. But I have a better idea—"

From out of the tangle of their baggage piled on deck, he drew a glistening new sign lately bought in Lewisham. It showed a man in a scarlet coat, a yellow cockade in his hat, large brass pistols in his hands—but no face.

"I didn't like to think of Master Welt having it left on his hands," Tom explained. "And *I* could fill in the face. Then Harry the Horsepad wouldn't be offensive any more, eh? Don't you think that would be a good name for it?"

"We will call it the Green Bells," said Molly.

"Yes, dear," said Tom, as he put the sign back.

www.ingramcontent.com/pod-product-compliance
Lightning Source LLC
Chambersburg PA
CBHW020607260626
47157CB00003B/901